*Grandpère*

# *Grandpère*

JANET ROMAIN

CAITLIN PRESS

01 02 03 04 05 06 16 15 14 13 12 11



Caitlin Press Inc.
8100 Alderwood Road,
Halfmoon Bay, BC V0N 1Y1
www.caitlin-press.com



Text design by Vici Johnstone.
Cover design by Michelle Winegar and Vici Johnstone.
Edited by Susan Mayse.
Cover photo Erkki Makkonen.
Printed in Canada

Caitlin Press Inc. acknowledges financial support from the Government of Canada through the Canada Book Fund and the Canada Council for the Arts, and from the Province of British Columbia through the British Columbia Arts Council and the Book Publisher's Tax Credit.

Canada Council for the Arts  Conseil des Arts du Canada

BRITISH COLUMBIA ARTS COUNCIL
An agency of the Province of British Columbia

Library and Archives Canada Cataloguing in Publication

Romain, Janet

Grandpère / Janet Romain.

ISBN 978-1-894759-56-4

I. Title.

PS8635.O4468G73 2011    C813'.6    C2011-900472-0

*I dedicate this book to the ancestors,*
*who sometimes whisper wisdom in my ears.*

# Contents


| | |
|---|---|
| Chapter One | 9 |
| Chapter Two | 29 |
| Chapter Three | 46 |
| Chapter Four | 63 |
| Chapter Five | 81 |
| Chapter Six | 93 |
| Chapter Seven | 110 |
| Chapter Eight | 129 |
| Chapter Nine | 145 |
| Chapter Ten | 159 |
| Chapter Eleven | 174 |
| Chapter Twelve | 191 |
| Chapter Thirteen | 207 |
| Chapter Fourteen | 222 |
| Chapter Fifteen | 237 |
| Acknowledgments | 248 |

# Chapter One

I have my pen and pad on my lap, ready. I smile at my Grandpère. He is so old and smaller than me now, his once brawny muscles shrunken away, but his wits are about him as clear as day. His dark eyes still twinkle. He sits in his favourite chair framed by sunlight streaming in through the window. His ever-present cane, which he always calls a walking stick, leans on the side of the chair. It's covered with carvings of every animal in the bush. He is dressed in denim jeans held up by a flat-braided rope with its ends tasselled and beaded. His plaid bush jacket is tattered on the cuffs and looks as though it has seen better days, but he hasn't worn the new one I bought for him and says this one is still good enough for now. It's just like him, getting a little frayed on the edges.

I have promised to write some things down for him.

"Tell them," he says. "Tell them, Anzel. Start with the people." He pauses for a long time, closes his eyes and continues. "My childhood name was SiMon Wakim. It means Little Salt Brother. In English they named me Simon Walker. I still have that name." He opens his eyes, smiles and nods.

"My people were a family of three brothers living in a village with their wives and children. We had four elders, three of them women and one man. The old people were still strong, but we all looked after them, making sure they had wood in the winter and food. We were happy."

Grandpère is in storytelling mode, sitting up straight-backed in the chair, swaying gently back and forth with that look of detachment that tells me he is reaching somewhere for his words. His sentences are not coming out with the usual smooth flow that characterizes most of his stories. He loves to tell the old stories.

"We were living in the land of plenty," he goes on. "Sometimes we were hungry but we never starved, and we always trusted a higher power would end our hunger. When it did, we always gave thanks, and the skinny times taught us to rejoice in the fat times.

"The people were safer then. There were no jails, but there was justice. There were no drunks. There was rarely any sickness. Everybody was good at something, and everyone fit in.

"At our gatherings we had speeches and dancing. It all was important.

"The families and the tribes knew their place in the world, but things changed very fast when white people and their God came into our land. Contact with white men made us grow up fast. Do or die. Many died. No one survived unchanged.

"My life has been witness to many changes. Some are good, some are bad.

"There are so many things to tell, Granddaughter." He looks at me with faraway eyes. "I have to think for a while." He smiles and closes his eyes. He was out with me early this morning in the garden and will probably sleep in the summer sun for a couple of hours, till lunch at least. I have such love for this old man. He looms through my life in all its seasons, his presence always so much larger than his frame, now that it's shrunken in his late nineties, and very much still alive.

I leave him stretched out in his recliner in the breeze through the screen door, his hand on his walking stick, and go outside. The weeds in the garden are growing as fast as the young vegetables, and for the last two days I've been pulling them. There's only one end of a row left to do, and I decide to finish it. The soil is warm, and the weeds come out easily. It is enjoyable to be out in the sun, and weeding feels more like play than work.

I come in a bit late to make a lunch of fried eggs and toast; it's just going to take a minute. Grandpère is up already, sitting at the table. He mustn't have slept long, since it takes him a while to walk from the living room to the table. Once I offered to get him one of those motorized wheelchairs, but he answered me with a look of utter scorn and told me that if he couldn't walk from the window to the table, he would just as soon be dead. No arguing with that logic. No even mentioning it again.

He eats well, although lately he seems to do everything so slowly that I have a hard time adjusting. By the time I've cleaned the frying pan and counter, he's done with his plate. "Thank you," he says. "That was very good." It doesn't matter what kind of crazy meal I serve, he always says that. It always makes me feel good.

I take the eggshells and bread crusts out to the chickens. They scramble to grab the scraps, running with their snatched beakfuls to some quiet corner where they can eat without competition. Grandpère always leaves his crusts now. He says old men and babies don't need to eat crusts. I don't care. The chickens have never eaten as well as they have since he came here to live.

I bring in the eggs, seven today from just eleven chickens. It pleases me that these old hens are laying well. They have the run of the place, and out here in the country they are welcome companions, protected from the wild by the two guard dogs. A lot of coyotes and foxes in the bush are fond of chicken dinner, so Duke and Blue make it their business to patrol the yard. Duke is old, a husky-collie cross, and may be the best dog we've ever lived with. Blue is only three years old, a Pyrenees-heeler cross, and is the most peculiar looking dog. His coat is almost blue, his expression is comical and his energy is boundless. Duke and Blue are good company. We're friends, these two giant dogs and I.

Going back to the house by the long path, I pass the garden. It's glorious in its summer array. Over the years we filled it with perennial flowers from around the world, all blooming here in the centre of BC. The vegetables now take up the open places: spinach and young salad greens, radishes and green onions, all ready for the evening meal. Picking enough for a salad for me and Grandpère doesn't take long, but I see a few more weeds to pull and flowers for a bouquet, so when I get back to the house, I've been gone over an hour. I put the greens in cold water in the sink, set the flowers in a vase and go to visit with him.

He is back in the easy chair. He beckons me over and points at the notepad, smiling. "I am going to tell you the things I want you to write," he says. I grab my notebook and pen, and he begins.

"When I was young, before I knew your grandmother, I didn't know that life could be any different than it was. The older men went down to the Fort twice a year. They traded furs for coffee, flour, sugar, axes, knives, bacon, bullets and beads. Sometimes they brought back hard curled candy. I sure liked that candy. My mother went once, but she never wanted to go again. She never said why. She always wanted beads. Everything that passed through her hands got beaded. She told her stories with beads. The circles were us, and they had the right colours for the directions. She put a little bit of herself in every design, and her beadwork was treasured among the family and the tribe.

"The year I got to go to the Fort was the first and last time. I went with my two uncles and my father, and my older sister came too. She was two winters older than me, but I was taller and stronger. We helped with the packs. Two of our three horses had died in the winter of that year, so we needed more people to pack the trade goods. We had to trade for horses too that year, and Sister carried a pack full of baskets and beadwork to trade for blankets and beads. The women also wanted a steel pot. We were so excited to go that we planned for days.

"How can I tell you what I felt when I saw the Fort? It was huge. We came out on the bank of the Mighty Big Lake, beside the River that Brought the Pinks. Across the water was the biggest village I had ever seen. One of the buildings was huge. It would have taken all of us many summers to put up that building, and even then, none of us would probably have slept upstairs. My Uncle Tree, my father's oldest brother, said it was the new trading post they'd finished two summers before, after the old one burned down.

"We made camp on the beach and made a fire in the circle there. It was sandy and hot. We took off our moccasins and leggings and swam in the lake. We had fresh fish and eggs, and Sister made a fish soup with things she'd gathered up on the way. I can still taste that soup. It was like nothing that people make today. It has the flavour of my youth.

"In the afternoon a trade boat came over and got us. It was the biggest boat I had ever seen, and I was very happy to get to ride in it. We each took a paddle, my two uncles, my father and I. Sister crouched in the bottom with our trade bundles between three pairs of paddlers and the steering man at the end. The boat handled better than a small canoe with all that manpower on the paddles. We crossed the lake in a big arc around the river outlet so we didn't get pulled into the current. Sister and I stared about even though we knew it was rude. We couldn't help it and we realized that neither could the grown-ups.

"The men who came to get us could speak our language, not well but well enough to get by. One of them was named David. He had visited our village with his wife Louisa, whose sister was married to my cousin, and their daughter Clementine. My sister and Clementine were friends.

"David was happy to see us and invited us to camp the night in his lodgings. We took our packs to his place. He had a shed beside the lodgings with two big dogs, very wild, tied up to the door. We could not go to the shed till he moved the dogs, which were very quiet and gentle with him. We put our trade bundles in the shed except for the one my sister carried, and he retied the dogs.

"Their home was not made like our lodgings. It had a metal stove with a chimney and wood on the floors. The floor was covered with the nicest furs, the softest and best quality furs you would find anywhere, and Louisa cooked things we had never tasted before. My sister, Clementine and Louisa talked and giggled and played games with the little ones till they were all sleeping. Then the women curled up in a corner with the pack of things my mother and aunties had made. They told Sister how much each thing was worth and said they would help her trade. They made sounds of pleasure at everything in the pack. There were gifts for each of them in there.

"The men and I had a drink of whisky. My first, but it was sure not my last. My uncles had warned me it was a custom of the white man, and it was rude to refuse. They said it was like drinking horse piss, but it did not feel so bad once it was down. They said to only take one drink, for it was strong medicine that did not agree so well with our tribe, it was white-man medicine. I was not prepared for the warmth it spread through my body, nor the feeling of joy and appreciation that accompanied it. I found a love for my kin and even for Louisa's man that night, which seemed to surpass all that I had felt before. If my uncles and father had not been there, I am sure I would have tried much more than one drink.

"The men talked about the winter — they had been trapping all winter — and they told tales of the animals and where they found them. At that time the names of the lakes and rivers were all different than now. I liked to listen to the stories. The talk of the men was a living history of our people. When Uncle Tree said he had been to the place where the people came over the neck, we knew it was the neck of the giant who had fallen long ago in a quarrel with another of his kind. We could see in our minds' eyes the calm lake, the birch forest with the gigantic mountain peak behind stretching to the sky, mirrored behind with peak after peak making the giant's spine. There was snow on top of those peaks in the heat of the summer days, when old man sun stayed in the sky for most of the day and night. How I would love to see that place again!

"The next day we woke up early. One of the small kids had

been crying in the night and was hot and cranky in the morning. Louisa made some medicine and gave it to the child, and pretty soon he was sleeping. We went off to the big store where the trading was done.

"There were so many things in that store that I did not know what they were for. I was looking at some of them when a big white person dressed in very smooth clothes reached out and touched me on the hand. He moved in sign to say not to touch with my hands. I nodded and didn't touch anything else, but I looked at everything. I did touch one blanket, very gently with the back of my hand, just to feel its softness. I wanted it for my mother.

"The trader was happy with the furs. He said 'plenty big' and 'plenty soft' at nearly every skin. He tasted the pemmican and said, 'Very fresh, very good.' Our men were smiling a lot, and Louisa's man was helping them by saying the words in our language. The trading took nearly all day, but everyone seemed pleased when we got back to the house. The little one was still very hot, and Louisa took him down to the lake and bathed him in the cool water, then gave him some more sleeping medicine.

"We were in a hurry to start back, so the same men took us and our goods back across the lake. We caught the horse and took the other one that the men had traded for from the herd. No one had used that horse yet, but he knew the rope and followed our old mare willingly enough. He was one year old and a stud horse. My father said in the spring next year we would have one more horse, and I was glad to have more horses again. We slept there that night and in the morning we broke camp and headed back.

"Our loads were light on the way home, and we were full of

stories of the things we had seen at the Fort. We had a big metal pot for my mother, and in it was the soft blanket I had touched in the store, wrapped around many small packets of beads and even some seashells that had been traded in from the coast. The thought of my mother's joy made us all happy.

"We had two cases of bullets for both guns. They would last us a long time. Our mare's packs were bulging with flour, sugar, coffee, ten pounds of dried apples and two sides of bacon. The apples were so good that we ate them with dry fish on the trail and never cooked a meal till we were home.

"All the men had traded for steel knives with cases that slid onto our waist belts. I must have pulled my knife out a hundred times on the trail home. The handle was bone, and it was mounted on the blade with two bolts. The nuts were recessed into the handle on the other side. To tighten the handle there was a slot on the bolt to turn it. I was fascinated and proud that I had such a fine knife.

"The trail home took us six days. We had such a party when we got home. Our uncles and Father laid out everyone's things one by one, and no one was left out or disappointed. My mother shared her beads with all the women there, and every little girl had a fancy comb for her hair, and every little boy had a fold-up knife. The women cooked bannock, and we all drank coffee.

"The next day my uncles and their families went back to their own lodgings, and our village dispersed to our summer camps. Our family went one day's journey west to the berry grounds and started picking strawberries to dry for the winter. We were there for less than a week when my sister started sweating and became very hot to touch. She never got better, and after a couple of days, she broke out all over with red spots. No one knew what to do. We bathed her with cool water and tried to get her to eat, but she lost her connection with everything around her. One morning she did not rise. By the time she died, my mother, my father and both the little ones were fevered. I was the only one who did not get sick. Within two months our entire family had died. I took my father last to the woods and tried to understand the meaning of this. Our family had rarely been sick, but now they were all gone."

Grandpère pauses for quite a while here, and I scramble to keep my notes up with the story. I know I'll have to start typing it; no one but me could make sense of this scribble. Tears are leaking out of my eyes. We look at each other; Grandpère's eyes have matching tears. He continues on in a shaking voice.

"That summer went by in a haze. Even now, after all these years, I barely remember how a young boy put his family one by one into their resting grounds and tried to make sense out of his life. At summer's end, I decided to go to the Fort. I didn't know how to live all by myself, and my uncles' lodgings were bare and silent. No one came home to the village. All I could think of was to go to the Fort.

"I will tell you about life in that town next time, Grandaughter."

It's the first time in all these years he's told of his family. I look at him in astonishment, tears wet on my face. "How old were you then?" I ask.

He looks up. "Maybe fourteen winters. In my family I was already regarded as a man. Men grew up quicker in those days. That is one of the things I am looking forward to on the other side, seeing them all once again." His voice grows wistful. "After all this time, will they still know it's me?"

"Of course," I say. "You are you, and no one could mistake you." We laugh, and we both wipe our faces with our sleeves. That makes us laugh more. My grandpère is a tease and a practical joker, and his sense of humour has never changed.

We have dinner and then sit on the porch in the late evening sun. Grandpère is such good company for me, I think, as I knit a sweater for my baby grandson. I was so lonely for so long after my husband died. Lorne and I were married for forty-two years, and the heart attack that killed him was as unexpected as it was final. The first few weeks and months after he passed away were filled with family and friends, but gradually they stopped dropping by so often, reassured that I was "Doing great!" and "Recovering well." I wanted them to stop feeling pity for me, because I cannot bear pity.

I think back and remember those long, empty days. I planted the garden, tended the animals and bartered my tractor driving in haying season for winter hay for the two horses and my milk cow. The milk cow dried up, and I had the neighbour butcher her. Now even the horses are gone. One was my old saddle horse who lived till he was forty years old, and one was the colt meant to replace him, never broke to ride till he was middle-aged, and me still calling him the colt. I hear he's a roping horse now, and my nephew is winning money riding him. Good for him. But dogs and other animals do not fill the lonely place inside us that longs for human company, and when Grandpère's second wife died the following year, I was quick to offer him a place to live in my home.

We rock and make small talk till the sun touches the horizon, and then we make our way to our beds for the night. Grandpère tells me to let him get a head start, since I have a habit of turning out the lights before he gets settled. For such an old man he does well. He is fiercely independent, and the only time we butt heads is when I get too "mother henny," as he calls it.

The next morning is another warm, sunny day, and he is up sitting at the breakfast table when I get in from letting the chickens out and opening the greenhouse windows. The cucumbers, peppers, zucchini and tomatoes are all starting to bear, and I have my shirt held up like a basket filled with the makings of an omelette.

He is impressed with the things I grow to feed us. I am Métis. Our ancestors taught us to be self-sufficient, and I am proud to say if the trucks stopped coming tomorrow, we would not starve, just eat a little more plainly.

"Good morning." He nods at the vegetables, stretches his nose out with a little snap, then winks and smiles. It's a language without words, like when my big dogs sniff their appreciation of the supper smells.

Grandpère says, "I had a dream last night. I was really awake, but it was not here and now, so I know it was a dream. I was in a hotel, and I couldn't find my room. I kept thinking I had found my room, but every time, strangers that I almost knew came in, and I knew I was in the wrong room. They were so familiar, but I couldn't quite put a name to them." He stops briefly and shakes his head, looking puzzled. "After many wrong tries, I found a teacher. He took me to a room with a round table, and all the people whose rooms I had been in came in too. He asked us if we knew who we were, and I suddenly realized that they were all me. Then everyone disappeared except one young woman who was annoyed with me for still being in her room.

"I said to her, 'Do you see? We're all in each others' dreams.'

"'I am awake and at work and I am not dreaming,' she said, and then she disappeared too.

"What can that mean?" he asks.

I believe that dreams have their own reality and meaning, so I give this query some consideration but all that comes to mind is the phrase from, I think, the Bible. "My father's mansion has many rooms," I say to him.

He tips his head as though he's caught some meaning from this, and we are silent till we're done eating. He tells me that he wants to walk to the old sawmill landing this morning. The landing is about a quarter mile from the house. Lorne had a small sawmill set up there when we were developing the property and building the house. Now it's just an opening in the woods. There's still a big pile of sawdust on one side and a mountain of slabs on the opposite side. There's a good trail to it, and it's a delightful walk, so off he goes, and I feel free to do whatever I want. I type my notes, trying to put in the right punctuation and perk up my rusty typing skills.

By noon I'm up to where he left off, and I'm not having to look at the keys anymore. I type directly into the computer. How I love to use backspace and delete and move sentences around! This is surely one of the good things of this age. Computers and hot running water; easy to come up with two good things.

We have sandwiches for lunch of green pepper, onion and baby lettuce. Both of us have false teeth, so we can chew anything now. We never see each other without our teeth in; it seems unfair that teeth don't last as long as bodies do. I have a sudden image of a skeleton with false teeth, still bright and pink, and it makes me chuckle. He wonders why I'm laughing, so I tell him. He laughs too. It takes little to amuse us, two old fools.

He has brought in the eggs and watered the greenhouse. The walk and these small chores have tired him, so he goes to the easy chair to nap. I finish knitting the sweater and decide to embroider the circle of life on the back. I put one feather and one arrow inside the circle, one for bravery and one for rightness, and then I embroider a small flower for tenderness. When the kids bring the new baby on the weekend, the sweater will be ready. He is my tenth grandchild, and they have named him Seth. It is an old name, and its time has come again. I like the name.

I wander into the sunny room. Grandpère is awake and wants me to read him what he said the day before. I do.

Then he closes his eyes and says, "The Fort. It was just as I remembered. I put my pack on the ground and lit the fire. I turned the two horses loose and waited on the lakeshore. Pretty soon a small boat with only one man came over. It was David, Louisa's man. I told him of what happened, and tears came to his eyes. He said it was measles. He'd heard measles were killing the people but hadn't thought it was true. He told me that I could live with them, for he had plenty to do and he could use the extra hands. I was grateful, and for the first time in months, I felt like my life could go on.

"It was very different living in town. Louisa's father was Métis and had come west from Manitoba when there was trouble there, bringing his two daughters with him. He settled with an Indian woman who came from the bush up north, and they built a wooden lodging just up the lake from the Fort. He spoke French and English and a bit of our people's tongue. Louisa and her sister could speak all three languages well and taught their children to read and write.

"Louisa and David made me feel like part of the family, and

there were a lot of chores. I did them willingly. Everything was so new to me, and they made me feel good with their praise. They were not happy that I could not speak English or French, so that winter they all taught me those languages, and I sat with the small children and learned to read and write English. It was a gift to me that I respected all my life."

And indeed that is the truth. Grandpère always has a book handy. When he moved in with me, he came with ten big boxes of books. We filled two bookshelves in his room with two rows on most shelves. I still haven't finished reading his books. He has some classics in there. He's read *Don Quixote*, and I saw him laughing when he was reading it.

He continues, "Their children all had lived through the measles; they said the white blood in them knew how to live through it. I guess no one was immunized then. It was a topic never discussed around me, for I was trying to put my grief behind me.

"It was your grandmère, Clementine, who was the kindest to me. It was not long before we had a special closeness that did not go unremarked. We were still just teenagers, but a longing grew in me to have her for my wife. I could not ask, having nothing to give but the horses, and David had many horses already. The only things I brought from the bush were my knife, my father's gun, my clothes and bedding, my mother's metal pot and a bag of my mother's that she had just finished beading. The pot I had given to Louisa and the purse to Clementine. The gun I kept.

"The next summer was a time of much activity. One of the happiest days was when a boat brought my Uncle Tree with his furs. He was as happy to see me as I was to see him. Not all of his family had gotten the sickness, but he knew my family was gone, for he had seen the ash pile and a fresh cairn of rocks among the trees at the berry grounds. He just hadn't known who survived. He offered to take me away with him, and while I was tempted, I did not want to leave David and Louisa's house, nor did I want to leave Clementine.

"So I stayed. The news around the Fort was that we could cut fir, float it down the river and get paid in coin. There were six of us who cut down trees all summer, David and I, his oldest son who was one year older than me and three Canadians from the town. There were a lot of Canadians living in the Fort, mostly half-breeds, French and Indian. They were hard workers. It took a long time to fall a tree. Those were big trees. We had to be able to get them into the lake, so they had to fall just the right way. We cut the wedge with axes, then used a long saw. It took two men all morning to cut a tree, and the rest of the day to cut it to the right lengths. We used poles to roll the trees into the lake, where we lashed them together four across and boomed them.

"When it was time, we opened the boom and let the trees go down the river. It was hard to get them moving, but once they were in the river, they took off fast. The Canadians went ahead in two boats so that they could catch them downriver for the mill. Before the snow fell, they were back. They brought us three bags of coin. I didn't even know how much money it was. I put it on the table and said it was for Clementine.

"David just laughed and gave it back to me. He said, 'If you want to have Clementine, you're going to need this.' That was all he said. He laughed, and Clementine would not even look at me. She told me after that I should have asked her first. But she would have said yes anyway, she said. That winter we worked on a house for us. We made it wooden, just sixteen feet wide and twenty feet long, but it seemed like a castle to us. We were married by the Catholic priest even though we didn't attend the regular services. Louisa insisted, and we went along just to make her happy.

"The next years were very good. There was work around the Fort, and I made friends with some white men. Louisa's father played fiddle, and how they all loved to dance! We rolled up the furs, and they danced on the wooden floors. They took turns dancing, one by one and sometimes two at a time, keeping time to the fiddle. I never could get the hang of that fiddle, but I could keep rhythm on the drums.

"One of my white friends was named Sven. He had golden hair and bright blue eyes and a real sense of fun. He liked to drink whisky and get roaring drunk, as he called it. The first few times, I drank too much and threw up, but then I could drink till my memory of things was hazy. I drank a lot when our first boy was young, but I still did my work in the day. Clementine spoke to me about it twice, but I didn't listen. Then one morning after a wild party, I woke up at my friend's house, and I was sleeping with another woman. I couldn't remember if we had sex or not. I was so ashamed. I crept out of the furs and started home. I was just about to our house when I saw our door open and my Clementine kissing on my friend Sven, who was leaving.

"I was enraged. I could not speak to them, so I crept out of sight and kept walking till I was deep in the woods. Then I lay down and cried like a baby. I stayed there for two weeks, arguing with myself. Who was to blame? My Clementine? Did I not just wake up in the arms of another woman who I cared nothing for? My friend Sven? Maybe, for he saw opportunity in the arms of a lonely woman. Me? Yes. I had been drinking instead of paying attention to what mattered most to me, my Clementine, our son and our life together.

"Finally, when I had it all straight, I went home. First I stopped and told Sven he was no longer my friend, that we were enemies from that day on, and that if I saw him, I would try to kill him. I never saw him again. I went home, and no words passed between Clementine and me about anything for some time. Ever since, though, I've never been drunk. I won't say I never had another drink, but something in me would make me stop.

"I stayed home a lot that winter, and Clementine and I learned to love each other more. The following year your mother was born."

His voice comes from deep inside him, the words booming around the room, as I strive to keep up with his story in my peculiar shorthand. It takes a while for my head to absorb what the words mean. My mother was born the following year? My blue-eyed mother, impossible in her dark-eyed family? My mother, who was always teased about being a throwback to some unknown Scottish ancestor? Is Grandpère telling me that he was not my blood? That my blood grandfather was some blond man named Sven?

I can't speak. I can hardly think. I just look at him. My thoughts are a jumble. I think of the family tree I treasure, with all the names of the ancestors hanging from the branches. Now in my mind's eye a broken branch stretches rough and jagged above the canopy.

He looks steadily at me. He answers my unspoken questions. "I'll never know. Maybe she was a throwback. I know I loved her more than the rest. She was a sunshine girl, my Annie, always smiling and dancing. She never lost that. But my story today was to tell about drinking. It is one of the bad things in this world. Days and years can go by in a haze. Some of the young men did not have as much to live for as I did. My cousin spent his whole life in a bottle, and his only reward was to die young with no pride and no friends."

He seems unaware of the emotions swirling around me. He yawns and says he thinks he will catch a nap. I take my notepad to the office and fire up the word processor. But I cannot type. I make stupid spelling mistakes and soon I quit. I go out into the garden and crawl along the rows, pulling up weeds. Inside I am seething with emotion. I feel that a firm foundation has crumpled, as though who I am has been compromised. I try to tell myself that it doesn't matter, but right now it does. It matters to me to know who I am. I feel this has changed who I am at some basic level.

With difficulty, I make myself think of other things. I try to notice the birds singing and to feel the heat of the late afternoon sun on my back. I think of my children and their children, and again I am overcome with the feeling that this has changed who they are. Lorne and I had five children, every one of them with blue eyes — not surprising with my blue-eyed Irish husband's genetics, even less surprising now. I must be truly distracted, for I find I've pulled vegetables along with the weeds.

Giving up on doing anything useful, I take the dogs for a walk. There is a hill behind the house with a path to its top — we call it the lookout — where I scattered Lorne's, my parents' and my two lost children's ashes. I always feel at peace when I sit up there. As we climb, the mosquitoes buzz around us, but they are the fat lazy ones that hatched recently and they don't bother to land or bite. At the top of the hill is a smooth rock. I like to sit on it and admire the view. Today it is especially pretty. The light green of the new poplar leaves contrasts with the dark spruce and fir. The dead pines stand purple against the horizon to the west, and the dark green patches interrupting the forest in every direction are hay fields. Far off to the east, a tractor drones around a patch; from here it seems to be plowing.

Sitting on the rock, a peace comes over me, and I say firmly to myself that it does not matter. What makes a family is love, not genetics. I repeat this every time I think of Grandpère, and by the time I am ready to go down to make supper, I am calm.

After supper I decide to do some baking and make an apple crisp and a rhubarb-strawberry pie. The rhubarb has gotten very large, and the strawberries are just getting ready. We still have strawberries from last year in the freezer, and I remind myself to make them into jam pretty soon.

By the time I am done, Grandpère has gone to bed. I decide to finish typing his story and now I can do it quickly. The house is clean, and the guestrooms are made up for the kids' visit. My oldest son Clint is coming for the weekend with his wife Patty. The new baby is their fourth child, another boy. They were hoping to have a girl, but they knew for months it was a boy. They showed me the pictures from the ultrasound and pointed out his tiny balls. It is a marvel to me still that we can take pictures of babies in wombs. It seems to take away some of the anticipation of birth, but at least I knew what colour to knit the sweater.

# Chapter Two

In the morning Clint, Patty and the boys arrive in a new car. Clint is very happy about it being a four-wheel drive and he shows it to me and Grandpère.

"Do you want to go fishing today, Grandpère?" he asks.

"I sure do," Grandpère answers. They go to the shed and get the fishing gear.

"We can take the car right to the river." Clint is excited. He is very handsome with his long, dark hair tied behind his head in a ponytail. He is tall and slim and has an easy smile.

He asks the boys if they want to come. The two older boys, Ryan and Jayden, want to go, so I take them into the house with me to make a picnic lunch. We make tuna fish sandwiches and put together a bag of tiny baby carrots, and I send one of the pies. Patty throws in some juice boxes and some packets with cheese and crackers. Then the boys climb into the back seat and do up their seatbelts without being told. Sometimes when I take them to town with me, they tell me to do up mine. It is the only time I ever wear one. I don't think the government has the right to tell me that I have to wear it. It's my car, my life and my decision. I recognize my rebellion here, but it pleases me to do as

I please. I am glad that the children wear them, though.

"Have fun!" we yell as we wave them off. We look at each other and laugh, for we yelled in unison. Patty is tall and slim, even now after just having a baby. I compliment her on how she looks, and she says, "I only get pregnant in my stomach. After the baby is born, I'm almost able to put on my old jeans." No doubt running around after three lively boys helps keep her that way.

"I used to get pregnant even in my face," I tell her. "Even when my last baby was born, I gained thirty-five pounds. It took me six months before my jeans fit."

Patty laughs and says she can't imagine me heavy. Standing beside her I feel tiny; my head doesn't reach her chin. We are good friends, my daughter-in-law and I. Her mother lives in Ontario, and she does not see her very often, and our relationship is like a mother-and-daughter one. She is a good mother to the boys, who are well behaved and polite. She and Clint look at each other with such love that it sends a pang to my heart for my own lost love, gone from me these past four years. Sometimes I miss him so.

The baby is still sleeping, and the three-year-old, Pierre, is sitting on the four-wheeler. He loves to ride it, and last time he visited, he figured out how to turn the key to make it go. I have the key safely hung inside the door now, so I get it and we ride round and round the yard. He keeps telling me to go faster, and I think his dad must go a lot faster with him than I do. I tire of the endless circles long before he does, and I distract him with feeding the chickens. He loves to get the eggs and wants to pack the bucket. He drops it and breaks two eggs. His little face is crestfallen, and he says, "Eggs broken." I tell him that dogs like broken eggs, so we feed each dog one egg, and they delight him by eating the shells too. He laughs, "Silly dogs, not supposed to eat shells." He is talking well now. He is sturdy and strong, his brown hair is long and curly and his blue eyes remind me of my own children's. They were so like him.

When we go into the house, Patty is nursing the baby. He is tiny, his little fists curled tight, and sucking as though he is starving.

"Is he good?" I ask.

"So good," she replies. "All week now he's been sleeping for eight hours at night."

"It is a blessing," I say, and I mean it. Pierre was a cranky baby who refused to sleep through the night till he was over a year old. When he was a baby, they were here a lot. I spent some nights up with him, for I wasn't sleeping much at that time either. Patty must have been remembering, too, because she said, "You won't be up with this little guy, Mother. When he does wake up, he just wants a new diaper and a feed and then he's right back to sleep."

Pierre wants to hold "his baby," and Patty sets him on the couch with the baby's head propped up on his arm. I take some pictures to put in my album. I have an album to record each of my children's lives. Seth on Pierre's lap will be the latest addition. I love these new cameras; take out the memory card and you can print photos from the computer in less than five minutes. Patty is surprised that I know how to do this, and I tell her that Darcy and Faith's girls taught me to do it just last winter. They are my oldest grandchildren, and at fourteen and fifteen know more about computers than I ever hope to. They really like to show me how to do things; it's such a role reversal. I have to remind myself that one is never too old to learn new skills. What good teachers these young ones are!

Grandpère and Clint and the boys get home in late afternoon. They have three big fish that Clint and Grandpère agree are Dolly Varden, landlocked salmon. They caught them in the river, so I have my doubts, but I keep my doubts to myself.

We cook up the fish and visit around the table for a few hours. Grandpère keeps nodding off. He won't go to bed yet, since he doesn't want to miss anything. Clint surprises me when he says they're going partway back to the city tonight. The boys have a soccer tournament the next day, and they have to be there for the team.

"We'll be out again in a few weeks," Clint says. "Make sure you keep this old man busy. He was trying to sleep at the river, and now at the table."

"I wasn't sleeping, I was just making sure the back seat of the car was comfortable," says Grandpère, grinning at Clint. "Just the same, who was it caught all three of them fish? I might be old and sleepy, but somebody's got to teach you guys to fish."

Ryan breaks in. "You should have seen it, Grandma. Dad was holding the rod for a long time, then he gave Grandpère a turn, and just like that he had a fish. He let me reel it in. And he caught the other two, but Dad and Jayden got to reel them in."

Grandpère smiles as though he's won the lottery. He tells them, "Goodbye. Come again when you want a fishing lesson." When they drive out, Grandpère and I are both tired and head to bed before the sun has even gone down. It's nice to see the kids and their families, but we are not used to the noise and confusion that accompanies small children and are never all that sorry to see them go.

The next day I go to put the picture of the boys into the album. I stop at the page with the family tree. I take a pencil and draw a branch bent like a question mark above my mother's name and write Sven on it. Then I feel disloyal to the rest of those names and slip the album to the bottom of the pile.

We get a lot of company in the summer. Close family, extended family and friends all drop by for a visit, some for a few hours and some for a few days. We like to have visitors and make coffee and entertain them. Most everyone leaves with fresh produce, because we always plant way more than we can possibly use. I think all gardeners who have space to plant do the same thing. It's little effort to plant; tending and harvesting consume the gardening hours.

One of my friends drops by one morning. I have known Bella since high school. She married right after graduation. Her son and two daughters are the same ages as some of my children. Bella was always heavy, and now she can hardly get in and out of her car. It seems as though her younger self is peering out at me from the centre of a balloon.

"Did you know that Carrie went into long-term care?" she asks.

"No, I never knew. Last I heard was that she had a stroke and was getting rehabilitated."

"Well," she says, and I know she's going to tell me a story that's going around. Bella knows all the stories that go around. "You see, she just had that stroke because she was so mad about her husband leaving the business and the boat to the kids. I guess she thought she was going to sell everything that guy worked so hard for and live in luxury the rest of her life. It wasn't like he left her penniless, you know. He left her two grand a month to live on, but that place she's in is going to cost forty-five hundred. Those kids will have to cough up the rest."

There is a note of righteous indignation in her voice as she relates this story, and I wonder what she objects to: Charlie not giving all of his fortune to Carrie, Carrie not recovering from the stroke or the children having to pay.

Bella loves to talk about her children's successes, so I change the subject by asking how her John is doing.

"He got a raise this year. He makes three hundred and sixty thousand every year now. They bought a cottage down at the lake and a new boat, so of course they needed a new truck to haul it." She laughs gaily. "I can't ever keep up with all the things they're doing. This fall they're going to Italy and France. And all three of his girls are in university."

"What are they taking?" I ask.

"Environmental science, the older two, and little Isobel is taking general studies till she can find her direction." She prattles on about John's house and the last time she visited, what the furniture was like and what art they had. Only just aware of her story, I'm saying, "Really?" and "How nice!" in the appropriate places. I'm still thinking about Carrie and her stroke.

Can a person really have a stroke on demand? Who would deliberately want to become dependant? I force my attention back to Bella and realize she's giving me a look that makes me think maybe I missed a response cue. Grandpère is grinning from his side of the table. I smile sweetly at both of them and ask if they would like to come out to the garden with me. I am older than Bella, but she takes as long to move about as Grandpère does.

I take pity on them and bring the four-wheeler over. They sit beside each other, perched on the carrier behind me. They hold on to my sweater, and Bella squeals while Grandpère assures her of my careful driving. On the way out we talk about the bear that's been hanging around. I tell them if the bear charges, I'm the only safe one, because all I have to do is shut off the bike. I won't even have to run, because I can walk faster than either of them can run. You don't need to outrun a bear; you just need to outrun the slowest person there.

We pick a plastic tub full of vegetables for Bella to take, and new potatoes, onion and dill to make soup for dinner. Grandpère and Bella sit at the table and gossip about our neighbours. I cook, chop up the potato and onion, throw in the aromatic dill and a little salt and put them on to boil. No need to peel these fresh potatoes.

"Did you hear that Dixon boy is going to jail?" she asks him.

"Yes, poor kid, both of those other kids riding with him died."

"Well, it serves him right." Bella knows all the boys' parents. "I hope he gets a long time. You know, they get out after just a couple of months, and it's not even like jail, it's like a hotel with TV and telephone and everything."

What Bella knows about jail is probably what she learned from the TV. She seems to know all the characters in all the shows, and any lull in the conversation she fills with her accounts of reality shows: who's likely to win and how each show is progressing.

Finally she has to leave for a doctor's appointment, and even knowing better than to ask about any of her illnesses, I still inquire, "What's wrong?"

"Nothing. I'm going for a checkup. My blood pressure is high, and we like to keep an eye on my cholesterol," she says.

Pretty soon we're waving, and Bella's on her way, probably planning to visit someone else after the doctor to tell what she learned here, which wasn't much. If she has nothing interesting to relate, she may just make something up. An uncharitable thought. I chastise myself.

Grandpère says to me, "Your friend, she is going to the doctor when nothing is wrong with her but that she is fat and lazy and has nothing to do. If she had something to do, she would be a lot healthier."

Bella is my friend by reason of long acquaintance, not because we are soul sisters, and I feel no need to defend her, so I merely agree with him. Bella has put on weight like armour, ill health has plagued her all her adult life and while I have some sympathy for her, I can also see that many of her problems are largely self-inflicted.

"I don't like to see doctors at all," he tells me, as though I don't already know. Grandpère and I are both healthy; we eat well and stay active. We joke to each other that we're only ever going to see the doctor by accident.

He still isn't finished with Bella. "When you asked her how John was, she told you all the things he had, not how he was. I tell you, girl, that is a bad thing about these times. We've all been taken over by things. Things are so important to that lady that she doesn't know if her son is happy or not. She is measuring his happiness by how many things he has."

He is not usually so blunt. Normally when someone annoys him, he gets sarcastic and makes up little barbs that he throws around for a couple of days to laugh at. "Lyle Dixon is a good kid. He just got liquored up one night and had an accident, killed some of his good friends. The memory of that will hurt him all his life. He doesn't need that woman wishing him bad."

Now I understand. The Dixons are related to him through his second wife. He knows the boy. I placate him. "Grandpère, if it's his first offence and he's sorry, the judge will go lightly on him."

"Just the same, just the same," he answers. He doesn't say any more.

The summer goes by quickly, and before we expect it, the first September snow flies. The blossoms on the hanging baskets are frozen solid with all their colours intact, crowned by delicate powdery snowflakes. The air is frosty, and snow covers every surface, making everything look clean and sparkling in the fall sun. How dazzling it all looks. I love the first snowfall of the year.

The sun melts the snow to a muddy glop by afternoon, but frost has killed all the tender plants in the garden and the yard. I fall into harvest mode, making a list of the things I have to do before freeze-up. At the top of the list is firewood.

We have an electric furnace, but in the cold weather nothing throws warmth like a wood stove, so we need a fair pile of firewood. Often my sons cut wood for us during their visits. This year they were cutting up the slab pile on the sawmill landing; all I needed to do was get it to the woodshed. They had offered to haul it, too, but it's a chore both Grandpère and I like doing.

We take the four-wheeler with its trailer. It doesn't hold much, but with a few loads a day we soon fill the shed. Today we go for four trips, heaping the slab chunks so high that the trailer tires go half-flat. Grandpère tells me to go ahead and do what I want while he finishes piling it. None of it is heavy or needs to be split, so I go to the greenhouse to salvage what I can.

The tomato plants stand taller than I do. None of the green ones show that transparency that means frostbite, although the vines are quite limp and look kind of sad. I pick the tomatoes, for they will ripen one by one in the house all fall, supplying us with fresh tomatoes till Christmas or better. Peppers, cucumbers, zucchini and squash all need to go into the house. I go back to get the four-wheel bike, sure that the trailer must be empty by now. The dogs have been whining at me for the past half hour, and now they run ahead of me.

To my surprise the trailer is still quite full. No sign of Grandpère. The dogs are standing by the edge of the porch, looking at me. I say, "What's wrong, boys?" But as I get closer I see what's wrong.

Grandpère is lying in the wet grass, his hat on the ground beside him and his jacket open as though he's sleeping in the summer sun instead of in a puddle of wet grass and mud. I just stand for a moment looking at him, breathless, wondering if he is dead. Then I notice that his chest is moving. He's waking up. I go to help him up, wondering if he's had a heart attack or a stroke and what I should do.

He gives me such a blank look that I am immediately scared.

"Who are you?" he asks me. I'm still wondering how to answer that question when he asks in the same wondering tone, "Where am I?"

Now I know I can't answer, so I help him up to the house and into the bathroom. He keeps asking where we are and calls me Clementine. Then he calls me Annie. I answer to both. He's so wet and muddy that I tell him to take off his wet clothes and I go get him some clean ones. While I have been gone, he's made no move to undress and has wet his jeans. I help him undress, the first time ever, and he makes no resistance till I try to help him get the clean ones on.

"These aren't mine," he tells me. Scared that he's lost his mind, I tell him that they are my husband's, and that Lorne wanted to lend them to him. He lets me help him get dressed, telling me the shirt is mighty nice and it was mighty nice of Lorne to lend it to him.

I'm shaken but ask him if he wants a cup of tea. Why do I always think a cup of tea will fix things?

"Yeah, Granddaughter, I think I do," he answers. Within an hour he remembers who he is and where he is, and everything is just as though it never happened. I ask if he remembers fainting, and he just looks puzzled. "I was piling the wood." His voice trails off and he looks as though he can't quite connect all the dots.

Quickly I change the subject. I want to finish the wood and get the stuff from the greenhouse, but I don't want to leave him, so I putter around in the kitchen and make supper early. He has a healthy enough appetite, and after the meal I feel a little better about leaving him to nap in his favourite easy chair.

He's gone to bed when I get back in the house, so I take the phone to my room and call my friend Rose, a registered nurse who has worked at the retirement home for a long time. Rose is what I call a real healer; she's not just an RN, she's skilled in healing touch, massage and reflexology and keeps learning new methods of healing. She is amazingly gentle and good. She is one of my soul sister friends.

Rose tells me not to worry, it was probably just a ministroke, which the very elderly sometimes have. The brain quickly reroutes the memory, and minutes later they are fine. It may never happen again or it may happen lots. It's the big strokes that kill, she says, and it seems to be as good a way to die as any. One day you're fine and the next you're gone. She is very matter-of-fact about this, and I feel comforted by the time we say goodnight.

In the night I get up three times and stand at his door, listening to see if Grandpère is okay. Each time I am reassured by the gentle snoring that comes from his bed. In the morning he is his usual self, and I tell myself that he worked too hard yesterday. I vow to myself that I won't let him do that again.

The fall days get progressively shorter and colder, and we spend less and less time outside. Every day in the early afternoon we go outside to feed the chickens and get the eggs. I bring in a wheelbarrow load of wood for the stove, and if the weather's nice, we go for walks. We don't walk together; he goes too slowly for me. The old dog always goes with him, and the young one comes with me. Often I'm home before he is.

The evenings are long, and after supper we play crib — usually four games — then settle down to our own pursuits. He whittles little chunks of wood into bird and animal shapes, and I braid rugs, knit, bead and quilt.

Tonight I'm braiding a rug. This skill was passed down over generations from the European grannies; it calls for four strands of rag strips woven together into a circle or an oval. I reflect that the old grannies would be pretty happy today with the fabrics and colours in front of me.

Grandpère says, "Get your book, and I will tell the story from Louisa's father."

"Sure thing." I go and get it. "Fire away."

He closes his eyes and begins, "Louisa's dad came here from Manitoba. He could read and write and had more education than most people. He looked completely Indian, but he was half-white. He spoke mostly French. His wife had been English, but he blamed the English for the deaths of her and his other children. I don't know that whole story, but sometimes when he was drunk, he would cry for her and them and curse the English. He came west with Louisa and Francine when they were about ten and eleven.

"He built a house beside the old Fort, made a garden spot and planted it. They built a deer fence with poles and in the hot days packed water for it. The first winter they had enough extra to trade. Many people in town depended on that family to have enough food to get them through the winter.

"Louisa's father got a wife from up north, and she came to live with them. She and the girls would go to the Catholic church, but he would never go. He said the Catholics and their god betrayed his people. Over and over. This is his people's story.

"His ancestors were from France. They came with the army to fight the British, three brothers in the same unit. They fought beside the native people, then they left the army and moved north by Three Rivers. They married native women and made their own village.

"The part of the family that Louisa's father belonged to worked in the fur trade and pretty soon came out west to Manitoba. They were fine horsemen, those Métis. They loved to hunt the buffalo.

"They brought the church with them. They were all Catholics. They called the priests Father. They trusted the priests would represent them to God and to the government. But something went wrong, and by the time Louisa's father was a young man, the buffalo were all gone, and the people were in hiding. Some lived with the tribes, and some, like Louisa's family, lived in the settlements in the northern States. The men were afraid for their lives and for the safety of their families.

"After some time Louisa's father and mother decided to come back to Canada, but enemies found them and killed her mother and brothers. Louisa's father just kept coming west till he felt he they were safe. He said he had a pardon, but it was a useless piece of paper. He never threw it away, though, because he showed it to me. He would only speak of it when he was drunk. Sober, he never told anyone anything."

Grandpère opened his eyes and looked at me.

"Do you see, Anzel, everybody's story is the same. It is like all the people were children once in their innocence, then they were taken over by empire builders. It doesn't matter if it is an empire in heaven or an empire of land, each one needs people. When we give away our power, it's not good. When you are following someone else's vision, you can't be your own person."

It's a topic we agree on. My husband was Irish, and the same sort of story came down from his family. They were starving when they immigrated to Canada. Lorne's family was scornful of those who wanted to get rich, calling them down for not knowing what enough was. Never in need of a handout, Lorne was proud that he could provide for us, letting me be a stay-at-home mother and buying us our forty acres in the woods. He is still providing for me on my pension; I get a widow's benefit.

"You know, there is something that I'm glad of," I say. "We're pretty free, you and I. We don't have to go to work anywhere, we get plenty from the gardens and we live pretty well on what we get."

"Yeah, well, you just remember that taxes are coming up, so you better save a little for that."

He's always reminding me to save up for bills, it's a habit from living with Esther, his second wife, who would consistently spend more than they had. She loved bingo and gadgets, and she must have owned every electrical kitchen appliance known to mankind. She was never above phoning and asking for loans to cover the power bill or the car repair. I don't think Grandpère ever knew how much we loaned her for keeps.

But as he does more and more lately, he answers my thought. "I know you sent Esther money more than once. I want to thank you for that. She was kind of crazy for a long time."

"No need to thank me. You helped us too when we needed it."

"But Lorne repaid me every cent."

"And you're repaying me for everything I ever gave and more by making my life here good," I say.

He gives me a smile. "I'm not so much help around here now. I think it won't be too long before this old body goes to sleep the big one."

It's the first time he's brought this up since the day he moved in. He told me then that he was an old man and he might die any time, and if he died, he didn't want a big fuss made. At the time I just laughed him off, but now I want to know what he wants.

"When you die, I will take care of things. What do you want me to do?" I ask.

His reply startles me. "I want to go the old way. You make a log pile like a nest, and you line it with moss. You dress people in their best clothes and give them gifts to help them get to the spirit land. You say your last words, then you light the fire. When the fire gets low you heap more wood on it till the bones turn to ash. Then you take whatever is left and you put it in a box. You take it to a spot they liked and leave it there under another pile of sticks."

"You know that's illegal. You can't just bury people wherever you want," I say.

"When has legal ever bothered you so much?" he asks. I laugh, for I am fond of saying there are so many laws a person can't help but break two or three every day just by accident.

"I'll think about that," I tell him and change the subject. "I think I will have the kids home for Christmas this year."

"That would be nice. I haven't seen all of them together for a long time. It might be the last time. Anzel, I am serious about my going. I can't bear the thought of this old body going to strangers who will poke and prod and try to find out why I died. I will die because I am an old man, and I want to go the old way."

He is not going to let me off the hook. "Have you picked out a spot?" I ask him, half in jest.

"Yes, I started building the pile at the sawmill. I wanted to have it ready in case I didn't make it through the winter. But it isn't big enough, it takes a lot of wood to send a person to the other side."

I think about his long walks in the fall. So that was what he was doing for such a long time out in the woods. The thought of the old man building his own funeral pyre makes my eyes fill with tears.

"Don't be upset, Granddaughter. I am at peace with death." He reaches over and pats my knee. "Nearly all the people I have known in my life are there waiting for me."

"I am not crying because you will die. It's the thought of you out there piling sticks for your own grave that bothers me. No one should have to do that. Don't do it anymore, please. When the time comes, I will do what needs to be done."

"Do you promise?" he asks.

"Yes."

He leans back in the chair, contented. I wonder what kind of a crazy promise I've just made. Can I really do what he asks? I decide to talk it over with Clint when he comes at Christmas.

We go to bed, and my dreams are full of fire.

# Chapter Three

The preparations for Christmas are fun. The tree is a fake one, and I don't even take the decorations off it from year to year, just tuck it in the storage shed. The tree is covered with decorations that are mostly homemade by two generations of children. I know who made every one of them. I don't take the Christmas lights off the house, so it's just a matter of plugging them in.

My three boys say they can come, and my daughter's husband and his new wife will come Boxing Day. My daughter Nadine died in a car accident when the girls were tiny — a senseless crash when she was driving to the store for milk — but Faith is a lovely woman who keeps close to our family, for the girls' sake as well as for mine. Darcy was a lucky man to find her. Tammy and Sarah are my oldest grandchildren, both throwbacks to the Native and French side of our family. Both have black hair and eyes, and they are beautiful and smart.

The days leading up to Christmas are cold and windy. Grandpère never seems warm enough. His chair is almost on top of the wood stove, and he is constantly putting another stick of wood in. It is too hot for me, so I move my work table over by the window where it is cooler and gets better light. We while away the hours making gifts for everyone. Grandpère whittles away, making a whole row of ducks and some horses, bears and even a moose. He has trouble with the moose horns, till finally he whittles them right off. He says it's winter, and the horns fall off anyway.

I laugh at him, knowing he will tell the little ones stories about each animal. I bake butter tarts and mincemeat tarts, shortbread and cinnamon rolls and freeze them. I make bread, cabbage rolls, chicken wings and shepherd's pie and freeze those too. When all our company comes, I shouldn't have to cook much. The root cellar is full, and we have lots of the garden harvest stored — more than we can possibly eat in one winter — so I make a mental note to myself to make sure all the kids take stuff home.

The first ones to arrive are Parker and Kristen with their three boys Ezra, Cameron and Coby. The boys are seven, eight and nine. They look as alike as three peas in a pod, all blue-eyed with dark brown hair. They want to go outside and slide down the driveway as soon as they can, so they gulp down their soup and pile on their outdoor clothes. The dogs are so excited that I fear they'll trample the boys, but Parker and Kristen aren't worried. They tell me it's three on two, so the dogs might get trampled instead. We watch them from the window, and I see that the boys have the dogs well in hand. Coby walks back up the hill with his arm draped over the young dog's back.

Kristen is tiny, smaller than I am, but she is a bundle of energy. Now that the boys are in school, she works full-time in an office building in the city. I don't really know what she does, but Parker is proud of her work.

"Kristen got a promotion and a raise for Christmas from her

boss. She is going back in January as head honcho in the office," he tells us.

"I am already head of the office," she grins. "They just finally decided to acknowledge it and pay me what I'm worth."

"She makes more than I do now," Parker says. "Pretty soon I can just stay home, and she can support me in the style I'm accustomed to."

"Try that and you'll soon be looking for a new woman," she retorts, and we all laugh.

They bring in their bags, and I put them in my room. They object to putting me out of my own room, but I show them the bed in the office, and they can see it's comfortable, so they're okay with it. I put a foam mattress and an air mattress on the floor in their room so the boys can all fit in easily. We don't blow up the mattress; the boys can do it.

We are just finished this when Jesse and Jessica arrive. Their truck pulls up honking, and we go to the window to wave. They have one four-year-old boy, Aaron, who is sleeping when they arrive. He wakes up on the way into the house and won't come to me, he just clings to his mother, hiding his face in her shoulder. She says he won't be so shy when he finishes waking up.

I get supper ready, and we have to call the boys in. They've made tracks in the snow all over the yard and a long line of snow angels, made by falling backward into the snow and waving their arms and legs. Jesse has been out with them, pulling them up carefully so as not to smudge the angel prints. His little boy didn't want to go out — he wanted to watch TV — but Grandpère and I haven't had TV for several years. He couldn't hear it unless it was blaring, and I don't care to watch TV. We have some movies, though, and Aaron is content to watch *Cinderella* on the computer screen in the office, curled up on my cot and sucking his thumb.

Jesse and Jessica married when they were in their thirties, and Aaron was born when Jessica was thirty-five. I think it is old to have children, but more and more young women are working through their twenties and having kids later. I have a hard time liking Jessica. She doesn't have anything nice to say. When she talks about things, she tells everyone what she doesn't like instead of what she likes. She has already told me what a bad job the road crew is doing, how bad the restaurant meal was on the way here, and all about her friend Jackie, who is going through a messy divorce. Jackie came with them last time, so I know her. It seems she and her husband are fighting about everything, doing it through lawyers and the courts. Jessica sounds quite self-satisfied as she relates their squabbles, and I think it's mean to talk to me about her friend's personal business. She is my son's wife, the mother of my grandson, and I want to like her, but I just don't.

Kristen seems able to distract her, and they talk about the kids. Jessica says Aaron has been to the naturopath, and he is allergic to wheat and milk. I wonder what I am going to feed him, but Jessica has that under control. She has brought soy milk, juice boxes and a box full of packaged things for him to eat. At the supper meal she lets him watch the movie while we all sit around the table. I hope he isn't getting supper all over my bed, but I don't need to worry, since he hasn't touched any of it.

After supper Kristen and I do the dishes, and when we get to the living room, the older boys are hanging around Grandpère's chair. They want him to tell a story.

"I will tell you of the battle of the giants," he starts. "Once long ago, when there were few people on the earth, there lived a race of giants. They were living all over the earth. One day a land bridge came up from the bottom of the sea, and a giant walked across to this country. The animals and the people were afraid, but the giant made friends with them. The giant would walk around, and his tracks would leave lakes and ponds behind. He would lie down for a nap, and when he woke and moved on, grassy meadows were left behind. His name was Ice Fisher, and he was bald because of his head brushing the sky.

"Ice Fisher and the people lived in peace for many years, but the giant was lonely for others of his kind. He went back across the bridge and was gone for a long time, and when he returned, he had a woman with him. Everyone rejoiced to see him. He was not back for long when another giant arrived. He came with a storm, ripping up earth with his giant hands and wanting to fight. He wanted the woman giant. Ice Fisher and the stranger fought for many days. They made thunder in the skies, and their weapons made slashes in the earth.

"In the heat of the battle a Dené man, a friend of Ice Fisher who was very brave, came close to the strange giant and cut the back of his leg with an axe. The bad giant fell back onto the land with his feet in the western sea and his head in our northern lands. Over time the giant's body became a huge mountain, and the caribou used his body for migration.

"Our people lived below the head of the giant, where they would meet the caribou. Every year the caribou came and gave themselves to the people for meat and clothes, thread and horn and bone. The people grew strong and spread out all over the land."

Ezra asks, "What happened to the good giant and his girlfriend?"

"I don't know. The time of the giants was long ago. They probably went to the other side."

"What other side?"

"The spirit side, where everyone goes when they are done living," Grandpère explains.

"Is that where Grandpa lives now?" Cameron asks.

Kristen looks at me to see if this question bothers me, but I have made peace with Lorne's passing, and I answer him myself.

"Yes. Grandpa is having fun with his friends there."

"Thank you for the story, Grandpère, I hope another giant comes here so I can see one," puts in Coby. He thinks for a minute and adds, "I hope it's one of the good giants. If it's a bad one, I'll chop him down."

"You better get big and strong before you chop down giants," Grandpère tells him.

"I am strong already," he says, bending up his arm to show us his muscles. I reach out and squeeze his upper arm.

"Wow, you sure must work hard," I say to him.

"Yep, I sure do. I help my dad a lot, and me and Cameron and Ezra go to tae kwon do."

Now the other boys are hauling up their shirt sleeves, and we have to admire everyone's tiny muscles.

Aaron comes out of the office and says he is hungry. His mother opens a package of noodles and pours hot water over them. She explains that the noodles are made from pea flour and this is one of the things he really likes. I want to feed him some real food, but I let it go for the time being.

Happy now, he sits on my lap while the noodles soak. "Do you know Santa is coming here?" he asks me.

"Yes, I do. I sent him a letter and told him that we will have eight boys here, so he doesn't need to go to your house this year."

"We got you a yellow sweater, but we wrapped it up so you can't see it," he tells me cheerfully.

"Aaron, you aren't supposed to tell her what it is," the three older boys say in a chorus. He looks crestfallen, but I snuggle him in closer and tell him, "I guessed anyway."

Parker laughs and says, "He keeps a secret as well as I do." Parker was always the one who couldn't wait to give his gifts. I don't think there ever was a Christmas when he was young when his gift was a surprise.

Aaron eats the noodles and goes with the other boys to blow up the air mattress. The pump is foot-operated, and they squabble about whose turn it is and how long each of them gets to use it. Pretty soon they decide to count the pumps, and each one gets ten. Almost as much air leaks out between personnel changes as they put into it. We laugh from the other room, knowing that by the time the mattress is pumped up, they'll be ready to use it.

We talk of the farm, what a good harvest we had and what a beautiful fall it was. Jesse asks me if Grandpère and I got enough wood in.

"Yes, we brought two bike-trailer loads in every morning," I answer, but the thought of the wood and Grandpère's fit, and the use he wanted to put the rest of the slab pile to, set my heart and mind racing, and I quickly change the subject.

We all go to bed pretty early. The kids are worn out from travelling and playing, and Grandpère and I usually don't stay up late. I've made up a bed for Aaron in the room with his dad and mom, but he gets into bed with them. That's why I put them in the room with the queen-sized bed. He always sleeps in their bed. I guess it's not really my business, but it bugs me. I feel sorry for Jesse. What kind of a sex life can they have with a four-year-old kid in between them? Not your business, I sternly remind myself.

In the morning Grandpère and I get up at six-thirty. We are being really quiet. We haven't spoken, but we have been communicating. I think he has taught me sign unconsciously, because I understand him when he tells me all my children are slugabeds. I sign back that my grandchildren are too. We don't laugh, but grin at each other as loudly as we can.

He lets me know we should eat when the kids get up. He points to his mouth and his stomach, and his hand indicates the table with seats all around. Then he holds up his hand in a wait gesture.

I shake my head no. I point to the clock, indicate both hands up, and shrug maybe.

We roll our eyes a bit, and I get us each a spoon and a bowl of berries with yogurt. All the berries are good this year. I've thawed out huckleberries and raspberries. He gives me a nod of thanks, and we have just barely begun to eat when Ezra and Cameron get up. They tiptoe out of the bedroom and come to lean on me.

I whisper to them, "Do you want some berries and yogurt?"

They both nod. It seems they know quiet talk too.

By the time I get their berries, Coby has emerged, rubbing his eyes and stretching. I give him my bowlful of berries and go off to make breakfast. Those boys will not be quiet for long.

Today is Christmas Eve. Clint and Patty expect to arrive before noon. The boys are all in a state of high excitement by the time breakfast is over. Their cousins are coming, and they will get to see the "new baby Seth," as they call him. The last time they were all together was at Easter, as they've never managed to coordinate their visits all year.

Aaron eats bacon but can't have pancakes because of the flour in them. He can have berries but can't have yogurt, no milk products even. He can have goat milk, but one swallow is enough for him. He shakes his head, sticks out his tongue and shudders. "Yuck. I don't like that. Goat milk is gross."

"It's good for you. It will make you grow big and strong," says Grandpère.

"I'll drink it," says Coby, taking the glass and drinking it all.

Jessica brings Aaron a glass of soy milk, which he drinks down with no problem. I tasted it one time when they were here and had much the same reaction as Aaron had to the goat milk. I guess it's all in what you get used to.

Clint and Patty arrive, and we set them up in the biggest room. They've brought a playpen for the baby, and the older boys have their own sleeping bags. They say they are going to camp out in the living room tonight and watch for Santa. The other boys say they want to do that, too, so I say they can all sleep there if they promise to go to sleep, otherwise Santa won't come. For now they should put their bags in the room with their parents'. Off they race.

Patty hands Kristen the new baby, only he isn't such a baby now. He is like a little butterball. We put him on the floor sitting up with pillows all around in case he crashes. The boys lie around him for a while, trying to make him laugh, which he does. He seems to think his brothers and cousins are the funniest things he has ever seen. He sits there and laughs and smiles and slobbers, leans over too far and crashes into the pillows. The older boys think this is hilarious, and they're all giggling, so the baby thinks it's funny and he laughs more. We laugh at the boys laughing, and the world feels good.

Soon they tire of playing with the baby and want to go outside. Jesse, Parker and Clint want to get their dad's old snow machine running, so they bundle up all the older boys — even Aaron and Pierre — in their snowsuits, toques, mitts and winter boots. Cameron complains that his boots are cold, so Parker feels them. The felt pack is sopping wet; he must have filled them with snow yesterday. Grandpère tells Cameron to bring him the insoles, and he will get them dried over the stove. I go and get two pair of woollen socks and put them on over Cameron's. "We'll pretend it's a double insole," I tell him. He looks skeptical but shoves his foot in his boot, wiggles around a bit and nods.

"Thanks, guys," he says and races out after the others.

"I'm a guy too," Kristen says in answer to my raised eyebrows. "It's an honour, so get used to it. At least he remembered to thank us." We laugh.

The day passes quickly. Grandpère and my sons have the heater going in the shop and the kids want to roast hot dogs in it. I don't have wieners but I have lots of moose sausage given to us by Lorne's hunting partner. He knows how we love moose meat and brings us some every year.

I give the boys a big coil of sausage, some dinner buns, ketchup, mustard and a jug of juice. They take it out to the shop for a picnic. "Don't forget to make some for your dads," I yell after them. Jessica takes some soup out for Aaron, who can have the sausage but not the bun.

A couple of hours later I hear the high-pitched whine of the snow machine, and Jesse pushes Aaron and Pierre, both crying, into the house. They are scared of the noise, he says. I take their outside clothes off and give them cookies.

"It's just like the four-wheeler. It's fun to ride and it goes fast," I tell Pierre, thinking of how much he loves the four-wheel bike.

"Too loud," he says, putting his little hands over his ears.

We watch through the window. The men have piled all five kids on the car hood that Lorne called his sleigh, and Parker and his brothers are taking turns pulling them around. Lorne used it to get firewood in the winter, but it seems to work fairly well as a sled bus too. We watch Parker take Grandpère for a gentle circle around the yard, sitting behind him on the snowmobile, then he brings him right up to the door, where he crawls off and doffs his hat. He reaches out and shakes Parker's hand.

Jessica comes over to look out and realizes that Aaron has a cookie. She snatches it away, ready to rant at him or me, so I tell her I made the cookies with buckwheat flour; Aaron can have it. He gives me a grateful look, and I am almost not sorry I lied about the flour. How can a tablespoon of wheat flour hurt a kid one way or the other? Then I realize it has milk in it too. Two sins in one cookie. I warn myself to keep an eye on him for a couple of hours to make sure he doesn't swell up or get sick. It's a good thing I keep allergy medicine in the cupboard.

After the busy day we all have a fairly early night, letting all seven boys line up their sleeping bags by the tree. When Aaron sees where the boys are sleeping, he wants to sleep there too. Jessica puts diaper underwear under his pajamas. I ask her if he still wets the bed. She says he doesn't, it's just a precaution. Poor kid; he's going to have issues with trust.

Christmas Day is one of those perfect winter days when the sun is bright and the reflection on the snow sets a million sparkles to shining. It's just below freezing with no wind. After the gift unwrapping mayhem in the morning, we take everyone outside. Even Seth rides in a backpack on Clint's shoulders.

Grandpère thinks this is especially funny and calls him Papoose Man. I asked him if he never packed his own kids, for he had my four uncles and my mother.

"Never. Never. If a man packed a papoose like that, he might get called a papoose man. You can put down the baby, but maybe you have to carry that name forever. Your grandmother carried our babies."

We look at each other. So many people are gone from our world, yet here out in this yard are all these new people, exuberant and excited, growing toward their own futures. I feel so much love for all of them, and a contentment with life overwhelms me. I say a silent thank you to the universe for this life of ease and luxury.

Boxing Day brings Darcy and Faith with their girls Sarah and Tammy. I don't see them so much now because they live up in Dawson Creek, but when the girls were young, they lived with us for three years after the car crash. Time has lifted the sting out of my daughter's death, but there is still a grief pang in my heart that misses her so much. Sarah and Tammy help fill that hole; Tammy is so like her mom in looks, and Sarah is so like her in nature. They call me Anzel. I taught them to do that when they were young, for I couldn't bear it when they called me Mom. When Darcy told us he was going to marry Faith, all I could think was that I was losing my girls, but when I met her and grew to love her gentle nature, I was glad for them all.

The girls rush in, hugging everyone and passing out gifts all around. They've brought Grandpère a pair of moccasins; the tops are beaded solid with seed beads, and the toes have concentric rows of circles in a beautiful design. They explain that they went to the museum and saw ones like them, but they had to buy slippers and sew the tops on, or else they might have been the ugliest moccasins ever. And, they point out, the slippers have a nice grippy sole.

Grandpère puts them on and does a few fancy, but slow, jig steps. He grins at everyone and sits down. "Still remember the old steps, but I can't make this old body do them."

I think he is pretty tickled that he can still do any of them.

Darcy says they drove halfway last night so they can spend the whole day here. The man is a workaholic. He has his laptop with him, and after visiting with us for a short time, he disappears into the office to "just do a couple of things that I should have done before I left." His brothers-in-law tell him to do it fast, as the sled team is about to saddle up.

The women all decide to stay in the house, and we sit around the living room, playing with the baby. Faith says he is the cutest baby she has ever seen. Darcy had a vasectomy after Sarah was born, so there's no hope for Faith to have a baby by the time-honoured method. She claims not to care, that Tammy and Sarah are her girls, but she always seems to have a soft spot for the babies. I think she has called each successive nephew the cutest one ever.

It is colder out today, and soon the sledders troop back in, letting clouds of cold air billow through the doorway.

"You can use that sled any time now, Mom," Jesse tells me. "We got the electric start working. Dad had a brand new battery on the bench, so we just added the acid and charged it. You should take it out in the spring and recharge it next fall."

Jesse is under the impression that I can do anything. I probably can take the battery out of the snowmobile in the spring, but I probably won't. Parker tells me not to bother anyway, since he'll do it when he's out at breakup.

We make an early meal, mostly of leftovers from yesterday's feast remade into turkey soup, vegetable pie and four big casseroles. I bake the biggest moose roast from the freezer, which must be twelve pounds with no bone in it. Everyone loves it and laments that they never get moose meat anymore. When Lorne was alive, we always had moose meat and other wild game, but the boys have not gone hunting since.

Ryan, however, is just itching to get old enough to go hunting. Clint says Ryan's going to get his firearms licence and hunting licence in the spring. They're two separate courses, but only a couple of days each. Grandpère snorts at this and says it takes at least ten years to train a hunter, not two days. Clint holds his ground, though, and tells Grandpère it's not as though he's completely green, since he's gone hunting with his dad.

After supper Clint grabs Lorne's fiddle, and Darcy pulls out his. We pull all the furniture to the wall and take turns doing the jig. There are over thirty different steps in the jig, but we don't know them all, so our dances are usually a couple of steps each. Then we bow in front of another person, who gets up and does his own piece. It's fun, and some of our dance steps must be originals, but nobody cares if they're right or not. When it's Parker's turn, he holds his arms totally rigid at his sides, and uses a crossover step that tilts his upper body back and forth sideways. This is one of the traditional steps, and the young boys are impressed.

Each one in his turn tries to emulate him, with Grandpère tapping out the beat on the floor with the butt of his stick, the two fiddlers working their way through "Liza Jane" and "Whiskey Before Breakfast," then into "The Woodchopper's Reel," and the rest of us clapping out the rhythm. What a great way to end Boxing Day.

The girls sleep in the office with me, and we whisper to each other far into the night. They have boyfriends and cellphones and talk to each other sometimes about things that I know nothing about. Their cellphones connect to the internet and have hundreds of hours of music stored in little computer chips. They let me listen to their best song ever, but to me it just sounds raucous and tinny through the little earbuds. We have a great night.

In the morning everyone leaves right after breakfast except Clint and Patty, who have taken an extra day off. I pack them huge lunches and give them all bags of produce from the root cellar. We wave goodbye from the living room window, and suddenly four kids and four adults seems quiet.

It's warm again today. Grandpère falls asleep in the sun, and so does the baby. Patty goes outside with the three older boys, and Clint and I sit down to a cup of coffee in the kitchen.

He nods at the old man. "Feeling his age this winter, eh, Mom?"

I tell him quietly about Grandpère's little stroke but am quick to add that he hasn't had any more.

"You know you can call me whenever you need me," he says.

I know he's talking about when death comes calling. I'd planned to tell him what Grandpère wants me to do when he dies, but for some reason I don't.

"If he gets too much for you to handle, maybe Rose can get him into the home," he says.

"That's the reason he's here, so he doesn't have to go to the home," I reply.

"Mom, you're not getting any younger, and he is so old. All I'm saying is that maybe he will get harder to look after, and if that happens, we'll help pay for him to live there."

"That's very generous of you, Clint, and I thank you for the offer, but right now we're doing fine."

I give him a big hug, but he's not much of a hugger — usually a tenth-of-a-second squeeze and a couple of shoulder pats — but today he returns my hug generously and kisses my cheek. It makes tears come to my eyes, and I am surprised to see his eyes full too. I pat him some more and tell him not to worry about us, we're fine.

The next morning Clint's family leaves, too, and suddenly it's really quiet. It's still warm, so Grandpère and I put on our jackets to go outside. At least we try, but the sleeves of both our jackets are sewn shut. It sends us into giggles and much speculation about who did it. My bet is on Sarah, but Grandpère thinks maybe Parker.

The kids have brought us wire grippers to go around our boots, and we stretch them on. Wow! You could walk over glare ice with these on. I show Grandpère how I can run on the ice.

"I think maybe I will walk," he says, "but if you want, you can run circles around me."

I decline.

I haven't tended to the chickens for days, since the kids have done the chores. The chickens haven't laid well, and I think the commotion has put them off, but now I find the reason. One old hen likes to sit on the eggs in her nest and stay there while her friends crowd in beside her and lay theirs. Today she's sitting on twelve eggs, and I guess that none of the boys was brave enough to stick his hands in the nest for fear of getting pecked — and not willing to admit it to anyone either. I tell Grandpère we are having a lot of eggs tomorrow, and we laugh about the kids being scared of chickens.

# Chapter Four

New Year's Day is bright and sunny but cold. The thermometer dips to minus thirty, and we decide to stay home. We've been invited to Rose's for dinner, but I phone to cancel, and she understands. We promise to get together soon.

Grandpère says his New Year's resolution is to tell me more about his life so I can write it down for him, if I'm still willing. "I better get to it before I'm too old to remember it or too dead to tell it." He grins to show me neither death nor age is weighing on him very heavily. "There was always work to do at the Fort. I worked most of the time in the bush, but many of the people moved in from the bush. Louisa's sister, Francine, and her husband, my cousin Tsa'a'lax — that means Angry Eyes — moved in and built a place beside us. In town they called him Alex. Francine did not like to live in the bush, and Alex said it was getting harder and harder to find the animals that we always lived with in the woods.

"Many trappers who were not our people were taking all of them, he said. He said these people took all the animals they could find and didn't even leave any to make new animals for the next season. They would even steal from our traps, and did not respect our territories. We didn't feel safe in our lands. Alex and Francine had been hungry in the winter before they came in to town, and they didn't have many furs to trade.

"We made them welcome, and we all helped them build a home. Louisa and Francine's father was happy. We were all working. Sometimes we traded for goods in the store, and sometimes we were paid in coin. Always the store tried to trade rum or brandy to us, but we knew better. Some of our people traded everything for booze and did not have anything left for food when they sobered up. It was very bad. When the people drink rum, they lose all their sense. They work all the time to get furs to trade and then have nothing to show for it but a two-week drunk, and then they go hungry. Gradually our people moved in, family by family. Pretty soon no one traded.

"Some moved into town so their children could go to the school. If you didn't put the children in school, government men came and took them away, and you only got to see them in summer. My Uncle Tree had eleven children, all younger than me. He said the government was not going to get his children and moved far into the bush. But they found him anyway and took his children far away where he could not even find them. The four oldest died in the schools. They only left the babies, and when they got older, they took them too. It was very hard on Uncle Tree's woman, and when the last child was taken, she went out in the bush and hanged herself from a tree. She died, I think, of a broken heart.

"The children, who were very happy in the bush, did not do very well in school except for my one cousin who they called Joan. I don't remember what her real name was. She forgot our language and did not want to go to the bush even in the summer.

She stayed with our family the first few years when the rest went home. When she was grown, she helped at the Catholic school. She married a white man who was very mean, then she caught TB and died before she had any children. TB was a bad disease in those days — we called it consumption — and people would get thin and weak and cough up blood till they died.

"Uncle Tree moved in to the town and took up with a woman who drank all the time, and so did Uncle Tree. When the children came home there was not enough food or space. They would not build a house, because every year when he got the children back, he said they were going back to the bush. We did what we could to make it better for them. Louisa, Francine and Clementine had made the garden very big, and we always had more than we could eat. Many a time our little house had so many children in it that we were glad when the school started again. Our own children went to the tiny school in town, and they all went up to grade eight. They grew up in town, but the boys wanted to hunt and trap, and we always spent the early winters on the traplines. It was true that there were not very many animals left in the woods, and I would not have liked to try to live the way we always had, because we would have starved.

"The white people called us all Indians and half-breeds and did not pay us as much as they paid white men, but we always had enough. The English people called us savages, but the English were far more savage than any of our people, especially when they were drinking.

"I spent a lot of time logging with my horses in the winter. I had traded for two big mares that were quiet and gentle. I worked with a white man named George who had a wild team. We had a contract to bring in firewood for the winter, and we always had orders for square timbers for building. It was easy to do the firewood, which other men sawed to length in the town, but it was a lot of work to square off the building trees. We did it all with axes, and we could sometimes do four in one day. The boys could help us when they were done school. We would bring the trees to the landing in the morning and in the afternoons we would square them.

"One day George's team ran away when he was hooking up and ran over him with the log. He broke both his legs and was screaming. We came to him, and one leg had the bone sticking right out through his clothes. We put him in the wagon and pulled him to town, but he passed out when we moved him. There was a doctor at the town who set his legs. One leg got better, but the bad one never did, and the doctor cut it off right at the top. He could never work in the bush after that, and I finished the winter by myself.

"Alex came and worked with me, but he didn't like the horses, and George's team was too crazy for anyone else to use. We traded them to a guy down south, and they turned out to be good horses after he had them for a while. I think they were wild because George was wild. He was loud and mean with the animals, but he was very good with his axe. His timbers were always good. Alex was not so good at making the timbers, but he was very nice to work with. We finished the contract, but after that I only did logs for firewood. When the boys got bigger, they sawed the wood into lengths. We had a long saw with handles at both ends that two people pulled back and forth between them. It was a very fast way to saw, not as fast as a power saw, but almost.

"We had a barn for the horses, and they had colts almost

every year. The colts would be left in the barn when we worked the team, and by spring every year they would be gentle. None of them grew as big as their mothers because the stud was a saddle horse who was out with the herd in the summers. The people who travelled out in the bush always wanted them for packhorses because they were bigger than an ordinary saddle horse, and almost all of them had a quiet nature from being handled when they were colts.

"One year I kept two and gelded them for use on the sleigh. They almost looked the same, big red horses with white faces. Clementine used to harness them up and bring your mother and the boys out to the bush. In the summer we would use that team when we travelled out. We had a meadow just north of the town. The railway goes through it now. Every year we would cut that meadow and bring the hay in for the winter. We stacked it behind the barn and covered it. If we didn't have enough in the spring, we had to struggle to find food for them. No one liked doing that, and it would just be hard to keep them alive, since they can't do well on willow like the moose can. So we made sure we had enough.

"No one had equipment to do haying, so we cut it by hand. No tractor could have hayed that meadow anyway — it was soft muskeg — but the wild grasses grew as high as my head. We cut the grass and made loose piles, then when it dried we hauled it home in the wagon and made a stack. It wasn't hard work; it was kind of fun. We would pick berries lots of the times when we were haying.

"Things changed very fast as our old way of life disappeared, but the new ways made life easier for us. Many of the old people did not like the changes and tried to keep their traditions, but new laws and new ways made it hard for them. Many of our traditions became against the law. The Mounties had four men in the town and made a jail where many of our people spent a lot of their time.

"There was work building the railway, and the road south changed from a trail to a highway."

His voice fades out here, and I look up at him. He leans back in his chair and closes his eyes. He's silent for a long time, then he leans forward and tells me that's all for now.

He asks me to bring in a couple of the sticks he'd put in the shed in the summertime, as he thinks he will make some more walking sticks. I'm going out anyway to make sure the chickens' heat lamp is still on, for the bitter cold of the day is sure to be followed by an even colder night. I take the scraps out to them, and since their water dish is frozen, I scoop up a pail of snow. The chickens don't really need water in the winter if they have snow. There are only two eggs, frozen almost solid. I give one to each dog, and they pack the eggs in their mouths back into the doghouse.

In the shop there are about a dozen pine sticks. On spring days Grandpère wanders through the woods and ties the tops of young pine trees in a knot. Then the following year he cuts them. The top where he has tied them grows into a loop that makes a handle. They are all different shapes, so I pick out two with the nicest tops and take them in to him. He sets them by the stove to thaw out, and I get him a cardboard box to shave the bark into. I also bring in an armload of dry slabs to keep the fire going. He's moved his chair close to the fire, which crackles pleasantly and sends heat all through the living room and kitchen. We have the electric heat on too, and the house stays warm even in the far bedroom. When it is warmer, we turn the electric heat off, but in this cold we need both.

I go off to type up this last bit from him, but before I get started, I hear the dogs barking and go to the window to see what the commotion is about. It is Rose in her Jeep. Now she's walking toward the house, carrying a large picnic basket with handles. I greet her at the door with a big hug. She is one of my closest friends, and today she's supposed to be having a New Year's party and dinner.

"What are you doing here?" I ask.

"Everyone who was supposed to come phoned and cancelled because of the cold, so I decided to come here," she explains. "I only have two days off, and damned if I'm going to spend them by myself."

She has brought supper with Grandpère's favourite dessert, berry pie. She goes over to the stove and gives Grandpère a hug too.

"Well, you old reprobate, I hope you're keeping busy."

"I don't do much anymore, Rose. Anzel waits on me hand and foot," he tells her.

"There's nothing to do for him," I laugh. "He is so darned independent that I need to tie him in the chair so I can look after him."

She laughs and says to him, "Somehow I can't see you letting her tie you in your chair. You would probably cut your way out and hit her with a stick for being so bold."

We all laugh. She is the same age as me and could have taken early retirement when I did, but she is so good at the home that they asked her to stay on. She loves her job and is more than happy to keep working. She is tall and thin, with long grey hair that is wound up on her head in a bun and held with clips. She dresses and moves with style and energy. Today she has on a long skirt, and when I comment on the skirt being cold for the weather, she shows us that she has on two skirts, one overtop of the other, and a pair of woollen long johns underneath.

"I put these under my clothes in September and take them off in May. If it gets any colder, I'm going to double them up." She asks, "Grandpère, how did you live in the bush when it was this cold?"

"I don't think we felt the cold the way we do now. We had warm clothes made out of fur, and we didn't bathe so much. It was considered unhealthy to get wet in the winter, and we always had a fire. A fire heats a small space a lot better than it heats a big house like this. We had flat rocks that warmed up by the fire, and we rotated them around to keep everybody warm. All us children slept together, and when my father was trapping, my mother slept with us too. All winter we didn't let the fire go out, because it was too hard to get it going again."

"Oh yeah, no matches," Rose says.

"We made fire with a dry stick. You wrapped a thong around it and pulled it back and forth in a small hollow in another dry stick till you saw smoke. Then you held it to a small pile of dry shavings mixed with pitch. Then you blew very gently on it till you had a small blaze. Sometimes it would take a long time, so it was better if we made sure it never went out. You could heap the ashes on the coals of the fire, and it would still be hot even if you were gone for several days. But when it was cold like this, we always kept it going. My father had a flint that struck sparks to start fires, but more often we used a fire stick. I can remember the first time I saw a match. I thought it was so clever."

"That must have been a hard life."

"No, it wasn't hard. It was just the way it was, and we were happy to go and find firewood, it was just one of the things that people did to live. Although it would be hard to go back to that way after having matches and paper. Maybe I am just getting soft."

"No," Rose says. "You don't even know what soft is. Some of the people in the home are soft. They can't dress themselves or even walk. They need people to help them do every little thing. We need to spoon the food into them. They give up on even trying. That's soft."

"I wonder why they don't die, if they are that far gone?" he says.

"Actually, I think they are already mostly gone. Their bodies are still alive, but the essence of who they were is missing," Rose says. "Their spirit is gone, but their bodies continue to live, because the body has its own will to live, even when their soul has called the spirit home." She sounds positive about this.

Grandpère nods. "In the old times, when the Great Spirit called them home, sometimes the old people would disappear in the bush. Sometimes we found them and other times not. We would sing for them and burn their possessions to help them find their way."

"I think it was a better way," says Rose. "It's not very dignified to continue living when your body is alive but unoccupied."

"Well, I think I will keep body and spirit together for a while yet. I still like to be on this earth, even though this old body has seen better days," Grandpère says.

Rose spends the afternoon with us, and we have an early dinner so she can get home before it gets dark, which is about four-thirty at this time of the year. She has brought us a carrot salad and a whole roast chicken stuffed with rice. We three eat the whole chicken and still manage to put down the pie. We are content, and I compliment her on her good cooking. She tells me that it was not all that special, food just tastes better when you don't have to cook it yourself. She should know; she's been alone for over ten years now since her husband passed over. She seldom gets to see her only child, a daughter who lives in England. She went there for a holiday after high school and met and married her husband there. They have visited only three times, and Rose has been there twice. It think it's a good thing that Rose has a job that she enjoys, for it is lonely for an older person to live by herself.

She has been telling us about the Wii game that the lodge bought to entertain the old folks. She tells me that I should buy one, that Grandpère and I would both like it. It sounds weird to me, but I tell her I will look around next time I'm in town.

Rose keeps up on current events, and she is full of excitement that a black man is running for president of the USA. I'm impressed too; I never thought I would see the day. Grandpère says it would be even more surprising if an Indian was running. Rose is worried about the recession and says that people are losing all their savings.

"Serves them right, silly buggers, trusting the banks with all their money," he says. "Those banks are just stealing their money. The banks can print more money any time they want." Grandpère never did trust banks. He's more liable to put his money in a jar and bury it than to hand it over to a bank.

I'm inclined to agree with him. Lorne and I never did have any savings. He always said, "Money ain't got no home," and we spent any extra money we ever had. We didn't waste it; we paid for our home and car, and his shop is still full of tools and toys. Sometimes I think we should have a garage sale, but the idea of selling his stuff somehow seems wrong to me yet. I don't use much of it, but it's comforting to know that the things he treasured are still right where he left them. The boys use his shop when they are here and keep it tidy.

Rose says she has to go and gives us big hugs. I tell her to come again soon. She has a quiet word with me at the door to say that Grandpère looks great, and if I ever need her to just call. She is such a lovely person. I thank her again and tell her to drop by whenever she feels the notion.

What a great afternoon on this cold New Year's Day. We let the dogs into the porch for the night. It's cold enough in the porch but a lot warmer than outside.

Over the next week the weather stays cold, and we stay indoors except for brief jaunts out to tend the chickens and bring in more firewood. The weather finally breaks with a Chinook wind that brings rain and warmth. The snow slides off the tin roof with a noise like an avalanche, and the rain pours down, turning our snow into a blue sea. The driveway and the yard are covered with a thick layer of ice when it cools off the next week.

We have used more firewood than usual, and I decide to fire up the snowmobile to bring in another load from the landing. I hook up the car hood and strap my snowshoes behind the seat, just in case the snowmobile breaks down and I end up walking.

The electric start works well, and I'm soon on my way with the dogs running behind me. There is a good crust on the snow, and the machine doesn't break through. It is only a short jaunt to the landing, but when I try to turn around, the machine sinks through the crust and gets stuck on something. A big pile of wood. I put on the snowshoes and pack the snow down in front of the snowmobile. Then I see the problem. The ski has hooked under a big slab sticking out from the pile. It is frozen in place and will not budge, even with all my strength and a pry pole. I snowshoe back to the house and get a hand saw.

The sun is out in a blue sky, and even though it is cold, I am sweating like a hog by the time I get back with the saw. It doesn't take very long to cut off the log, and then I have no trouble getting the wood piled high on the car hood. With the weight behind the snowmobile, it plows through the crust the whole way back, sending frozen spray over the hood that stings like needles on my face.

When I get back to the house, Grandpère is out in the yard. He was getting worried about how long I was gone and was coming to look for me. I tease him for worrying about me, and he laughs back, but I can see he is relieved that I am safe and sound. He helps me unload the wood into the shed, and we are just going back into the house when a taxi pulls up.

It is unusual for a taxi to come out here, so we both just stop and stare. A young girl gets out of the back. She looks vaguely familiar, but I can't quite place who she is. She comes up and asks me if my name is Anzel O'Flaherty. I tell her yes.

"My mom told me you were my grandmother," she says. "Can I stay here for a while?"

The girl looks like she's on her last legs, and even though I'm pretty sure I don't have any grandchildren I don't know, I tell her, "Yes, you can."

She pulls a ratty suitcase out of the taxi and pays the driver. He waves and drives off, and we are left staring at each other.

I tell her to come in and get warm. Many questions are burning in my mind, but first I tell her that I'm going to make lunch and she should put her stuff in the bedroom. She comes back and sits at the table, silent. Her hair is long and dark, and her eyes are as blue as the sky outside the window, but she has dark circles under them and her face is covered with pimples. Her clothes are not clean, but her jeans are patched neatly and her blouse is buttoned right up to the neck.

I ask, "Who is your mother, dear?"

She speaks so quietly I can barely hear her. "Jane Moberly."

I stare at her, and the name comes shooting up through my memories like a dart. Jane was my youngest son's girlfriend when he died. I look closely at her and realize that the reason she looks so familiar is that she looks like Ben. Her hair is dark — his was reddish brown — but the shape of her face and those blue eyes are his. Jane moved away after the accident, and I haven't heard of her since. That was over thirteen years ago.

"Does your mother know you are here?" I ask.

"No," she replies. "She doesn't care about me. I ran away. I didn't know where to go, but I've had your address for a long time, and it was the only place I could think of to come." She dissolves into tears, and I sit beside her and put my arms around her. She is as tense as a wild cat, and she sobs as though her heart is breaking.

"Now, now. Now, now," I keep whispering. Inside I am astonished that a little piece of Ben has returned to me after all these years. This distraught teenager is one of my own. What am I going to do with her?

Grandpère comes and sits on the other side and pats her knee. She pulls away from him, and I shake my head, no. He nods and goes into the living room. She finally calms down and relaxes a bit. I dish us up the hot soup and call Grandpère back into the kitchen. She doesn't talk but eats as though she's starving, downing three bowls of soup and two sandwiches before she's finished.

"Thank you, that was very good," she says, and she says it just as Grandpère does. I smile at her and ask if she wants anything else. She says she is really tired, she has been on the bus all night and hasn't slept. If it's okay, she would like to have a sleep. I tell her to sleep if she wants, and she goes into the bedroom and shuts the door. Later on I try to look in on her to see if she wants some supper, but the door is locked, and I don't knock. I just let her sleep.

Grandpère and I talk about her, wondering why Jane never told us about her. He agrees that she looks like Ben, and he says the Great Spirit must have sent her here. He never calls the Great Spirit by the name God; he says that God is cruel and unjust, but the Great Spirit is a kind and good provider who would never do the things that God has been credited with doing.

I wonder why this girl thinks that Jane doesn't care about her and why she's run away. She still hasn't gotten up by the time we go to bed, so my curiosity will have to wait till the next day. We don't even know what her name is. I mix up some frozen orange juice and put some cookies on a plate and set them just outside the bedroom door.

In the morning she is up before I am. When I get up, she is looking at the pictures of my children and their families on the living room wall.

"Is this my dad?" she asks, pointing to the picture of Ben on his graduation day.

"Yes," I tell her, and take down the picture. She sits at the table and looks at the picture for a long time as though she's memorizing it.

"I only have one picture of him," she says, getting a picture of Ben out of her wallet. It is dog-eared and faded, but it is a good picture. He's laughing and sitting on the picnic table in this yard. I can remember the day the picture was taken. It was in the summer, before the accident. Jane is sitting in front of him, and they look young and carefree. His shining hair is long and blowing in the wind, and he is smiling down at her, his hand resting on her shoulder. Her face is turned in profile to the camera, looking up at him. They were waiting for Lorne to come back from town so they could go fishing when Jane asked me to take a picture of them with her camera.

"I think I took that picture," I say. "Where does your mother live now?"

"In Vancouver. I can't go back there," she says with such a look of anxiety that I reassure her right away that she doesn't have to.

"I think we should phone and tell her where you are, though. She must be worried," I say.

"She probably doesn't even know I'm missing," she says in a tone of utter dejection. "She hasn't been home for a week."

I just look at her for a minute. Poor little thing — she's been looking after herself. Where the hell is her mother? My heart goes out to her. No wonder she ran away. "You must have a name," I say. "If you are going to live here, I can't just keep calling you 'girl.'"

"My name is Angel, but most everyone calls me Angie," she says.

"Well, my Angel, let's make breakfast," I say.

I put on some bacon and mix up some pancake dough. I tell her she can set the table and show her where the dishes and cutlery are. She sets everything around, and Grandpère shows up just as everything is ready. I've thawed out huckleberries to put on top of the pancakes. She asks what they are and says that they're good. For such a little thing, she packs away groceries like a logger after a hard day's work. She doesn't talk any more till she's done eating, then she offers to do the dishes. I wash and she dries, and we put them away together. Then she just sits silently at the table.

I sit down at the end of the table with a cup of coffee and ask her, "Do you want to talk about it?"

She shakes her head, no.

"What do you want to do?" I ask her.

"I want to know about my dad," she says.

I can talk about Ben now. Her coming here has released a flood of memories.

"Ben was the youngest of our children. He liked being outside, he liked to ride the horses and the bikes and he was always messy. His room always looked like a cyclone had hit it, and he didn't like me to clean it up. He was always teasing his brothers and getting into trouble, but he was so funny that no one stayed mad at him for long.

"Once, when he was little, he crawled under the house where the dog had puppies and went to sleep with them. Everybody looked for him for hours. We thought he was lost in the bush and had the whole neighbourhood looking for him when he finally woke up and crawled out. I was so mad at him that day, but we were so happy to see him that I got over it fast.

"He didn't want to go to school at first — he wanted to stay home with me — and he cried every day at the bus stop till he made friends with another boy at school. Then he always wanted to go, not to learn but to play with his friends. All his report cards said he was disruptive in the classroom, but he did well on all the tests, so he finished school on time." I pause. What else can I tell this girl about a father she never knew?

"What grade are you in, Angel?" I ask.

"I'm in grade eight, but I missed so much school this semester that I won't pass," she answers. "Why is your husband so old?"

"You mean Grandpère? He isn't my husband, he's my grandfather."

Her face gets red, and I can tell she's embarrassed. "No need to worry, it is a natural mistake," I tell her and go get the picture of Lorne and me that I keep on my nightstand.

"This is my husband," I say. "He passed on four years ago. Grandpère came to live with me after that. We don't really know how old he is, but near as we can figure out, he will be ninety-eight this year."

"Is he Indian?" she asks.

"Yes. When he was young he lived in the bush. He never lived on the reserve. He married a Métis woman, your great-great-grandmother. She was French and Indian. She has been gone for many years now."

"Am I part Indian then?"

"Yeah, you are," I tell her and watch to see how she feels about that. I'm pleased to see the ghost of a smile cross her face.

"My mom told me I was part Indian," she says.

"Angel, people will be looking for you. Young girls cannot

just disappear without someone worrying. Shouldn't we tell someone that you're here safe?"

"I can't go back. My mother does drugs and she hardly ever comes home. There is never any food in the place, and last week the power got shut off. Her old boyfriend came looking for her and he didn't believe me when I said she wasn't there and he pushed open the door and then he said I would do just as well and he, he . . . " Her voice catches with a sob and she puts her head down on the table and cries in great wracking sobs that shake her body.

"He just did it to me, and I couldn't get away," her muffled voice comes from under her arms.

I move over to the chair beside her and put my arm around her. "It's not your fault. You did right to come here. No one will ever hurt you like that again. I promise you," I say to her. I hope that I can keep this promise.

# Chapter Five

Angel cries for a while, and when she gets her composure back, she says, "My friend Carly gave me money for the bus ticket to get here. We could call her."

I hand her the phone. She dials the number and says, "I made it. Nice. Okay. Bye."

"Satisfied?" she asks, handing back the phone.

"Good enough for now. Come on, I think you should come and meet the chickens and the dogs."

We go to the door, and I realize she doesn't have boots or a decent warm coat, so I dress her up in some of my clothes, and we go out to the chicken house. She holds her nose while we tend the chickens and doesn't want to collect the eggs, but she likes the dogs and pets them. We walk around the yard, and I show her the shop and the woodshed.

"Is this all yours?" she wants to know.

"Yes. I have lived here for over thirty years. Your dad lived here from the time he was three years old," I tell her and ask, "Did your mother not get married?"

"No, but she lived for a long time with Robert. He was nice to me, and I thought he was my dad, but then they were fighting all the time, and when he left, she told me he wasn't my dad. She didn't let me go with him and didn't let me see him anymore. She was drinking a lot then, and it was getting bad. Later, after her boyfriends were all smoking coke and they didn't sleep or eat, it got really bad then." Tears start pouring down her cheeks again. "I don't think my mother cares about me," she chokes out, her face crumpling.

I reach out and hug her — she doesn't shrink away — and her muffled voice comes from my shoulder. "She just doesn't care about me."

I am angry as hell. What kind of a mother would expose her child to the things that this girl had seen? If Jane were here now, she wouldn't be safe from me.

"She told me your name when Robert left, and Carly and I found your address on the internet," Angel says, sniffing back her tears.

"My name is on the internet? How?"

"It's in the telephone directory."

"Well, I'm glad you had the sense to come here. Your mother is not your only family," I say to her as we head back into the house. "Do you want to have a shower and get cleaned up?"

"Can I have a bath?" she asks.

"Certainly, you can do whatever you want." I take her into the bathroom and show her where everything is, and she takes her suitcase in with her. While she's in the tub, I fill in Grandpère on what I've found out about her.

He is as angry as I am that such a young girl has had such a hard life already. He says to just be quiet about her being here and wait and see what comes of it.

"If I was younger, I would go hunt down that fellow and kill him," he tells me.

"Well, in that case, I'm glad you are old and decrepit, else I would have to defend you on a murder charge," I retort. He swings his cane at me, and I duck.

"No one would ever figure out what happened to him," he says. "I would come and go like smoke."

Angel comes out of the bathroom with wet hair and wearing different clothes, but these ones are, if anything, in worse shape than the ones she had on before. She asks if we have a laundromat close by.

"Even better than that, we have a washer and dryer right here," I say and show her how to use them. She dumps in the whole suitcase load, saying everything in it needs to be washed.

I wonder how I am going to entertain a young girl but I needn't worry, since she asks if she can read a book. She goes into the office and chooses a big book, then settles down on the couch to read it and soon dozes off. Grandpère and I play crib silently. He wins all three games and is in a fine mood when we put the cards away. He loves winning our crib games. Angel wakes up before supper and comes into the kitchen. She peels the potatoes while I make a meat loaf, and we both chop vegetables for a salad. She is fast and efficient, and I am impressed with how she cleans everything up, then sets the table without being asked.

"What about school?" I ask her.

"I don't want to go to school anymore."

"But Angel, nowadays you have to get at least your grade twelve to get any kind of a job."

"Please let me just stay here and don't make me go to school.

In the fall maybe I can start again," she says, her eyes pleading.

"Okay, but it might be kind of boring. Grandpère and I live pretty quietly here."

"I don't care about quiet. It's nice here," she tells me.

After supper I work on a braided rug, and she sits beside me, watching. After a while she asks if she can try it, and I see that she has watched closely enough that she can do it without any further instructions. I start another one, and soon we are both happily braiding away.

When we are ready to go to bed, she goes too, taking the book with her. I get up in the night to go to the bathroom, and her light is still on, but the door is locked again. She doesn't answer my soft knock on the door, so I guess she is sleeping with the light on.

In the morning she is still sleeping, so I take the opportunity to call Clint and tell him about this latest development in our lives. Surprisingly he agrees with Grandpère, tells me not to phone and report her whereabouts, to just wait and see. He says they will be down as soon as they can get away. I tell him there's no rush, it's going to take us a while to get to know her, and she seems content here already.

When she gets up, I ask her if she meant to sleep with the light on. "Yes, it's too dark without it. I turned it off, but I couldn't even see to get back in bed. I've never been in that much dark. In the city there's always light, and I have — I used to have — a night light in my room."

"Do you want a night light in your room here?"

"Do you have one?" she asks.

"Yes, your cousins like to have one when they stay here." I go and get the night light and plug it in by her bed.

"How many cousins do I have?" she wants to know, so I take her to the living room and point out which pictures are her cousins.

She spends a lot of time looking at the pictures, then she goes and gets a piece of paper from beside the computer and writes down the names of all her cousins in the order they are in the pictures. I tell her she must be a little bit younger than Sarah and that I expect they will be good friends before long. I ask her if she has any cousins on her mom's side. She says she doesn't know. Her mom doesn't get along with her family, and she's never met any relatives. She says she had some cousins who were Robert's brother's kids, but she hasn't seen them since he moved away.

I feel badly for her, and I am surprised again that she came here. If Jane didn't keep in contact with any family, how did Angel know to trust an unknown grandmother? I send a silent thank you to the universe for arranging this.

I tell her I have to go into town to get dog food and chicken feed, and I think she should come too, because if she is going to live here, she needs winter boots and a warmer coat.

"I don't have any money to buy that stuff." She looks anxious.

"I am going to buy them for you," I tell her.

Grandpère says he is staying home and will do the chores, so we have a quick bowl of porridge, then Angel and I get ready to go to town. The car hasn't been started since before Christmas, but it starts right up, and we head into town. We first stop at the feed store, where Angel says she will stay in the car, then over to the grocery store. I ask her if there is any particular thing she wants, but she says she likes everything and doesn't need anything special. Our little town has only two clothing stores, one a cheap chain store and the other a nice but small clothing store.

We go to the chain store to buy boots — the other one doesn't carry boots — and we buy a pair of felt packs. It's January, and everything is on sale, so they're cheap. Angel looks at coats, but I tell her wait till we see what they have at the other place.

There are stickers all over the window of the little store. Inventory Blowout! Super Sale! Up to seventy-five percent off!

"Oo-hoo! Shopper's paradise," I tell her.

Angel looks at everything in the store. There are nice warm jackets, and we choose a hip-length, pale lavender down-filled jacket. They really do have everything on sale, so I get her to try on some jeans. When she's in the dressing room, I pick out three long-sleeved T-shirts and some socks and underwear and put them with the coat. She comes out with the jeans on. They're a perfect fit, but long in the legs. I say that we'll hem them up at home and tell her to find a toque that she likes. She picks out one with a brim, almost the same colour as the coat, and we leave the store with our purchases. The whole bag has cost less than the jacket alone would have cost in December.

When we get home, she takes out the jeans, jacket and hat and hands me the bag with the rest of the stuff.

"No, no, those aren't for me, they're for you," I tell her.

To my surprise, she bursts into tears.

"What's wrong?" I ask.

"This is the most new clothes I've ever got at once. I'm happy, that's all."

"Happy people laugh, they don't cry," I say, grinning at her.

"Haven't you heard of tears of joy? These are tears of joy," she blubbers. Then she smiles back at me. I think it's the first time she has really smiled since she got here, and it transforms her face. I realize that she is a beautiful girl.

"Go try your stuff on, and we will pin up those jeans so we can hem them."

She goes into the bedroom and tries everything on, coming out to show Grandpère and me each new shirt. It is the most animated I have seen her, and I'm happy that the shopping trip was a success. I get her to stand on the coffee table so I can pin up the jeans. She says she knows how to hem, and within the hour she's finished. She sews with a neat stitch. Carly's mother showed them how to sew, she says.

We go into her bedroom and empty out the dresser so she can put her clothes away. The dresser has an odd assortment of Lorne's old work clothes, stuff the kids left here and linens. Lots of this stuff is just rags, I tell her, and she says she'll cut them up for our rugs. It tickles me that she already looks at rags and sees rug material.

Her bed is neatly made, and a small teddy bear is tucked in at the pillow. I say he's cute.

"I've had him all my life. He always sleeps with me. His name is Pooky. Mom says I got him when I was born."

I look at her closely, wondering if mentioning her mother has made her feel badly, but she doesn't appear to care one way or the other.

"What do you want to do with the rest of the day?" I ask.

"What would you do if I wasn't here?"

"Oh, Grandpère and I would probably play a few games of crib, then I would knit or bead or braid or read a book till it was time to make supper. Or I might put the snowshoes on and go for a walk in the bush."

"I would like to do all those things," she says.

"Too hard to do them all at once. You've got to pick just one."

I'm teasing her a bit.

"Oh Grandma, I didn't mean all at once. Let's play crib first. I like to play cards and I already know how to play crib."

So we play three-handed crib. Our board has three rows, so we play every man for himself. Angel does know how to play crib, and she counts difficult hands with ease. She even notices once that I forget to count a point for having the jack in my hand, and reaches over and moves my peg up one. Grandpère makes little rhymes with his counting — fifteen two and the rest won't do, fifteen four and the rest don't score — and Angel picks it up. Pretty soon they're making rhymes for everything, and she's laughing along with us at the goofier ones. They're having a great time, and when I excuse myself to make lunch, they keep right on playing.

One by one the other children call, expressing wonder that their brother left a child and that she should find us. They are all apprehensive about what will happen down south when no one can find her. I tell them not to invite trouble.

I am becoming fiercely protective of this girl, and I am determined that no one else is going to hurt her, for I can see that she is a lovely girl; she is respectful, ambitious and quick to learn. She wants to know how to do everything and is always at one of our elbows watching. She's making our lives much more fun, for she laughs at her mistakes and tries again. Grandpère is as taken with her as I am.

The last one to call is Faith. She has a friend who works in child protective services and will inquire behind the scenes what we can do to make sure we can keep Angel. Faith tells me not to mention her name online, even in a private email.

I tell her that isn't a problem, since I seldom go online. Faith says, "I know you don't, Mother, but make sure she doesn't use her email."

"Okay, thanks."

"Bye, love you," we say and hang up.

It hasn't entered my thoughts before. Angel accepts that we don't have TV and hasn't even asked to watch any movies, though she knows we have some. She hasn't asked to use the internet or even to use the computer. She hasn't got a phone or one of the music players with headphones that the teenagers wear now. When I think back to my own kids packing around their boom boxes, I'm grateful that someone figured out a way to keep the noise pollution to a minimum. But boom box or iPod, Angel is simply not doing any of it.

That night at supper I ask her if she has an email address. "No, Mom could never afford to keep a computer. We had one when Dad — I mean Robert — lived with us, but he took it with him when he left. We had one twice after that, but she took the first one to the pawn shop, and the next one got stolen. No one would email me anyway."

"Don't you have friends?" I ask, and am instantly aware that I've asked a somewhat rude question. But it doesn't faze Angel. "Carly is my friend. She helped me run away. She had her own money and she gave it to me to get here. That was her money I paid the taxi with. We used her name on the bus ticket. She's as good a friend as anyone could want. Carly and I know we can't talk to each other for a while. We made a pact."

She smiles at me and says if she hasn't learned anything in thirteen years, she's been wasting her time.

I am overcome. My scalp prickles, and I feel kind of dizzy. Grandpère must feel the same, for he starts to sing, *Ah, ah, ah, ah, eee.* He chants this very slowly, for a while, his voice going high and squeaky on the Es, and then I start singing with him too. Angel looks back and forth between us, and then she joins in. We're all grinning at each other while we're chanting, and my whole body is prickling. We end it on a long note, *Eeeeeee.* Then we all crack up, clapping and stomping and laughing.

"If everyone measured their age by learnings, some old people would be pretty young," Grandpère observes. I agree with him. I can think of a few people who would still be in their infancy.

The next week Grandpère turns one of his walking sticks that he's carving into an arrow. He cuts off the loop at the top and says he is going to carve that one into a pistol. Sure enough, when you hold it up by the stem, it is shaped just like a pistol.

The arrow that he's making must be entirely ceremonial, for the amount of carving he puts onto the shaft would make it fly pretty badly. It is beautiful at one end, the one with the point, and the faces all point toward the tip. On the other end all the faces point toward the feathers, and they are ugly. One looks like the devil, complete with little horns. He asks me to saw a nock on the end so he can put in some feathers. I do it and ask what kind of feathers he wants. Rooster feathers, he tells me, tail feathers.

I always save feathers — I have pretty ones sitting around in vases — and rooster feathers are easy to locate. Grandpère splits the feathers lengthwise and pushes them into the cross. Then he puts the arrow into a pillow case, wraps it up and starts carving on the twisted end that he's cut off to make his pistol. He chants a little song as he works.

Angel offers to tend the chickens. She still holds her nose every time she goes into the henhouse but she likes to get the eggs now. When she comes back into the house, she has a puzzled look on her face. "Grandma, I think the chickens have been smoking pot. I can smell it really strong in their house."

I look at her, and she is entirely serious. The thought of the chickens trying to roll a joint with their beaks sends me into gales of laughter. I think I know what she's smelling; a pack rat must have moved into the chickens' house. Every winter when the snow gets deep in the woods, some of these wood rats abandon their bush homes and try to move into warmer, dryer places. The chickens will kill any mice that move in, but the rats are too big for them. The dogs will kill them if they get the chance, though they never eat them. Instead they roll on them, getting the pungent smell on their hides. It is like dog perfume for them. I have been around country growers who pass off the smell of their cash crops by saying it must be rats. I explain the smell to Angel and tell her we'll put a trap under the house to catch the rat.

We go out into the shop and get down a number four wolf trap. I show her how to set the trap. These traps are illegal now for trappers. Meant for a leg hold, they're cruel for a large animal. If its leg gets trapped in the steel jaws, it might die of starvation or chew off its captured limb if the trapper takes a long time before checking his traps. For pack rats the traps are ideal, though, for the trap usually catches the rat's body and kills it quickly.

We cover the bait trip with tinfoil before setting the trap. These rats like shiny things, which they save in their nests. I have found whole socket sets stored in their nests. They make nests with bark and grasses and bits of odd things in a great pile. The rats are as industrious as they are filthy, leaving a trail of turds wherever they go and peeing on everything they encounter. They reek with the same smell as skunkweed.

The set trap we place in a short length of tin stovepipe, as the rats can't resist running through tunnels. We slide the whole thing under the henhouse, anchoring the end of the chain attached to the trap to a nail sticking out of the wall. I tell Angel that tomorrow morning a fat rat should be in the trap. She looks dubious.

# Chapter Six

Faith calls me in the afternoon and asks if Angel would be willing to press charges against the man who raped her. She says it will be easier to get custody if it can be proven that she is at risk living with her mother. I say I will ask. She tells me Darcy and she are going to come on the weekend.

After supper I bring up the subject.

"Angel, the man who hurt you, do you know who he is?"

"Yes. He went out with my mom after Robert left, but I hate him and I never want to see him again."

"If you will say what happened to you, we can get the papers that let you stay here."

"Will I have to see him?"

"I don't think so, dear. I think that you just have to tell a judge or a child worker."

"I don't want to. I just want to forget about it."

I actually don't know the process that gives custody of a minor to someone other than a parent. I tell her not to worry, even though I'm a little worried myself; if there's any way to get legal custody without telling about the rape, we'll do it that way.

"You have to go back to school in the fall, and we can't

register you without the world finding out where you are. The only reason you're safe here now is that no one knows you're here."

She understands this, and we talk about her going back to school. She says she did well in school till this last year when her Mom started doing so many drugs. She starts crying again, and I worry that talking about this is going to set her back. I hug her for a while, then change the subject and say, "Let's hear a story from Grandpère about the old days."

He nods, and we go sit in the living room.

The fire is going nicely in the stove and I open the door and put the screen in front of the blaze. All of us like to watch the fire. I get my pad and pen and sit beside Grandpère. I think it's time I wrote down some more of his stories.

Angel sits on the floor a few feet in front of us, and Grandpère begins. "There are two mighty forces in this world. You can call them God and the Devil, but your Grandmère Clementine, she called them Gitchi Manitou and Matchi Manitou. She said Gitchi Manitou was good. It was this being who brought the fish up the rivers, brought the summer back each year and looked after the well-being of the people.

"Matchi Manitou was not good. All the bad things that happened were the fault of this one. All Clementine's family left things in the bush to try to be the friend of him. That way she could make sure he didn't bring his bad ways to our house. Sometimes she would throw good stuff in the stove and say 'Matchi-Manitou, take this bad away.'

"When I was young, the elders would talk about that time before the black robes, before the priests of God. My mother did not like them to tell us about the old times, and she told us not to talk about the old times. She told us God was our father now.

She was always excited about priest days."

Grandpère is quiet for a minute and seems lost in thought.

"What were priest days?" Angel asks.

"In those days the priests travelled around. When they would come, we would know for weeks ahead of time where they were coming to. Everyone would go to the priest days. The priests would perform ceremonies for the people's weddings, the births of new children and the funerals for the ones who passed on. Sometimes the only time you would meet all your relatives was then.

"It was a big celebration when the priests came. All year long my mother would talk about the priest days. Whatever the priests said, she believed. She was very afraid of the devil. She told us the devil could hear us thinking.

"She told the elders to quit telling those stories, that God could hear them and the devil would get us all.

"We didn't have a sweat lodge ceremony like they do on the reserve now, not like the one you went to," he tells me.

I think back to the sweat I went to. Rose had phoned and asked if I would like to go to a sweat with her. I was surprised to be asked and had gone mostly out of curiosity.

"You went to one? That is so cool. Tell me what happened," Angel asks.

"We're supposed to be writing down Grandpère's memories, not mine!" I laugh.

"No, Anzel, I can't tell the girl about that. I think it was only in the fifties when that kind of thing was allowed again. Potlatch and everything, it was all against the law long before I was born. You tell her about the sweat."

I smile at him. We talked about the sweat for days after I

went. He wanted to know every little detail. I wonder if I'll remember all the teachings they gave us that day.

"Well," I begin, "it was late in the fall. I remember the drive up there with Rose. The leaves were all turned colour, and it was a beautiful day. We were told beforehand to bring a dress or long pajamas to wear inside. When we got there, we went and changed in a shed in the yard. A huge fire was blazing in the backyard, heating up the rocks. They were red-hot. There were stones in a path from the fire to the little conical mound that was the sweat lodge, which was all covered up with blankets and had a blue tarp over the top. They explained to us that the lodge was like a womb of the mother earth, and the fire was tied to the lodge by the rocks like an umbilical cord. We were told to walk clockwise around the fire to enter the lodge.

"We went into the sweat, both men and women. The first round was the welcoming round. The hosts were modern medicine people who told us about some personal challenges in their lives and how they overcame them. They talked about a more holistic view of health and how the spirit has to be healed at the same time as the body. They talked about how the ancestors were always there to be relied on for advice. They told us the rocks they brought in signified the wisdom of the ancestors, and when they brought them in, we should acknowledge their presence. The significance of the building was explained as a circle to denote the circle of life, with nine rows of saplings, one for each month the child is carried in the womb of the mother. They are bound together by four horizontal rows that signify the four ages of humans. The rows of twigs leave a round opening at the centre peak. This circle is crossed by tied twigs oriented in the four directions. Hanging from the centre is a large eagle feather.

"The four ages of humans start with infancy, from the time you are born till about twelve or thirteen. That is the time of being looked after. Childhood begins then, and that is the time you learn to care for others and be responsible for yourself and others. Childhood lasts different times for different people. The next stage is adulthood, which you are in for the longest period. Adulthood leads finally to being an elder. The elders are the ones who have learned to turn knowledge to wisdom. Adults and children have to look after infants and elders.

"They passed the pipe around. It was huge, just like the peace pipes in old movies. You could either puff some of the tobacco in it or just touch it to your shoulders when it came by. It got passed around three times, always clockwise.

"They told us about the four sacred elements — earth, air, fire and water — that were all there with us in the earth we were sitting on, the air we were breathing, the fire in the hot rocks and the water sprinkled on the rocks.

"They brought in the hot rocks one by one. The first one went in the centre, then the next four went in the four directions. They got sprinkled with a nice-smelling herb when they came in. Then they closed the door, and it got incredibly hot in there. At first you could see the dull red glow of the rocks, and then when they sprinkled the water on, it was so humid that the sweat just poured out and so dark that you couldn't see the hands in front of your face. The people who held the sweat started singing, and Rose and I were singing too, even though we'd never heard that song before. It repeated itself four times.

"Then they opened the door, and the cold air rushing in felt nice. There were four rounds of putting more rocks in; they brought in seven each time after that. Between rounds they would give us more teachings. After one round they passed a bowl of fresh berries, and after the next some rat root, which some people call sweet flag or calamus. It was a really wonderful experience. The message of healing was strong, and their belief that people are able to heal both the earth and themselves left us both feeling refreshed."

When I stop talking, Angel says, "I didn't know they still had sweat lodges. It sure would be sweet to do that. Maybe someday I can go to one."

I can see that Grandpère is far away, so I ask him if there's more about the priest days he wants to tell us.

"No. In the long run, the priests didn't do us much good. My father didn't believe in the priests like my mother did. Now the priests can just be forgotten," he declares, and on that note we all retire for the evening.

In the morning we have indeed caught the pack rat. I pick up the trap by the chain and take it to show Grandpère and Angel. Disgusted by the limp body hanging from the trap, she makes a "yuck" face and backs away. I take the rat out of the trap and throw it far into the woods, hoping the dogs won't find it. But of course they do and pack it back into the yard like a treasure. When they're finished playing with it, I steal it back, put it in a garbage bag and stow it in the shop. If Darcy brings the pickup on the weekend, I will get him to take a garbage run for me; there's getting to be quite a pile in the shop.

I reset the trap in case there's more than one rat out there. When I get back into the house, Grandpère asks if the trail up to the top of the hill is good enough to take the bike up. I tell him I don't know, but I'll give it a try. The bike starts well, and I see if I can make it up the trail. It's fun to drive the bike in the snow — it slides around goofily — and it goes right up to the top with no trouble.

The morning fog has burnt off, and the sun has some heat in it. Yesterday's wind has knocked all the snow off the trees, and the world looks clean and sparkly. The lookout is down to bare rock, and I spend a few minutes admiring the winter view. The poplars are bare, but their bark is turning that green colour that holds the promise of new leaves. The fields are patches of clean white, and the contrast of the dark evergreens makes it look like a postcard from a winter wonderland. I take the bike up and down the hill a couple more times to pack in the trail.

I come in the house and tell them how beautiful it looks, and Grandpère says, "Let's all go up to the lookout." Sounds like a good idea to me.

We have a quick lunch and put our outside clothes on. Angel wears a pair of my old snow pants with her new coat and hat. Grandpère puts on his old patched coveralls, and we all pile onto the bike. He has a pillowcase full of stuff that he straps onto the front of the bike. I raise a questioning eyebrow at him, but he pretends he doesn't see it. It takes only a couple of minutes to climb the hill with all of us on the bike.

When we get up there, Grandpère unloads his pillowcase. He has paper and kindling in it to start a fire.

"Good idea," I tell him. Angel and I go break off dry branches from the trees close by and feed them to his fire.

"This is a fire for you, Angel," Grandpère says.

He sits her down in front of the fire, and takes his carved arrow out of the pillowcase. He holds it up in front of him and points it in the four directions, asks their guidance and blessing. Then, chanting the same little tune he sang while he was carving it, he sticks it point down in the ground in front of her. "Close your eyes, and think of all the good things and the bad things in your life. Each time you think of a good thing, you send it down to the point, and every time you think of a bad thing, you send it to the nock. When you are done, you cross your arms.

"You, Anzel, you help me sing."

Angel looks at him skeptically but does as he asks. He sits across from her and motions me to stand behind her. He starts chanting his same little song, and I sing along with him. She is silent and unmoving except for once when she flings out an arm and points straight at the arrow; I think she points to the bad end. After a while she crosses her arms. Without losing his chant, Grandpère laboriously gets to his feet and picks up the arrow.

"This arrow carries Angel's good and bad things." He breaks the arrow in half and tells her to hold out her hands. He gives her the halves, the good end in her right hand and the evil one in her left. "The bad things need to be gone. Take the bad things and give them to the fire so they will trouble you no more."

She looks at the two pieces, then reaches out and shoves the ugly end in the fire. We all watch silently while the arrow burns. It doesn't burn like the tree branches — the flame is iridescent and swirly as though the fire is reluctant to burn it — but soon it is nothing but a red coal that suddenly crumples to nothing in the heart of the fire.

"These things will trouble you no more, my granddaughter," he says. "Let's go. The end of that arrow that you still hold will draw good things into your life from this day on. It is part of your good medicine."

Angel looks from the arrow point in her hand to his face and back again. She stares at the fire for another moment, then takes off her new hat and throws it in the fire. "For Matchi Manitou," she says.

I am surprised that she has burned up her new toque, but Grandpère nods in approval, and we climb back on the bike to ride back down the hill. When she gets off the bike, she goes around and helps him off.

"Thank you, Grandpère. I don't know how you did it, but I feel better than I have for a long time."

He nods and says, "Do not speak of it anymore. It is done."

On the weekend Darcy and Faith come in the pickup as I hoped. They don't bring the girls, who Faith says are dying to meet their cousin, because they've promised to babysit for some friends. Faith and Angel hit it off right away, and I feel comfortable leaving them while Darcy and I take the garbage to the dump and make a run into town. I want to go to the store and buy a few groceries, and I stop at the clothing store and pick up another hat for Angel. This time it's black, the only colour they have left in that style. I buy her another pair of jeans and two new summer tops that have just arrived.

Darcy quizzes me about her during the trip, and I tell him what a lovely girl she is and what a rotten time she had before. He says that I shouldn't worry about her, that Faith is figuring out how to make sure she never has to go back to that life again.

We stop at the feed store to get dog food, and in the window a poster of missing children catches my eye. I step closer to look at it, and my heart drops. Angel's photo is right in the centre.

I catch Darcy's eye and motion him over. He looks at it, then grabs my elbow and steers me away. He gives my arm a little shake, which reminds me to gather up my scattered wits and carry on. I barely make it back to the truck before I dissolve into tears. He drives around for a while till I'm composed enough to go home. It's a good thing that I've got myself back together, for when we got back home, Bella drives in behind us for a visit.

Of all the people I want to see right now, Bella is at the end of the list. I shoot a look of panic at Darcy, but all he says is, "Easy, Mother, take it easy."

When we get into the house, I put the groceries away but don't give Angel her new stuff. I tuck the bag in my room, wondering how I'm going to explain Angel to Bella. Darcy takes that worry out of my hands, introducing Angel to her as his niece who came along for the ride to visit her cousins' grandmother. I think it's a little thin, and both Faith and Angel look confused. Darcy asks them to come out to the shop with him to give him a hand for a minute, and out they go.

I'm not able to give Bella my full attention, but she doesn't seem to notice. She doesn't need a conversation, mostly just an audience to listen to her, and I'm relieved when she only stays for a short time and leaves.

After she's gone, I tell them about the poster and how worried I am that someone will recognize Angel from our trips to town. Grandpère says that old busybody is probably the worst danger, meaning Bella, and after some talk we decide it would be best if Darcy and Faith take her home for a while. Faith says it might be boring, as the girls are in school, and Darcy and she both work, but Angel says she's well used to staying alone and it won't bother her.

"But I want to stay here." She looks as though she's going to cry.

"It will only be for a couple of weeks," Faith soothes her. "Your cousins are just a little bit older than you, and they'll be so happy if you visit us. We need to get going on the custody. It's the only way you'll be safe. I have a friend who will help us, and you can phone here whenever you want to."

I remember the things I bought her and go to get them. "These are for you. I hope you like them."

Now she does start crying in earnest, and none of us is dry-eyed.

"There's no need for any of us to worry. We'll have this straightened out in no time. Now is anyone around here going to make some supper?" Darcy asks.

"How about a cup of tea for mother?" Faith seems to know that a cup of tea usually makes everything right in my world.

I give her a grateful smile, and sure enough, after a cup of tea I put myself back together and help get dinner ready. After the meal we pack Angel's meagre belongings into my good suitcase so they can get going early in the morning. I notice that her arrow point is packed in the suitcase along with her Pooky. Somehow this makes me feel better about the whole thing.

Darcy, Faith and Angel leave after breakfast the next morning so they can make it home to the Peace River before supper. They say they will call every day. The house seems empty and quiet again with just the two of us there. Grandpère and I are both out of sorts. He is whittling as though he's angry, and I can't get up any enthusiasm for doing anything. Finally I take a book, curl up on the couch and read the day away.

At night I lie awake and toss and turn, trying to let sleep overtake me, but weary as I feel, it's early morning before

I finally get to sleep. In my dream I am astride a huge warhorse. I am fighting a battle, and there is noise and confusion everywhere. I have a battleaxe that I swing with rage, cleaving heads. My horse rears up and smashes my enemies before I can reach them. Then suddenly I am at a lake in the mountains, washing the blood off myself and my horse. My two dogs that I have in real life are there, and it is calm and quiet. Someone I know walks across the water toward me, and I run to meet her. When I almost get to her, we both sink under the water, and then I am swimming hard for the shore.

I wake up more tired than when I went to bed. Grandpère is still sleeping, so I make a pot of coffee and drink most of the pot before he gets up.

"Sleep well?" he asks.

"No. I hardly slept at all."

"Me neither. I was wishing that girl was here safe in her bed."

"Oh Grandpère, what if they find her and send her back to her mother?"

"We'll have to hope that won't happen. She has good protection now. You have to imagine everything will work out right, because that will make it happen. The more you worry, the worse you make it," he tells me.

It's the power of positive thinking, I well know. The more bad things a person imagines, the more they draw unfavourable circumstances toward themselves. However, it's easier to apply that theory to someone else's worries than to your own. I decide I will try to imagine it all working out. Each time a worry thought comes into my head today, I will make a positive statement. What should it be?

"Angel is safe now and she will continue to be safe." I say it out loud once, then repeat it in my head a bunch more, trying to convince my skeptical mind that it's true.

"Atta girl, that's more like it." He smiles, and I begin to feel better already. I give him a hug.

The day is bright and sunny, and the dogs are wanting to play. I check the trap when I go out to feed the chickens. It's still empty. There was probably only one rat there, but I leave the trap set just in case there are more. I check the shop for sign, but there are no little droppings anywhere. We've kept mouse poison under the bench ever since the little vermin chewed all the wires off the battery charger, so there haven't been mice in the shop for a long time. Grandpère doesn't approve of poisoning the mice, but I don't approve of them living in my space, so I quietly bait them all to death. I figure what he doesn't know doesn't hurt him.

I decide to go for a walk in the woods with the dogs, so I strap on the snowshoes and walk around the perimeter of the property, checking to make sure all the wire is up on the fence line. We live in an open range area where the cows from the ranch down the road can freely go anywhere that isn't fenced. It has always been open range here; if you don't want cows in your garden and your yard, you have to fence them out. New people who move in are always outraged that they have to fence the cows out at their own expense. They've formed a committee and are trying to make the government or the rancher build or at least maintain the fences. They've tried to get the range permit taken away from the rancher, but the department of forests and range didn't co-operate, and one fellow who shot a cow right in his carport got charged for doing it.

I can see both sides of the argument. Raising cows doesn't

make much economic sense, and the ranchers need all the help they can get. On the other hand, having to fence cows out of private property is expensive, and maintaining a fence is a chore. So I stay away from their committee and look after my own fence. Lorne and I built the fence to keep our cows in. We had one milk cow and always raised her calf for beef as well as two or three calves each year that the ranchers would sell us when they were born. They would seldom keep both calves if the mother had twins, and if there was no cow they could graft the unwanted twin onto, they sold it to us, knowing we would bottle-feed it. Our kids always liked to look after the baby calves, and many a summer they would have calves following them around outside.

Today the fence is in perfect shape, with no trees down or staples pulled out anywhere. The dogs are delighted to go for such a long walk, bounding through the snow and investigating every rabbit trail and track we come across. A chipmunk scolds us from his perch on a tree branch, likely telling us that we are not welcome in his domain. There are a lot of rabbit tracks everywhere, and I think this summer we'll have to make sure the garden fence has good two-inch-mesh page wire around the bottom.

By the time I get back to the house, I'm in a great mood. There's a message to phone Faith, and I call her right away. She has good news. She has taken Angel to see her friend who works in the child services branch, and her friend has gotten a really good lawyer to get the custody case moving. I tell her that I will pay for the lawyer, but she says, "No need. Every good lawyer takes a few cases of this kind every year for free. It's called a pro bono service." She explains that it is an ethical responsibility of lawyers to help those who can't help themselves in cases like this, and he will do a far better job than a legal aid lawyer.

Best of all, he will do it for free.

"What about her mother? She's reported her as a missing person. Won't the police take Angel back to her as soon as they know where she is?" I ask her.

"No, child protection now knows that her mother is part of the problem, and they can protect her from having to go back into that situation. That's why I took her there, to make sure that won't happen. We don't know what her mother has told the authorities, but Angel's side of the story is on record now. They told me the police will contact us but won't remove her from our home. We have temporary custody."

"Is it safe for her to come back here?"

"Just leave her here till this all shakes down. Don't worry, Mother, she is safe and happy here, and she's already friends with her cousins. They were so happy when she came home with us, and there are lots of things they want to do. I could hardly convince them to go to school today, and I have taken the week off work so I can deal with all this."

I thank her. I am so relieved that Faith has taken over the reins on this. I trust the system far less than she does, and in my distrust, I would have been hesitant to do the things that she has already done. When we hang up, I'm feeling quite good about the whole thing, and when I tell Grandpère, he is also pleased.

We keep grinning at each other, and our funk from the previous day is quite forgotten. Not for long, though. In the late afternoon a police cruiser pulls into the yard, and two officers get out and come to the door. They ask if I am Anzel O'Flaherty.

"Hi, Todd," I say, for the younger one is well aware of who I am; he is one of Jesse's friends. "Have you forgotten what I look like?"

"I have to ask for the record," he says, and sure enough, the other one has a notebook and is writing down what we say. I don't like the other one. When Lorne was still alive, we had a run-in with him over Lorne's unregistered gun lying in the back seat of the car when he was stopped for a speeding ticket. They confiscated it and still haven't given it back.

"Did you come here to return my husband's gun?" I ask him. He doesn't look up at me and pretends he doesn't even hear me.

Todd answers, "No, Mrs. O'Flaherty, we have a report of a missing girl who might have been seen here."

"There's no girl here. You can look around if you want," I tell him.

"Who was the girl you were in town with last week?" says the other one.

"That was my granddaughter who was visiting me." A half truth is better than a lie, I believe. "Why would you think a missing girl would be here?"

"A taxi driver told us he brought a girl out here last month. If you don't mind, I think we'll have a look around," Todd says.

I look at him with my eyebrows raised, make a little bow and wave my hand in a "help yourself" gesture. They make a half-hearted search by looking in the bedrooms and bathroom.

Todd comes back and says, "Sorry, but we have to follow up on all reports. If you did know where she was, you would tell us, wouldn't you? Her mother is very worried about her, and we are using up time we don't have in following leads."

"Who was the girl the taxi driver brought out here?" the other one asks.

"It was my same granddaughter who was visiting me last week," I answer.

"Thank you for your time. Sorry we had to bother you.

Come on, Dave, she obviously isn't here," Todd says, and I watch out the window till they pull out of the yard. My held breath comes out with a big whoosh.

Grandpère is shaking his head, laughing at me. "I think Todd knows. He's pretty smart. I saw him look at the *Archie* comics on the coffee table, and I think he would remember that Jane Moberly was Ben's girl. They didn't even ask your granddaughter's name, eh? He knows if we have her, she's okay."

I don't think he does know, but I haven't lied to them about anything, unless lying by omission is the same crime as telling an untruth. I sure am glad that she wasn't here when they came. Thank you, thank you, I say in my head to whatever god is looking out for us right now. I call Faith and tell her about the cops coming, and she says she'll phone the lawyer and tell him.

Angel gets on the phone, and I ask her how things are going. "They are so nice. Tammy and Sarah gave me a whole bunch of clothes that don't fit them anymore, and we are going to walk to the mall after supper so we can meet some of their friends. I never had my own cousins before, and I am the only girl cousin they have. We're already friends. We are going to go ice skating tomorrow because Auntie said they could have one day off school to show me around." She sounds so bubbly and happy that now I am sure we did the right thing sending her home with Darcy and Faith. "But I miss you and Grandpère already," she says before she hangs up.

At bedtime, I fall asleep when my head hits the pillow, and if I have dreams, I remember none of them in the morning.

# Chapter Seven

The following week Rose phones and tells me that the people who run the home want to start a vegetable plot there for the old people to tend. She says that they have the funding to build raised beds so that even the ones who aren't able to walk can still get out and tend them from their wheelchairs. When they were wondering who could manage a program like that, she thought of me. Am I interested?

"I sure am," I tell her.

Rose wants me to come and talk to the board. "We're having a birthday party for Mrs. Daly, who is turning one hundred, and some of the board members are coming tomorrow. That will be as good a time as any," she says. "Bring Grandpère. He might like to visit with some of the old folks."

When I tell him we are invited to the home for a birthday party, he is not really sure he wants to come. Then I explain about the garden, and he approves and says he might as well tag along.

I find my gardening books and read over the sections about raised beds. I want to refresh myself on how to manage raised beds, as this is not a practice I use here at home. It seems as though the only problems are keeping enough moisture in the soil, as the beds tend to dry out quicker in the heat than soil in the ground, and making sure they're deep enough for root crops to develop.

When we head out the next day, Grandpère has taken more care in dressing than usual. He's even put on his new bush shirt, the first time he's worn it. "Are you trying to look good for anyone in particular?" I tease him.

"You never know, one of those old girls might want me," he tells me with a straight face.

When we drive up to the home he is surprised. "Looks more like a fancy hotel than a home."

The home is new, and there has been no expense spared in the building. The door is locked, and we have to ring a buzzer to get in. A young nurse answers the door, and she looks from me to Grandpère, probably wondering which of us needs admitting. Before she can ask any questions, I introduce us and tell her we are here for the birthday party. She smiles at us and asks if we want a wheelchair for Grandpère.

"No, girl, I walk a little slow, but I don't need wheeled around quite yet," he answers for himself.

She guides us past the desk, points out the washrooms and invites us into the common room. It is decorated with streamers and balloons, and about twenty people are already sitting at the small tables placed around the room in a semicircle. A guitar and amplifier are set up on a stage at one side of the room, and a banquet table on the other side is filled with trays of fruit and vegetable platters, fancy sandwiches, cookies and squares.

It is very warm, and both Grandpère and I take off our outer layers and hang them on a coat rack. We take a seat at one of the tables where two people are sitting. The lady, who says her name is Bertie, has a round face creased with smile lines and is very talkative. She introduces the man on her left as Jack, but adds that he doesn't often remember who he is.

I introduce Grandpère. "This is my grandfather, Simon Walker, and I am Anzel."

"Are you coming to live here?" she wants to know.

"No, we're just visiting," I reply, and I can tell she is disappointed.

Jack shakes our hands, then drifts out of the conversation, his eyes kind of blank and unfocussed. Bertie ignores him and tells us about Mrs. Daly. "Do you know, she got a letter from the prime minister, congratulating her on turning one hundred. She has been here — not here in this place, but here with the home — for twenty-two years now. She can't walk anymore, and most of the time she thinks she is back on the farm. When she could still walk, she used to run away all the time till they put a bracelet on her that beeped when she went through the door. But she hasn't tried to run away since I got here. No one can run away now. The doors don't open unless a nurse opens them."

I don't even dare to look at Grandpère. I can imagine what is going through his head. I try to engage Jack in our conversation by asking, "How long have you been here, Jack?"

"Eh?"

I repeat my question, but he just looks puzzled and shakes his head.

"Where am I?" he asks.

Bertie pats his arm. "You are right here at home, dear," she tells him. "We are going to have a party."

He smiles at her, then drifts off again.

"We don't ask him things that will upset him," she explains to me in a disapproving voice.

Just then I spot Rose in the doorway and excuse myself to go and say hello to her. Grandpère and Bertie are talking, so I feel comfortable going with Rose to her office. She shows me the plans for the gardens. They want to build eight beds, each four feet wide by eight feet long. They will be built up three feet high and filled with soil to the top, and they will have automatic sprinklers on timers. A paved pathway surrounding them will make it easy for the old people to wheel their chairs around. It sounds really nice.

"What exactly do you want me to do?" I wonder.

"We are hoping you'll start the plants, then come in once or twice a week to supervise throughout the summer," she says. "We'll pay you twenty-five dollars an hour, plus forty-two cents per kilometre for your travel. You will keep track of your hours and bill us bimonthly. We'll pay for any extra equipment you need, plus you need to keep track of the time and money you spend on the bedding plants."

"That is very generous. I think I'll like doing this. Do you hire me, or do I need to talk to someone else?"

"There are only two people who need to approve my hiring. They will both be here later on." Rose grins at me, and I know she has already convinced them to go along with her wishes. She doesn't exactly manipulate people, but usually everyone is willing to do whatever it is that Rose wants them to do.

We go back to the common room, where the chairs around Grandpère are all full. He waves at us to sit wherever, so we sit down at a table across the room from him.

"Where is the birthday girl?" I ask Rose.

"She wasn't too well this morning, so they'll bring her out when it's time for lunch," she replies. "In fact here she comes now."

Two orderlies walk in, wheeling a chair that holds the caricature of a human. An intravenous stand is rolled along beside her chair with a steady drip connected to a tube in her arm. She is shrunken into the pillows that line the chair, and her head bobs forward as though her neck is made of rubber. Her shrivelled skin is discoloured with brown patches, and a large dressing covers most of one cheek. A line of drool traces the deep line from her mouth to her chin, and the attendant solicitously mops it up when they come to a halt in front of the centre table. Her eyes are glazed and unfocussed.

"Here you are, dear. It's your birthday party!" the orderly cheerfully tells her.

There is no reaction from Mrs. Daly. She seems completely unconscious of her surroundings, and to me it seems entirely inappropriate to be making such a fuss over someone who is so out of it. I feel quite sorry for her, and turn to Rose to express my dismay. She is smiling away as though it's perfectly fine, so I don't say anything, but it feels kind of creepy.

A young guy comes in to turn on the amp and spends a couple of minutes tuning his guitar. Then he stands up, strikes a chord on his guitar and says, "One hundred years old! A new centenarian!" and he plays "Happy Birthday." Everyone joins in singing, and a cook complete with chef's hat rolls out a trolley holding a huge cake lit up with one hundred candles. It looks dangerous, more like a small bonfire than a cake.

At the sight of the cake and candles, Mrs. Daly comes around for a moment. "Birthday cake," she says, and her voice, like her body, seems rusty from disuse. Then her head falls forward again and the light goes back out of her eyes.

They cut the cake and serve it to everyone who lines up around the buffet table. The ones who can walk are picking up extra platefuls for some of their more stationary friends. Nurses wheel others around and help them to dish up food, which they place on their laps for the ride back to the table. Some of the nurses sit down and spoon-feed the more helpless old folk. The whole scene makes me shudder, and I look to see what Grandpère makes of this place.

But he's not looking at me. He and Bertie are chatting away. She is laughing at something he said, and he looks kind of pleased with himself. Bertie has a plate of food for Jack, and when she hands him each thing and tells him to eat, he does. Two other old ladies are sitting with them, and they and Grandpère look as though they're having a lively conversation. I leave him be and tell Rose about Angel. She is delighted for us, and says she thinks Faith will set everything to rights.

"We will have faith in Faith," she says, and we laugh at her play on words.

"I'm going to start some plants next week," I say. "The moon is dark right now, and as it rises, it will be time to start the peppers, tomatoes and onions." I'm already planning how much extra to plant for the home. "The squashes and pumpkins don't need to be started quite yet. They'll get too leggy if I start them too soon." I'm suddenly excited about gardening by a different method than I'm accustomed to.

"I knew you were the right one to organize this." Rose sounds excited too.

"Do you think you can talk them into building a greenhouse too?"

"Rome wasn't built in a day. If this works out well, maybe that can be the project for next year. I've been trying to talk them into this garden for a couple of years, but this is the first time any funding has been set aside for it." She sounds pleased with herself, and I know her well enough to know that she is the one responsible for getting this project going.

"Should I plant flowers too?" I ask.

"No, the flower beds are done by the groundskeepers — it's part of their contract — and we don't want to step on their toes. It's enough for you to do the vegetable part." She squeezes my arm. "There are the board members now, Anzel. Come on, I'll introduce you."

We follow the man and woman to her office. Bill appears to be in his forties and Tracy is about our age. Rose introduces us, and I ask them if they have any questions for me.

"No," Tracy says. "Rose has told us you'll be able to help us get this program up and running. We trust her judgment."

Bill seems to be the one who has put the funding together, and he and Rose need to discuss other things, so I thank them for hiring me and take my leave.

The young guy with the guitar has been playing softly throughout the meal. Now he turns the amplifier up louder and sings "Home on the Range." Lots of the old people sing with him, but others just sit and stare with blank faces. I look at one old man who hasn't spoken to anyone; a nurse fed him each bite from her own hand. He is dressed neatly and still has a full head of hair, the wiry kind that defies the comb, but it's tidy, and his hands stay crossed on his lap in front of him. It's his stare that's disconcerting, for he looks around constantly, letting his gaze stop here and there as though he's looking for something that he's not finding. He doesn't look sad or happy; he looks lost. I notice his foot is tapping in time to the music, though, and I reflect that music still gets through when most of the other connections are missing.

The guitarist breaks into another song, and with some surprise I realize he's singing a John Prine song that Lorne used to sing:

*Please don't bury me down in that cold, cold ground.*

*No, I'd rather have them cut me up and pass me all around.*

*Throw my brain in a hurricane, and the blind can have my eyes . . .*

*Send my mouth way down south, and kiss my ass goodbye.*

I am somewhat surprised by his choice of song, and some of the staff must be too, for a couple of heads poke around the corner and look at him. He just smiles back with such an infectious grin that they shake their heads and grin back. He sings for about an hour, and everyone looks as though they're enjoying the music. I watch some of the ones who seem to be missing in action, and they're all connecting to the music, some of them swaying, some tapping a hand or a foot. It seems they are, in their own limited way, enjoying themselves.

Except for Mrs. Daly, who seems to have gone quite to sleep. The nurse has put a party hat on her head, and it has slipped down on one side. Her head leans sideways on the pillows, and her untouched cake sits in a plate on her lap. It's sliding dangerously down her lap, and the nurses have left her propped up in the place of honour beside the cake trolley.

I decide I should go rescue the cake before it hits the floor. I walk over and reach for the cake just as it slides over onto her blanket. I turn it right side up and go to grab a napkin to wipe up the icing just as a nurse comes to help. We both scrub a little bit, but she says it doesn't matter, they'll get a clean blanket right away. Mrs. Daly could be a plastic doll in a carriage; she neither wakes up nor moves through the whole procedure. The nurse wheels the birthday girl out of the room, and the kitchen staff start clearing off the buffet table. It must be the cue for the party to end, as everyone gets up and starts dispersing down the hall.

I go over to Grandpère just as Bertie says goodbye. "Come and visit any time, Simon," she says to him, and keeps turning around and waving till she rounds the corner.

"Ready to roll?" I ask him.

"You bet, sooner the better." He's already going for his coat. He's walking faster than he usually does and seems in a big hurry to be leaving.

When we get to the car, I ask him how he liked it. "If I ever get to the stage of some of those wrecks in there and don't notice, just put me out of my misery. I don't want to live like that." He's quite agitated and hits the dash with his fist to emphasize his words.

"Not all of them are spaced out, Grandpère. Bertie seemed pretty with it and nice," I say to him.

"She is nice, but she's only lived there for a year. She's only seventy-five. They look after them too well; they don't know when to die. That old one with the birthday, she's mostly gone already. She must have known what was going to happen when she tried to run all those times. It's awful. Why would she want to be alive? In the old days people who couldn't look after themselves died. I'm not talking about people who got injured or sick; of course we looked after them. But people who were so old they forgot who they were and how to do the simple things like getting food into their own mouths — they died. No one would be such a burden. But these places, they get paid to keep you alive, so they do it. I don't think it's good. I would rather be dead than live in both worlds at once. It would be a kindness to that old lady if she could take the long sleep." He is vehement in his displeasure with the old folks' home.

"Well, Grandpère, I can't say I completely disagree with you. It gave me the creeps looking at those ones who were so vacant. I don't ever want to be like that either." A little shudder runs down my spine. I don't know how Rose can work there so happily, but probably it's like everything else; once you get used to the way things are, you get more comfortable with them. "I said I would go there once a week this summer to help them with their garden project."

"Well, you'll be going there without me. I am never going there again."

"Not even to see the cute little Bertie?" I can't resist the urge to tease him a bit.

"Nope. You could bring her out here to see me once in a while if you want." He leers at me, and we laugh the rest of the way home.

True to her word, Angel phones every week. She sounds happy and tells me what she did every day. She's teaching her cousins rag rug braiding, and it sounds as though they're becoming fast friends. Faith and Darcy have temporary custody granted to them, and they want to know if they can put Angel in school there to catch up on the last semester that she didn't finish in her old school. They are both on the phone, making a hollow echo on the line.

"If that is what she wants to do, by all means do it," I say, knowing that means Angel won't be back till summer holidays. "It is important to me for her to get her education, and it will be easier for her to go to school with your girls than to face a strange school alone. Are you sure you want her to live with you that long?"

"She fits in here like a hand in a glove," Darcy claims, and Faith says, "You know how much I adore my girls. Well, three is even better than two."

"What about the police?" I want to know.

"We have contacted the police here, and the missing child report is down." Darcy sounds pleased with himself. "We filed a restraining order that doesn't allow her mother to see her, so she's quite safe."

I ask to talk to Faith privately, and my last worry is laid to rest. Angel has started her monthlies. I feel as though everything is going right, and when I get off the phone, I am humming a little tune and dancing around. Grandpère laughs at me, but when I catch him up on the progress, he's just as pleased as I am.

"That girl is fine. That girl is safe." He does his own little dance.

The following week I clear the bed out of the bedroom at the end of the hall and set up rows of bricks standing on end with planks between the rows to make shelving, then hang florescent tube lights from the planks. This year I make three rows of shelves to accommodate the extra starts for the home. I use the same set-up every year to start the plants, so it's easy to do. The staples are still in the planks to hang the fixtures, and over the years I've replaced all the lights with full-spectrum bulbs to give the little starts the best conditions to flourish. I plug the lights into a power bar and plug the power bar into a timer. I give the plants fourteen hours of light each day. During the winter I save the plastic containers that fresh greens come in. Now I fill them with soil and sprinkle the seeds over the top. The soil I dig from the greenhouse, but it's still a little too cool to put the seeds in, so I put the plastic tub full of soil over by the heater to warm up for a day or two. I round up three kinds of lettuce seed, onion, pepper, two kinds of tomato and some flowers for myself. The lettuce and the flowers can go in the greenhouse when it gets a little warmer, and the other things will get repotted into plug trays after they germinate. None of the seeds are new, so germination rates may not be the best, but I find that planting them this way lets me get the longest possible life out of the seeds.

Grandpère says if I would like to write them down, he will tell me some of the things his people knew. Once more I gather up my notebook and pen.

He begins, "This is what my own grandfather told me about the beginning.

"Once the world was just one big shining ocean. There was no land anywhere. The only inhabitant of the world was a mighty bird whose eyes were fire. When he looked about, his glances were lightning, and when his wings beat the air, thunder sounded. His name is the Immense One or the Thunderbird. One day the bird flew right into the ocean, and when he rose, he brought up the land with him, and the land stayed on top of the water. He called forth all the animals to inhabit his new land, and man was called into being at the same time. The bird gave the new people a special arrow and warned them to leave it undisturbed. Some of the people were so crazy as to carry it away, and since that time, the bird can no longer be seen.

"Sometimes a person can find the bird in the dreamland. It is a power dream that shows you the bird. In the dreamland, the bird is a huge grouse. If you find the grouse in the dreamland, you should pay attention.

"Throughout time the bird shows his anger with the people's ways by destroying the world and making another world. The people try to survive by going to the top of the tallest mountain, but the earth catches on fire and burns the mountain. The people are rescued by the bird, who brings them to his new world.

"The new world is abundant, and all the people live in harmony for many years, but then once again disharmony comes to the people, and they quarrel. When they fight, the bird causes the sea to rise into the lands, and he tells a man to build a boat. On his boat the bird tells him to take the animals, all except for the very large ones. They drift on the waters for many days, then the man releases a raven to look for new land. The raven doesn't come back. He must be feeding on all the dead people and animals, for he survives, and there are always ravens among us. After this time the people and the animals can no longer understand each other.

"Soon afterward the man releases a white grouse, which comes back with a willow shoot in his beak to show the people he's found the new world. The boat full of survivors follows the bird back to the next world. It is once again abundant, and the people and the animals live in peace for a very long time. The people know to only take some of the animals for survival, and the animals share freely of themselves to keep the people full and clothed.

"This is the world we live in now. But the people no longer respect the world, and it will soon be time for the next world to come into being. The Creator is impatient with the people, who do not respect the balance. The bad things that happen are the fault of the people, who no longer respect the earth. The world can only go so far out of balance before it is time to remake it.

"This is the story as the elders of our people knew it."

"Grandpère, the flood is the same story as Noah's ark," I say, wondering if this story was adapted out of the Bible.

"When the elders told us this story, it was before the time when the people could read or had even heard of the Bible," he replies. "It is proof of the flood that other peoples have the same story." He pauses for a minute. "When I first heard of Noah's ark, I thought the Christians had taken our story and used it for themselves. But now I understand the story is all over the world. It is a true story, but the world is big, and many different people survived the flood.

"You know, Granddaughter, when I was young, people did not fear death. They knew their spirit just uses the body to live on this earth. They knew when people's bodies wear out, the spirit will leave. When the body dies, the spirit will leave and go on living. The spirit is meant to move on when the body dies; the body is gone, but spirits are separate. They have choices. They can live with animals or even with trees or they can be born again in a new body. When someone dies, their body is destroyed so the spirit won't try to stay. After the body is gone, no one speaks the name of the dead, for to speak the name would hold the spirit from moving on.

"The songs we sang for people who passed over were to encourage them to go on. The songs told them that the ones they left behind would let them go and promised to join them when the time was right. Sometimes the grief of the people who were left was too much, and they would kill themselves so they could journey together. This was not encouraged, but if it happened, there was respect for that person's decision, and it was not considered a criminal thing. It was usually wives who did it, for if a strong man died and left his wives behind, they were considered slaves of his family for two years after the death of their husband. Some wives were too proud to be in that position."

"I am glad that some of the customs have changed," I tell him. "My husband's family wouldn't have known what to do with me."

"Those ways will never come back, but the understanding of those ways is important. If you imagined your husband coming back to you each time he left, if you imagined the next year with him, and always pictured your life together, there would be a good chance you would bring that future toward yourself. We knew there were many paths available, and if you chose a future without your husband, it was your fault."

I am slightly indignant. "Do you mean it's my fault Lorne is gone?"

"No more than it is mine that my Clementine is gone," he answers.

We look at each other for a minute. "But it was the wife's responsibility to make sure her husband returned," he says, then with a twinkle in his eyes, "Back then men and women were equal. Men walked in front to protect, not because they were more important."

It is a theme that I've always expressed, that men and women are equal but different. We should walk beside each other; neither one deserves to lead or follow. He knows full well that

I believe this and offers it as a balm. I accept it, put my notepad aside and go to get supper on.

The next week is very warm. The temperature stays above zero every night and soars to ten degrees Celsius in the day. The melting snow sends little rivers through the yard, and we go out every day to direct them where we want the runoff to go, I with the hoe and Grandpère with his walking stick. The snow has lost its pristine whiteness and looks dirty and tired.

The dogs are running around, happy in the warm weather, but my older dog, Duke, has developed a stiffness over the winter that makes him move with a strange gait. His hips seem to be stiffening up, and his front end always seems to be waiting for his back end to catch up.

I take some bones out of the freezer and the dogs hide them from each other in the snowbanks. It is funny to watch them trying to be unobtrusive, affecting an air of nonchalance to each other, then each burying its bone quickly while the other one is out of sight.

I put two chairs out in the sun, and we take our tea sitting in them, both of us shedding our coats in the heat of the late February sun.

"This won't last, so we'd better make the most of it while it's here," I say.

"Springtime never comes in February," Grandpère agrees. Sure enough, by Friday the wind starts blowing, the temperature plummets and a snowstorm brews up and dumps another six inches of snow to usher in March.

I plant the seedlings in their containers, and everything germinates but one package of leaf lettuce. I always mean to write the year on the seed packets when they arrive but seldom get around to it, so I don't know how old the seeds are. Too old is my guess, and I add leaf lettuce to the list of seeds that I need to order from the supplier. The last to germinate are the peppers. I like to grow the red-hot chili peppers that bear the pods above the plants. They're pretty and dry well for storage. Sometimes I store the seeds, but because the plants are hybrids, the seeds don't always grow the same plant as the ones they're harvested from. These ones are from the seed company.

Clint and Patty phone and say they will come down from Edmonton for Easter. They've been up to visit Darcy, Faith and the girls, and they're as much in love with Angel as the rest of us are. Easter is in April this year, and the week before is the children's school break, so they plan on coming on the Wednesday. They'll have to leave on Easter Sunday.

"No worries," I tell them. "We'll have Easter dinner on Saturday." I love it that they always try to come for Easter.

After they hang up, I call Parker and Kristen and ask if they can come for Easter too. Parker says they'll try, since it isn't too busy at his job in the sales department of a big car dealership. His company has laid off some of the salespeople already, he says, and they'll be happy to give him some time off. He says Kristen is really busy in her office. "The tougher times get, the busier she gets."

When I phone Jesse, he says they just can't make it this year. Jesse has already been laid off, and Jessica doesn't want to take any time off because they're having a hard time with only one salary. He doesn't get as much on employment assurance as he made when he was working. When I ask if he needs a loan, he laughs. "We aren't destitute, Mother, we just have to watch our spending a little more. Nothing to concern yourself with, we're a long way from needing a handout." But I think I hear a little worry beneath his bravado, and before he hangs up, I tell him how much I love him.

Before the receiver has cooled down from my talk with Jesse, Darcy phones and tells me the girls have made a plan to travel down on the bus so they can spend the whole week of their school break here. Will that be all right with me and Grandpère? I assure him that it's more than okay with me, it's a wonderful plan. He tells me how well Angel is doing in school. She's so bright that the teachers say she'll be caught up to the rest of the class before the year ends. I'm pleased to hear this, and I'm so eager to see my girls that I'm fairly dancing with excitement when I get off the phone.

The next weeks pass quickly. The temperature rises again, and all the greenhouse soil needs to be turned. I do it with a wide shovel, double-digging to bury last year's topsoil underneath and bring the underlying soil to the top. I sprinkle bone meal on top, and Grandpère stirs it into the soil with his walking stick. It feels exciting to get the soil ready, and I'm full of anticipation to see what the new season brings.

My old dog seems to be getting worse. His hips are not moving easily, and he has trouble getting to his feet. I read in an animal health journal to give him Tylenol to help him move more easily, so I start giving him a couple each morning, and it seems to help. Grandpère tells me that he thinks I should give him a couple each morning as well. "If it works for an old dog, it will probably work for an old man." So he takes them along with the dog.

"Do you need yours tucked inside a wiener?" I ask him, because that's the only way I can trick Duke into taking them.

"No, I think I can swallow mine with water. No need to be sneaky with me," he replies. It seems to help him too.

I start all the other plants in the flats in the bedroom and add a halogen light to the room. The tomatoes and peppers are big enough to pot, and they need the extra light. It is so bright that I put on sunglasses when I tend to the indoor garden. Grandpère thinks this is hilarious, and he says the sun is shining brightly inside even on cloudy days. The ballast for the light makes quite a loud hum. We can hear it anywhere in the house but soon get used to it and after a few days don't even notice it. The plants are all doing well. When they start to get crowded in the flats, I transplant them into plug trays, so that when I set them out in the garden they will have strong, healthy roots. Tending the tiny plants takes a lot of time, but they hold the promise of warm weather and garden bounty. It's something I really like doing, too, so it's more like play than work.

The soil that I brought in hatches fungus gnats, and the annoying miniature flies are taking over the house. They seem to enjoy flitting in front of our faces while we're playing cards, eating or trying to do anything. I get some sticky traps to hang around the room, and pretty soon the flies are under control. The sticky trap papers are covered with tiny fly bodies, but I am glad they work, because the alternative is spraying insect killer, and I don't believe that's good for people to breathe. I phone The Bug Factory on Vancouver Island and ask them to ship me some bugs that control fungus gnats so I can mix them in the soil in the greenhouse before I plant the rest of the crops.

# Chapter Eight

The month passes by quickly, and before we know it, April is upon us.

My mother's cousin Alphonse from Saskatchewan comes by to visit. He brings his dad, my Uncle John, with him. Uncle John is one of Uncle Tree's children, the only one still alive. He is eighty-two years old and has been living with Alphonse since they went to the prairies. He looks a lot like Grandpère, small and alert with twinkling brown eyes. We are happy to see them. They didn't phone and tell us they were coming, just stopped by as though they were living next door. I didn't know who they were till I opened the door, alerted to the fact that someone was here by the dogs baying.

"Well, for heaven's sake," I greet them. "Didn't know you still knew how to find us."

"Dad got restless this winter, and I promised him a trip back to the old stomping grounds before spring planting," Alphonse tells us, then adds, "I knew you were here, because we didn't hear otherwise. No news is always good news, you know. Bad news travels fast."

"John, how good to see you." Grandpère hugs them both,

and I go to make something for lunch. They sit in the living room, and I can hear them laughing and talking a mile a minute. I have leftover meat loaf and some boiled potatoes in the fridge. I spread the meat loaf in the bottom of the pan, pour a can of cream corn over it and slice the potatoes thinly on top. I stick it in the oven and make a salad. By the time the salad is made and the table is set, the dish is heated through. I call them to the table, and they all come to the kitchen.

Alphonse is a nice guy who makes everyone feel good, and today is no exception. "That's the best meal we've had for two days since we left home, Cousin," he tells me.

"Leftovers! You're just getting leftovers, nothing special."

"It might be, but it is still good." Uncle John confirms Alphonse's opinion. "We stopped a lot along the way. I am already tired of hamburgers and fries. Never thought I would see the day I was tired of French fries, but today is the day."

They are heading back up to the old Fort, where two of Alphonse's sisters still live. They say the snow is just about gone from the prairies, and it looks as though it will be a good spring for planting. It's been too dry for the last two years to have a good harvest, but with the eternal optimism of prairie farmers, they're expecting it to be a good season this year. "If it remembers to rain," adds Uncle John.

"Surely you can do a rain dance when you get back," I tease him.

"If a rain dance would help, it would have helped last year and the year before. Dancing, praying or threatening, nothing seemed to budge the rain out of the sky. The clouds would build up, then pass us by and go rain on Ontario, where they really don't need all that rain," he says.

I ask Alphonse where his wife is. "She couldn't come.

She had to stay and look after the cows and the chickens. She isn't much of a one for travelling. She told us to take pictures, and she will look at them when we get home."

That makes me laugh. It sounds just like Pearl. It's a wonder he talked her into moving to the prairies at all, and I don't think she's been back since they moved. Alphonse gets his camera from the car and takes pictures of me and Grandpère, then takes one of the room full of plants, then goes outside and takes one of the dogs. "That old dog looks like his hips are giving out," he tells me when he comes back in.

"I know, he is pretty old." I do some quick calculations in my head. "He was just a pup when Sarah was a baby, so he must be near on to fourteen years old. In dog years he must be the same age as Grandpère."

"Yeah, we walk about the same speed," Grandpère says.

They can't stay long, as their family is expecting them before supper, and we're soon saying goodbye. We wave at them from the step till they're out of sight, and when we turn to go back in, I'm surprised to see tears in Grandpère's eyes.

"It's probably the last time I'll see that old bugger," he says.

I don't ask whether he's feeling his own mortality or John's. I ask him if he would like to play some crib, and he wins all the games, so he's in a good humour again long before supper.

"Sure was nice of them to come by," he says quite a few times, so I know their visit has touched him.

Rose calls and says the garden beds are almost ready. Would I come by next time I'm in town and have a look at them? I have to go to town anyway, so the next day I stop by to see the progress.

The home is built in a U-shape, and they have built the garden beds in the space between the wings that's sheltered from the wind. It is warmer than most places, a great location. The beds are well-built of posts squared on three sides and have dovetailed corners. They look great. Rose wants to know what soil they should get to fill the boxes.

"You can order a dump-truck load of compost from the Reimers," I say. "They have really nice compost."

"Oh, good idea." She grins. "I'll call them this week. Is it too early to start planting?"

"In this sheltered location we can start salad greens next week," I tell her, "as long as they get covered at night with garden blankets."

"Where can I get garden blankets?"

"I'm going to the feed store. I think I can pick some up there."

Rose tells me to save the invoice and bill one hour for my time today. She also reminds me to keep track of my mileage for coming to town.

"But I had to come to town today anyway," I say.

"Whenever you come here, you bill us for the mileage. It doesn't matter what else you do in town while you're here," she tells me with a smile. "We have a big budget for this project, and it's one of the good ones, so don't be bashful."

The feed store has garden blankets just the right size, so I pick up two. I notice dog food for "senior dogs" at the store, and I ask what the difference is. The clerk tells me it has been fortified with special ingredients that help old dogs' bones and muscles, and even though it's fifty dollars for an eighteen-kilogram bag, I buy one, hoping it will help old Duke regain his strength.

Suddenly I feel in a huge rush to get home, but I don't know why. I race through the grocery store and don't stop to gas up the car, even though it has only a quarter-tank left.

When I get home, the door to the house is wide open, and Grandpère is sprawled on the porch. I throw the car into park and run to the house. He is passed out, just like last summer, still breathing but unconscious. I try to lift him, but he's too heavy. I roll him onto his back, then get him into the house by lifting under his arms and half-dragging him over to the couch. For such a small guy, he sure is heavy. I get him up on the couch, but he is still out to the world. I bring a cool, wet cloth and sponge his face for a while. I cover him up with blankets and light the fire, for the house has cooled off. I think the door has been open for a while. His breathing is deep and even, but this is more than just sleep. It doesn't sound right. I wonder if I should call someone, but just as I'm deciding, he thrashes around a bit and starts to wake up.

"What the hell? What the hell?" he keeps muttering.

"Grandpère, you just had another spell," I say to him, but he doesn't seem to understand. I keep sponging his face till he pushes my hand away. He focusses on my face and smiles.

"Annie, my Annie, I thought you were gone," he says to me.

"I'm right here with you," I tell him.

He sits up. "Clementine, my love, get us a cup of tea," he says to the air beside him. "Look, Annie has come home."

I am totally flustered by this time, and I tell him just to wait, I'll be right back with the tea. He keeps looking at me with a tender smile as I race around getting tea ready. He sits on the couch, his hands in his lap, and watches me. He takes the tea. His hands are shaking. He takes a couple of gulps, then in a distracted voice says he thinks he will have a little nap. He lies back down on the couch, and goes to sleep. I know he is just sleeping now. The soft snoring reassures me that he's over his fit, and I think he's going to be all right.

I go out to the car and realize I never even turned off the ignition; it is still purring away in the yard. I unload the groceries and dog food, trying to do everything very quietly so I don't disturb his slumber. I remember last year when this happened; he slept for a long time and woke up fine. I water all the plants in my grow room and make supper. He finally wakes up and asks what time it is.

"Suppertime," I say. "Let's eat in the living room."

I set up two TV tables, and we eat side by side on the couch. He picks at his food, then says he thinks he'll make an early night of it. He wonders where his stick is, so I get it from beside the front door.

"How did I leave it there?" he wonders, but I answer him with only a smile.

I watch him closely as he goes into the bathroom, then into his bedroom. He is a little shaky and slower than usual, but he is doing okay. When I hear the bedsprings creak, I heave a big sigh and realize how tense I am. I start crying and cry till I feel like a snotty, blubbering fool. If tears can fix things, I have done my best, I tell myself. I stay up late reading a book and check on him every little while. He is sleeping soundly, and I finally make myself go to bed.

In the morning everything is back to normal. If he remembers anything about the day before, he doesn't mention it, and neither do I. I tell him the girls are coming on the bus today, and he says he thinks he will come with me to pick them up. I have no intention of leaving him home alone while I go in, so I'm glad he decides to come of his own will.

The bus is late, and we wait in the café at the bus stop till it arrives. A young woman with a tiny baby is waiting to get on the bus. Her baby is fussing, and she's trying to get it to take the soother, but the baby keeps spitting it out and crying. She looks tired, and I feel sorry for her. I ask if I can hold the baby for her. She looks as though she's going to say no, but then she changes her mind and says, "If you want to. He's not happy and won't settle down." I take the baby from her, put him on my shoulder and start rocking him back and forth. I hum a little tune that's always settled down my children and grandchildren, and he rewards me by wiggling close and going to sleep. She sits down at our table, and Grandpère asks if she's hungry.

"A cup of coffee would be nice," she says, and Grandpère waves over the waitress and orders one.

"Where are you headed?" he asks her.

"I'm going to my mother's. She lives two hours south of here, and I'm going to stay with her for a while. She hasn't seen my baby yet. He's only two weeks old."

"He is a very nice-looking baby," Grandpère tells her.

She explains that she'd been living here with her boyfriend, but he has a camp job at a mine up north and won't be home for a month, so she's taking this opportunity to visit her mother. "I never knew how hard it is to look after a baby. He hardly ever sleeps, and Mike can't stand it when he cries. I hope he learns to sleep better pretty soon."

Just then the bus arrives, and we all get up. The baby stays asleep while I transfer him back to his mother, and she thanks us and makes off for the lineup forming in front of the bus.

The girls are the first ones off, and they make a beeline for us, laughing and talking and hugging us both. Angel looks nothing like the bedraggled girl who arrived on our doorstep a few short months ago. Her skin is clear, her hair is shiny and she looks happy. The three girls pile their bags in the trunk and climb into the back seat, talking non-stop the whole while.

I keep glancing at them in the rear view mirror, hardly believing that they're all in my car and ours alone for one whole week. They're animated, talking over each other, telling us about Angel trying to skate, laughing about how many times she crashed, all the while Angel protests that she really did turn out to be a good skater. Her cousins tease her, "Yeah, but only when Ryan, the handsome Ryan, held her hand to keep her upright. But maybe she just tried to be wobbly so he would help her."

Grandpère says to me between snorts of laughter, "How are we going to be able to hear ourselves think for the next week, with this flock of ravens croaking steady?"

Squeals of indignation come from the back seat. "Grandpère, can't we at least be pretty birds, maybe songbirds?"

"Yeah, maybe robins or bluebirds?" says Tammy.

"Maybe hummingbirds?" says Sarah.

"I think we might be majestic eagles, soaring high above the clouds," says Angel.

When we get home, they want to all sleep in the same room. "We each have our own rooms at home, but lots of times we all sleep in the same room. Dad and Mom don't care as long as we get our homework done, and it goes faster if we help each other," says Tammy. "I'm the oldest, so of course I help these little girls with theirs."

More squeals from the other two.

"And how would you have passed math if Angel and I didn't help you?" exclaims Sarah.

They want to go outside as soon as they get their stuff stashed in the bedroom, and we go out to the greenhouse. Grandpère putters along behind us. When Angel sees how far behind he is, she goes back and walks with him. Tammy and Sarah immediately tell me how much fun it is to have Angel living with them. "She's more like a sister than a cousin. Everyone at school likes her, and she's so pretty that all the boys want to go out with her, even some of the ones in our grades."

"You're all too young to go out with boys," I tell them.

They groan. "Everyone in our school goes out with boys. They're the only thing that makes school interesting. You're just old-fashioned, Anzel."

By this time Grandpère and Angel have caught up. "Why do you call Grandma Anzel?" she wants to know.

"When they were little, after their mom died, I taught them my name so they wouldn't call me Mom," I explain.

"Well, you're just like I always imagined my Grandma would be, and I want to call you Grandma."

"You can call me anything you like, my sweet."

They're as excited as I am about the new plants sticking their heads up through the dark greenhouse soil. I show them how to turn on the hydrant and water the plants with the fine-spray nozzle. They cover the little plants with the blanket when they're done, and then they want to walk up to the lookout. I ask Grandpère if he wants to come, and he says, "Yes, but I will go up on the bike if you don't mind."

I tell them to start up ahead of us, and I go into the house and pack a picnic lunch. Grandpère is waiting by the bike, and by the time we get to the top, they're sitting by the big rock. The remains of Angel's fire lie off to the side, just a dusting of ashes left.

Angel tells the other girls about the fire, how she threw all her bad experiences into it and let the flames take them away. "I don't know why it worked, Grandpère, but it did. I still remember my old life, but it seems so far away, and it doesn't hurt to think about it anymore."

"It is a healing that my uncle taught me when I was a young boy and was very sad because of some things that went wrong."

"What things?" they ask.

"The things I threw away then are gone, just like this fire here is gone. It is not good to bring them back even by talking about them."

I say, "How about you girls get some dry wood, and we can light another fire. This time we'll use it to toast our lunch."

The girls run around to gather dry sticks. Grandpère shaves a dry twig with his jackknife, and soon we have a pretty little fire going. They borrow his knife and come back with willow sticks to cook their sausage over the fire. Grandpère sits on the ground like the rest of us. When I tell him to sit on the bike because it is more comfy, he tells me that the ground is the best place to sit up here because it lets him touch the earth.

"We never had wood floors in our homes when I was young. The first time I slept on a wood floor was in Papa David's house. I am used to it now, and I like my soft bed with a mattress, but the first time, it felt like I was away from an old friend. The earth sings you to sleep when you lie down on it." His voice sounds far away as though he's going to tell us a story, and I wish I had my notepad. But he doesn't, he just closes his eyes and rocks himself for a while.

Duke shows up. I had told him to stay at the house, but he must have followed us as soon as we left. He doesn't always do what I tell him. The young dog, Blue, is excited to see Duke and tries to get him to play, but Duke growls at him, and goes over and lies down beside Grandpère. He pats the dog gently and croons to him. Blue comes around to everyone, can't decide who to lick the most, then gets distracted by a squirrel in the bush and bounces off to his own pursuits.

"Let's camp up here one night," Tammy suggests to the other girls. "Can we, Anzel?"

"If you want to. It still gets pretty cold at night, but if you have warm sleeping bags, you should be fine."

"Tonight let's sleep in the house, but tomorrow let's set up the tent here and spend the night," says Sarah.

"I always wanted to camp out, but I never have. It will be fun," says Angel, and the girls start planning what they need to camp out.

Grandpère and I get back on the bike, and the girls say they will be down shortly. I try to get Duke to jump up on the back of the bike — he used to ride there when he was a puppy — but he doesn't want anything to do with it and follows along behind. I feel badly when I see him limping along, but short of manhandling him onto the bike, I don't really see any choice.

The next day I teach the girls how to drive the four-wheeler. They are all a little jerky on the throttle, but by noon all three know how to drive it. It has an electric shift and will only start in neutral, but sometimes the shifter doesn't work, so they have to know how to use the wrench to do a manual shift. Sometimes the electric start doesn't work, so they have to know how to pull the starter cord. Sarah listens to instructions best, so pretty soon she's the expert on the bike, and Tammy and Angel are content to let her do most of the driving. They make about ten trips up and down the hill.

They take the tent, three good sleeping bags, matches, paper, flashlights and enough food for a small army. I pack the food in a cooler and tell them not to take any food or the cooler into the tent at night; if a bear comes around he will smell it in the tent and try to get in. Then I wonder if I was wise to mention bears, but bears are a real concern, and it's better if they know how to avoid a conflict with one. I tell them to keep Blue with them; he will sleep in the tent with them and keep them safe.

They laugh and say not to worry, they'll be fine.

By suppertime they have their camp all set up, and I take a ride up with them to check it out. They have rolled a log over to the tent for a bench, and they have enough dry wood piled up to keep a campfire going for a week. I tell them it looks cozy enough to live in, and they're all pleased with themselves. They take me back down to the house, and off they go to spend the night in the woods.

Grandpère and I laugh about them camping. He bets they're all back in the house by morning, but I don't take him up on it. I remember my own kids camping in the backyard. I don't think they ever spent a whole night out — invariably they would be back in the house before daybreak — and it was always the other guy who got scared, his siblings were just coming in to keep him company.

In the morning there is no sign of them, but Blue is home in the yard, and we are both surprised. By noon I am no longer surprised, I am worried. I decide to take a hike up there and see how they're doing. I ask Grandpère to keep Duke in the house so he won't follow me and set out on the trail to the top. The campfire is still smoking when I get there, and almost all the firewood is gone. There is no sound coming from the tent, but when I unzip the flap, they are all still inside, sound asleep.

The morning is hot, and the sun has really heated up the inside of the tent. My unzipping wakes up Sarah, who bolts to a sitting position, wide-eyed. When she sees it's me, she visibly relaxes and asks what time it is.

"High noon. I was wondering if you were coming down for lunch."

"Noon? It feels like I just went to sleep," she says, reaching over to shake the other girls awake. "You guys, it's noon already."

They look as though they had a hard night.

"How was it?" I ask.

"It was so scary. We stayed out by the fire way after dark. Then when we came in, Blue wouldn't stay in the tent, so we let him out. He went out growling and barking, then he got farther and farther away. After that, we kept hearing noises outside, and we didn't know if it was Blue or a bear, so we started singing really loud and sang for a long time, and then it was quiet out. But when we tried to go to sleep, someone would hear a noise, and when we listened, we could all hear noises, and we were afraid to go to sleep, then we started telling stories to each other, and then we got even more scared, and none of us went to sleep till it started to get light." Tammy is talking a mile a minute.

"Why didn't you jump on the bike and come back to the house?"

"We were scared to come out of the tent, and none of us knew how to turn on the headlights."

It makes me laugh to think of the girls huddled in the tent, scared silly, and I can't keep myself from laughing. They look at me indignantly, then all three of them start laughing too.

"Well, here it is noon already, and you all lived through it. Do you want to come back to the house now or are you ready to camp out the rest of the week?"

"Back to the house. You'll miss us too much if we stay out here," Sarah says earnestly, and we all start laughing again. They have the tent down and are all packed up in record time.

"Don't tell Grandpère how scared we were. He'll think we're a bunch of wusses," Tammy says.

I promise not to tell. I've been looking around in the soft ground, but there are no tracks other than the dog tracks. I tell them they must have been imagining sounds, and they agree that sounds are a lot scarier in the night than they are in the day. I am still chuckling when we get back to the house with the three campers perched behind me on the bike and all the camping gear piled into the trailer.

Later the girls help me transplant seedlings from the flats into the plug trays, and the job is quickly done. It is most pleasant working with them. They are full of stories of the camp-out, and I notice that as the day progresses, they remember less about being scared and more about how much fun it was.

They all have iPods with them, even Angel. When I ask her about it, she says, "Auntie bought it for me. She said it was a late Christmas present. And we have a really nice computer that we can use any time we want. I have my own email address. It is Anzel at Hotmail. Do you know Anzel means Angel in Carrier? All the Angel names were taken, so I used yours."

"Yes, my dear, I did know that. I don't know if your mother knew it when she named you, but I'm glad we share our name.

How did you find out about Carrier language?"

"It's an elective course in our school. The teacher told me my name in Carrier. It's a fun class, but we still can't speak the language, we just know some of the words."

I am amazed that the school is teaching Carrier, and when we tell Grandpère, he starts talking to them in Carrier. They don't have any idea what he's said, so he gives up and tells them they have a long way to go.

"We took it for fun. The teacher is really nice, but none of us can understand her yet."

"I think you have to grow up speaking it to ever really understand it," I tell them.

At one point when I was young, I wanted to learn it, but with no one to speak it to, the few words I did learn are gone from my memory. Grandmère Clementine could speak English, French and some Carrier, but my mother and father spoke only English to us, and except for a few swear words in French, English is all we learned.

It is so much fun having the girls here that the days fly by. They want to learn everything I do, and since it is warm and the frost has gone out of the soil early this year, I decide to rototill the garden and plant some of the hardier seeds. My old Rototiller fires into life at the first pull, and I start at the top end of the garden. Sure enough, the ground is dry already, and the tiller churns up rich black soil. It is an amazing transformation. The dry, cracked clay that's on top of the ground after the snow melts disappears beneath the tines, and behind us is lovely, soft garden soil. I keep tilling down until the soil starts clumping, which shows me the rest of the garden is too wet yet, so I quit and put the tiller back in the shop.

With Grandpère directing, the girls have the seeds planted in perfect rows almost as soon as the ground is ready. By the time I've put the tiller away, the job is complete.

"The rest can wait a few weeks till I know it isn't going to snow any more," I tell them, for a freak snowstorm in April is not unheard of here.

Just as though I've called it into being, the next morning we wake up to a blowing blizzard, and before it's over, there are four inches of fresh snow on the ground.

"What about the seeds?" the girls worry.

"They're snug in the ground, so it won't hurt them a bit. This snow will melt away in a couple of days, and they'll get a fresh drink to help them wake up," I tell them. "Aren't you glad it didn't do this the night you camped out?"

"That would have been quite the story to tell our friends. Hey, you guys, let's make a snowman before it all melts away," says Sarah.

They all put on my winter clothes and make a giant snowman. They dress it in a huge straw hat and a scarf and throw a shawl around the shoulders, not to keep it warm, they explain, but to keep it cool.

# Chapter Nine

It is early on Wednesday when Clint and Patty and the boys arrive, and as a wonderful surprise, they've brought Jesse and Aaron. It was a last-minute decision, Jesse explains. Jessica had to work and they'd decided not to come, but when Clint stopped there, Jesse decided to come along.

The snow has all melted, leaving behind mud that sticks to our boots in great clumps and makes walking a chore. The trees are starting to bud, and the moisture has started to turn the lawn green. The boys are full of energy after being confined in the Jeep for hours.

It's the first time Jesse has met Angel, and he keeps looking at her with curiosity. "You look so much like Ben but in a girl body," he tells her, and I can see she's pleased to know that.

"Anything you want us to do while we're here?" Clint asks.

"No, I'm caught up on everything here. The girls and Grandpère started the garden already, and the rest of the yard is still too muddy to work on. Let's just visit."

Patty has brought the boys' Lego, and all five boys are playing with it. Baby Seth is walking, though he still falls down a lot. The older boys spend half their time keeping him away from the castle they're building, but he wants to play too, so they give him his own pile of blocks and try to distract him from wrecking theirs. He likes the little horses, so they give him some of them to play with. He still puts them in his mouth, and they are disgusted to find his slobber on them. "Not to eat, Seth," Ryan keeps telling him. The girls tell us they're going to make supper. They don't want any help, since they tell us they are master spaghetti cooks.

"Go to it," I tell them. They may be master cooks, but the kitchen looks as though it will need some master cleaners when they are done with it.

"That's the reason we should have had some girls," Patty tells Clint.

"Well, we can keep trying," he answers. "But with our luck, we will probably have ten boys before a girl pops out."

"Maybe we'll call it good and rent our nieces for the summers."

"Good idea, Auntie, we can come and be your slaves for the summer," calls Sarah from the kitchen.

"I'm coming to stay here for the summer," says Angel. "Grandma and Grandpère need me."

For the summer? I wonder, have plans been made that I don't know about?

The spaghetti may indeed be the best spaghetti I've ever tasted. They've made garlic toast and even an apple crisp for dessert. No one has denied Aaron any part of the supper, and I wonder if he's over his allergies. I don't ask in case Jesse suddenly whisks his supper away and replaces it with dried noodles.

After supper Patty and I tell the girls we'll clean up the kitchen, and everyone else sits around the living room and visits.

Patty asks me if Jane has tried to contact me, and I tell her she hasn't.

"Don't you think that's weird?" she asks.

Now that I think about it, it is weird. Jane must know by now where Angel is. Or maybe the restraining order prevents her from finding out. "She doesn't deserve to have that girl. She hasn't been any kind of a mother to her," I say.

"Mom, Angel is a sweet and good kid, and she didn't get that way on her own. Jane must have done a few things right for her. Most kids in her situation would be wild and doing who knows what in the conditions she was living in. I think we should give Jane a little bit of credit for how good Angel is."

I have been so angry at Jane that I never thought of it this way. "Well, I guess she must have done a few things right," I concede. "Just the same, I'm glad Angel got away from her."

We make a pot of tea, once the kitchen has been restored to order, and bring it to the living room. Clint, Jesse and Sarah have just finished playing crib with Grandpère, and Angel and Tammy are playing with Seth. Every time he laughs, they laugh too. He is still young enough to think that if his head is under a blanket, he's hidden. "Peek-a-boo," they say when they whisk the blanket off his head, and he laughs a little belly laugh. He's as cute as a button.

"Grandpère, will you tell us a story?" Ryan asks.

"What story do you want to hear?"

"Tell us a story about when you were a boy."

I get my notepad, and everyone wants to know why. "I'm writing down the stories so that after Grandpère is gone, we'll still have his stories."

"Where is Grandpère going?" Jayden wants to know.

"I am going where everyone goes when they are finished here on earth. It is the land past life," Grandpére says, smiling at the kids. "Let's see — how about I tell you the story 'Bear learns from his Mother'?"

The kids nod and settle to listen.

He begins, "Bear was born in the mountains in a little den behind a big rock. The summer before Bear was born, his mother dug the den deep into the hillside under the roots of a large spruce tree.

"In the summer Mother Bear ate everything she could find. In the spring she ate roots from the plants and new leaves, and in the summer her favourite food was berries.

"Later on in the summer, huckleberries would get ripe. She found her friend, Father Bear, in the huckleberry patch, and they spent long hours playing, eating and sleeping in the hot summer sun. They both grew fat and lazy, but bears need to be very fat because they sleep all winter long.

"In the fall the bears came down from the mountains to catch the salmon. They came to the river where they met all their cousins; they all came down to the river because there were so many fish, they could all share.

"The fish had laid their eggs in the river-bed gravel so there would be new fish to go downstream the next year. Then the fish gave up their bodies, and the bear did not have to catch the fish, just find them on the banks and eat. Mother Bear was grateful to the fish for giving their bodies to her.

"Eagle liked the fish, too, and one day while Mother Bear was sleeping with a half-eaten fish in front of her, a strange noise woke her. Eagle had taken her fish, and was eating it right in front of her. She jumped up, angry that Eagle had stolen her fish.

She growled and jumped at Eagle, but he just laughed and flew away, and he took the salmon with him.

"Mother Bear was angry that the bold Eagle had taken her fish, and she stood up and growled at him. She put her arms around a willow bush and bit it, wishing it was Eagle she was crushing. She wrestled with the willow bush for a while, then pulled it right out of the ground. Mother Bear was very strong.

"There were hunters in the bush, and they heard her roaring and growling, and they snuck up on her. They were going to hunt her. She smelled them coming, and she knew to run away when she smelled the hunters. She tried to sneak into the woods, but they had seen her, and before she got out of sight she heard the loud boom of the rifle and felt a crease of pain across the top of her back.

"She was hurt, but she could still run very fast, so she ran for many miles till she felt safe from the hunters. She found willows and ate the bark to help with the pain. She dug out the roots of other plants that she knew would make her better. For days she limped around, but soon she felt better.

"Then one day, after the frost had made the ground as hard as rock, when the clouds were heavy in the sky, Mother Bear went home under the spruce tree.

"Before springtime, while there was still snow covering the earth, Baby Bear was born. He was just a little, tiny baby. Mother Bear had woken up just long enough to lick him and his brother clean and then she went back to sleep. Baby Bear and his brother drank milk when they were awake. They wrestled and played in the darkness of their home and slept long hours snuggled in the fur of their mother, till one day she woke up and crawled toward the entrance of the den.

"After a while she left the den, and the baby bears followed her. She dug in the earth for a while, finding roots to eat, then she went and laid under the spruce tree that was growing on top of the den.

"While she lay at the bottom of the tree, the little bears tried out their sharp claws on the tree bark. To their surprise they found they could climb trees. At first they only climbed a little way. Then they would fall — *Crash!* — onto their mother. Pretty soon it was a game. Baby Bear found he could climb very well, and after a few hours he climbed almost to the top.

"His brother was asleep with his mother at the bottom of the tree. He was so high in the tree that it was too far to jump down. He didn't know what to do, so he just stayed there. His mother woke up and looked up at him. He knew she wanted him to come down, but he didn't know how. She sent him a picture of a bear slowly hanging on with his claws, backing down the tree. He tried to do it, but after only a little way, he slipped and came crashing down to the bottom. It hurt, but he knew he was all right, and he followed his mother and brother across the hillside and down to the creek at the bottom.

"When the cubs did something she didn't like, their mother would reach out with her paw and swat them. They learned quickly what they were allowed to do and what was going to get them a swat. Many times she would make them climb a tree, then make them stay there while she went off. She would send them mind pictures of them staying there, and most of the time they would do what she wanted.

"Mother Bear taught them all the things that bears have to know, where to find the good food, what smells are ones to run and hide from, and where it is safe to play. They met all the animals in the woods and became fat and sleek.

"When Mother Bear met Father in the summer, the two cubs stayed away, but when Mother and Father parted again, she let them come back and live with her. In the fall the two babies were almost as big as their mother, but the den was big enough for all three. The next spring the cubs left the den to go down to the creek and from there they kept travelling. They knew now how to live well and they did."

Grandpère finishes his story and looks around at us. I'm still scribbling like mad, trying to get the story down in his words, and Seth has gone to sleep on Patty's lap. It amazes me that these little ones are so quiet while Grandpère tells his stories, but now they have a dozen questions.

"How big was the bear? What colour was he? Why didn't the father stay with him?" come their voices all at once.

Jesse stands up and pretends he is a bear, stretching his arms out and growling. "This is Papa Bear, and he says you all have to go to bed right now."

We all laugh at him, but the boys get up and start getting ready for bed. Aaron says he and Pierre are going to sleep together; they've been playing together all afternoon and are fast friends. Jesse says they can sleep with him, and I notice with pleasure that Aaron doesn't have to wear a diaper to sleep anymore.

"Did you just make that story up for the boys?" Patty asks Grandpère.

"The words are not the same, but the story is. The stories for children contained all the children's lessons. It was through the stories that we learned how to behave. All year there were stories. Each place in the woods and the mountains would contain a story. The names of the places and the people would hold a story. All the places are renamed now, and the ones who kept their names have lost their stories.

"I sort of made it up, and I sort of remember the pictures the stories made in my young mind. I find in my memory that little boy sitting in front of the fire, imagining the two little bears blinking in the light at the end of the tunnel while their mother sleeps."

While he's telling us this, he screws up his face, pretending to be a baby bear sniffing the wind, his eyes squinting in the imaginary sun. He looks like a little bear, and we all laugh.

The girls are looking at my notepad. "It might as well be written in Greek. How do you know what this means?" I show them my method, and they are impressed that I can actually read what I've written. "When you get the stories written out, save them, and we'll make a book," Sarah offers. "The school has a binding machine they let us use."

"Cool," I say, and in my mind I see the broken branch of the family tree with the name Sven written on it. I wonder what the girls will think of that story.

Everyone goes to bed. I've moved to the cot in the office and am in bed reading for a while when there is a soft knock on the door. Jesse comes in.

"Hi, Son." I sit up and pat the bed beside me.

He comes and sits down, and I can see he wants to confide but is fighting himself to do it.

"What's wrong, dear? You might as well just tell it straight." I take his chin, look in his eyes and smile. He is my sweet son, the one who wears his emotions on his sleeve. I have saved wooden plaques with "I Love You" handwritten with varying degrees of readability, all from this boy.

"Oh Mom, it's Jessica and me. I don't think she loves me anymore. She isn't happy, she's angry all the time. She says it's not me, but I think maybe it is. Mom, I love her, but I sure don't like her sometimes."

Hearing that makes my heart hurt. I want to agree with him; I don't like her much either. But he chose her, and they have a responsibility to try to get along for Aaron's sake. "Don't forget, Son, you teach people how they can treat you. Can't you just ignore the anger and try to make her laugh? Angry people need to laugh more."

"She doesn't think I'm too funny anymore. Things she used to think were funny just make her go 'ha, ha' in a sarcastic way, not funny at all."

"Honey, people go through these periods when they look at their mate and think, My God, how did I end up with you? But the truth of the matter is that you learn the lessons in your life from the people who are closest to you, and no one is closer to you than your wife. You're teaching each other some important lessons. Instead of being mad or hurt, ask yourself, What am I learning? and maybe you'll get through it."

"Did you and Dad ever feel like this?"

"A time or two. We both had tempers and strong wills, so we butted heads once in awhile. But we could always make each other laugh, and we both learned to say 'I'm sorry,' so most of the time we were pretty much happily married. Just try really hard for a while, Jess," I beg.

He nods, swallowing a couple of times. "Thanks, Mom." He gives me a kiss on the forehead and quietly leaves.

It isn't news I want to hear. So many divorces now. I hoped for all my children to be able to raise their children in a two-parent home with parents who love each other. I know so many people who grew up in a home where the parents made it a battleground, and those people are invariably scarred deep. I believe that if people can't be nice to each other, they shouldn't be around each other. I cross my fingers and my hands in an ancient warding sign passed down to this modern age, a symbol for hope.

I have a hard time going to sleep, and I dream about the little baby bear lost and crying for his mother. In the dream the little bear turns into Aaron, and then I am sitting in a chair rocking him, and then he turns back into the little bear, jumps off my lap and runs out the door of the house and disappears. Then I'm looking for him in the bush, but he's a big bear now, catching salmon in the river, and I'm sad that he's forgotten he was a little boy. I wake up, still half in the dream. It's just as real for a while as the room I'm lying in, till my amazement that I am awake and dreaming at the same time snaps the dreamland out of focus.

The weather has been nice, but a snowstorm is forecast for Sunday, so the kids decide they should leave on Saturday. We decide to have Easter dinner on Friday and spend the day cooking. The boys take the saws and go cut up firewood. When they come back, they say we don't have to stack it like that, they can just cut it out of the pile, and I wonder what they're talking about. Then I remember Grandpère's pyre, and I look at him.

"Oh, I just did that last fall while I was puttering around," he says. I look down to hide my smile. He isn't about to admit to these guys what he was doing.

On Saturday morning they time their departure so they can take the girls to the bus stop. Eleven people are stuffed in the jeep. Good thing they have three rows of seats. As it is, three of the boys are sitting behind the back seat on top of the luggage. I hope they don't get stopped on the way into town, but they are all laughing with the fun of it when they leave.

Suddenly the house is too quiet, and Grandpère and I go outside. Blue comes running up and runs toward the greenhouse in little short runs, whining in the back of his throat. I know he wants me to follow him. I do, and when we get to the greenhouse, I see Duke lying in the little hollow he always sleeps in by the south wall. Blue runs over and pushes him with his nose, continuing to make little whimpering sounds. He runs back to me and sits down. "Come here, old boy," I say to Duke, patting my knees. He tries to get up but can't, and I see why Blue is upset. Duke can pull up his front end, but no matter how he heaves, his back end won't co-operate. I know what it is. I have read in the animal health journal about old dogs' hips suddenly becoming paralyzed. There is no cure. My dog needs to be put out of his misery. Should I take him to the vet? I wonder.

By this time Grandpère catches up. He stands beside me to watch the struggling dog. "Need to shoot him," he says.

"I can't do it. Maybe I should take him to the vet."

"It would be cruel to move him to the car, make him ride to town and take him in to the vet," Grandpère replies. "Just bring me the twenty-two. I can do it."

I go to the house, put Blue inside and get the twenty-two and Duke's dog blanket. I find a clip, put three bullets in it and bring it to Grandpère. "Are you sure?" I ask him, knowing he hasn't shot a gun for a few years now.

"This little gun, she don't even kick. You just go away and get the bike and trailer."

I get the bike and am hooking on the trailer when I hear the shot. Just one. Thank you, Grandpère.

"We'll take him to the landing, where the wood is," he says. I drop the tailgate on the bike trailer and drag Duke onto his blanket. Then I lift him into the trailer. He is lighter than I expect, and I keep patting his side. I curl him up in the trailer, then Grandpère gets on the bike with me and we make our way to the sawmill landing.

When we get there, Grandpère, who seems to have turned into the funeral director, tells me to start piling wood. There is a huge pile the boys have cut up, and while I pile up wood, he sits on a stump and whittles shaving strips into feathery shapes. "Stop," he tells me after I have made a pile about six feet across and three feet high. "Let's make a nest for him."

He points out two boards and tells me to lean them on the pile, then tells me to back the trailer up to them. We drag the poor dead dog wrapped in his blanket onto the boards, then, with Grandpère pushing and me pulling, we drag the dog and the boards to the top of the pile.

"Go get some bones," he tells me.

I drive back to the house and get a package of frozen bones out of the freezer. When I get back, Grandpère has built a little teepee out of wood over the dog. He puts the bones inside and tells me to keep piling wood. I add strips till the pile is as high as I can reach, then make it round like a cone. Grandpère takes his kindling strips and puts them around the pile in a circle, singing a little chant while he does it. He tells me to light every one of them, and I do. The fire catches right away, and in no time the whole pile is blazing. "Say goodbye, and come away now, Anzel," Grandpère says.

I think of the years I had with Duke and what a good dog he was. Happy trails, old buddy, I say to him in my thoughts, bowing my head for a while. Then Grandpère touches my arm and motions me toward the bike. I nod, and we climb back on the bike and go to the house. Blue must know something is over, because he doesn't want to go outside. He just sits at the table with his head on my lap while we eat.

After lunch Grandpère goes for a nap. I sit on the step, my arm around Blue, and watch the smoke curling in the air in the distance. I have a little cry for myself, and Blue snuggles closer and licks my face. "Pretty good, that old dog," I say to him, and he seems to agree with me.

The next morning Grandpère gets a little wooden box that he has made and tells me we have to go back to the landing. When we get there, the pile is completely burned up. Grandpère takes his walking stick and stirs in the ashes till he finds some bones. "Pick up the bones and put them in the box," he tells me, and each time he stirs one up, I add it to the box. There aren't very many, just some big joint bones and part of the skull with the teeth still in. When he doesn't find any more, we take the box to the shop and nail a top on it.

"Where do you want to put him?" he asks.

"Up at the lookout, I guess. That's where the rest of them arc." The thought that he and Lorne will be together again pleases me.

"Just walk around till you find the right place and leave the whole box there."

I take the box on the back of the bike to the top of the hill. I walk around the ridge, wondering where to leave it. I stand at the edge and spot a little shelf about six feet down. I can get right to it and suddenly I'm sure that's where I want to leave him. I get the box from the bike and climb down to the shelf. It recesses more than it looked like from the top, and I'm able to tuck the box right into the face of the rock. I go back to the top and hunt around till I find a flat stone about the same size as the box, then take it down and lean it up against the box. It looks like part of the natural landscape, and I am pleased with the location. "Rest in peace, my friend," I say to him, and I suddenly feel a lot better.

When I get back to the house, Grandpère lifts his eyebrows at me, and I nod to him. We don't talk about the dog funeral or the resting place. But the old man has a gleam in his eye that tells me he just showed me how to do things his way.

# Chapter Ten

Next week the weather turns balmy, so I phone Rose to ask if they're ready to plant some starts.

She says, "Come on Wednesday."

I talk Grandpère into coming with me. "You don't have to go inside, just help me get the beds right."

"Don't let any of those husky nurses throw me in a chair and start wheeling me around," he jokes.

"Just yell for help, and I'll hit them on the head with my shovel," I tell him.

We load up the car with plants and seeds. I have been taking flats of lettuce, Swiss chard, bok choy, broccoli, cabbage and cauliflower in and out of the house every day to harden them off, and now they're quite ready to be planted out. I bring along the garden spades and the two blankets.

I love this time of year when everything is waking up. As I drive to town, the poplars are just starting to turn green; no leaves are visible, but the tops of the trees have a greenish glow. The bright green of the new grass makes a striking contrast to the withered blades of last season that form great clumps along the roadway. The first arnicas are starting to bloom, their pretty yellow faces turning to the sun. The evergreen leaves of the Oregon grape are shining on the forest floor, soft in their mossy beds, and the sun is streaking through the pines. This is the decade when we learn to live with tall, dead pines. It may seem odd that dead things are beautiful, but the pines have gone through stages of red and purple and finally needle and bark drop. They remain beautiful.

On the way in we see three deer. They stand and look at us as I slow the car. They're not a bit scared, and we pass within ten feet of them.

"Sacrifice deer," Grandpère says. "They're saying 'Have me for lunch.'"

Lots of people are outside when we get to the home. It has a lovely yard, and there's a concrete path to the garden area. Two workmen in coveralls, with shovels and wheelbarrows, are filling the beds. A big pile of compost has been dumped at the edge of the paved parking lot, and the men have the beds I want to plant all ready.

The top rail has been painted and plastic stapled to the inside of the wood. The soil is beautiful — fine and rich. When I squish it in my hand, it makes a clump, which breaks when I drop it to the soil surface. Perfect!

I borrow a wheelbarrow to bring the flats of seedlings from the car to the beds. One of the workers offers me his, then insists on wheeling it over for me and returning to get the rest. I thank him when he gets back. He's a good-looking man of about my age. His hair is still mostly black, but I can see silver threads in it. He's wearing it long and braided under a baseball cap turned backward. He has a sunshine smile and bright, dark eyes. He tells me, "At your service, little lady."

I thank him, then realize I have already thanked him, get embarrassed and go off to start planting. Before I even realize I need it, he rolls out a hose with a fine nozzle. I thank him again, he just grins and inclines his head with the same gesture Grandpère uses for "you're welcome." I watch him as he walks away; he looks much younger just walking. Maybe I've misjudged his age. What a nice guy!

Some of the old folks have gathered round. Bertie is pushing Jack in a wheelchair.

"What happened to his legs?" Grandpère asks Bertie.

"He can still walk — he just can't remember from one step to the next where he wants to go, so it's easier to put him in the chair and take him outside. He likes it outside."

She parks him by a tree, and he reaches out and touches the tree. Then he sits motionless, his hand on the tree, smiling contentedly.

Bertie comes over and takes an interest in the garden. She goes and gets sticky labels and marks what is in each row. It's a good idea. We plant one bed with salad greens, one with broccoli and cauliflower and one with carrots and peas. The last bed I plant half with spinach and half with the hardened-off herbs. We put the garden blankets on the first and last beds, and I explain to Bertie that they need the blankets on if there's a call for frost or if the sun shines as brightly as it does today. She says she personally will check the weather forecast every night and make sure they get covered. I tell her it's okay to leave them covered up all the time, but she says they look too pretty to hide all the time.

The kitchen staff bring out tea and snacks, so we all sit down to enjoy them. The two workmen come over and sit with us. The one who helped us introduces himself as Jim.

"Have you lived here long?" I ask.

"Just moved to town last fall. I have a place above the learning centre."

The learning centre used to be a corner store, and the people who ran it lived upstairs. I was up there once long ago and remember it as a rabbit warren of rooms filled with stuff from China, where the store people had emigrated from.

"Are there still lots of rooms up there?" I ask.

"Yes. I only live in three of them. The rest are just empty. They said I could knock out some of the walls and remodel the place. I might do that. A person could make it really nice." Then he laughs. "They'd probably raise the rent if I did that."

"Are you a carpenter?" Now I feel as though I'm interrogating him, but he doesn't seem to mind.

"I've done a lot of carpentering over the years but I don't have a ticket. I'm sort of a jack of all trades. That's why I got this job. They need all kinds of different things done around here, and it's a good place to work."

Now it's his turn. "Do you live in town?"

"No, Grandpère and I live about twenty minutes west of here," I tell him. "We live on a farm, but it's not really a farm anymore unless you count chickens as livestock."

"If you have chickens, it's still a farm," he asserts. His eyes are black, and he has two dimples that show when he smiles. He is making me feel like a schoolgirl. I keep looking at him, and every time I do, he's looking back. After a couple of times, I quit sliding my eyes away and look directly at him. He smiles, and I feel as though I'm blushing. My God. Sixty-three years old and feeling like this. I smile back, then tell Grandpère we'd better go. He and Bertie are having a plant discussion, chatting away like long-lost friends.

I wave to Jack. "Bye now. See you next week."

He waves at us, then Bertie grabs his chair and wheels him back toward the door.

At the car Jim comes up and says it was nice to meet us. "Are you coming on Wednesday next week?" he asks.

"Yes, I'm going to try to come each Wednesday morning."

"I'll maybe see you then. Nice to meet you," he says.

I'm glad I'm not the only one repeating myself. I grin at him, and he waves till I turn out of the parking lot.

Grandpère is sitting in the passenger seat, just full of it. "Goo-goo eyes. That's what you have, Anzel, goo-goo eyes."

"I do not. I was just being friendly. Besides, if anybody has those eyes, it's you and sweet Bertie." The best defence is a strong offence, I believe.

"She is pretty sweet. She doesn't have to watch out for Jack; she does it because she's nice." He is unperturbed. "That was a mighty helpful man. I think he wants to steal my little angel." Give Grandpère an inch, and he's taking a mile. He's grinning away as though he has ammunition to spare. "I think we'll be seeing a lot more of that man."

"Oh, get away with you," I tell him. But I keep thinking about Jim all afternoon and that night I dream about him.

In my dream we're in a canoe — he's in the back — and we're going down a river. I'm kind of scared, but he's singing a song, and pretty soon I know the words and am singing along and am not scared anymore. We get to a bend in the river and beach the canoe. I have my wicker picnic basket and set out a picnic lunch, making a table out of a big rock. I cover it with an embroidered tablecloth and set plastic dishes and cutlery around as though I'm in a fancy dining room. He lights a campfire, and we're cooking marshmallows over it when I wake up.

I shake my head. I think maybe I have a crush on the workman at the lodge. I haven't looked at anyone else since I lost Lorne and feel disloyal for a minute or two. Then I laugh at myself. When I was younger, I thought passion died with age, but here we are, and this stranger has me thinking about things I haven't thought of in years. Could I even deal with another relationship? Something to ponder when I'm pulling the weeds out of the garden.

I miss Duke, and Blue is living up to his name, though when we named him, it was for his colour and not his mood. He's just moping around as though he's lost his best friend. He has, I guess. I decide maybe we should get another dog as company for Blue.

"What kind of dog should we get?" I wonder aloud to Grandpère. "Do you think we should get a house dog, one of those little ones that sit in your lap?"

"God, no. Esther had a little Shih Tzu when we got married. That dog never liked me and never let me forget it. We had him eight years, and he never learned not to shit in the house. He liked to do it on anything that was mine. Once he even crapped in my shoe. Dogs are not meant to be in the house." He thinks for a minute. "Let's get a Bernese mountain dog. I knew one once. It was really big and really smart. It was a guard dog but it wasn't mean. There were little kids there, but he was really gentle with them. I think that would be a good dog to have."

I buy all the *Buy & Sell* papers for BC and one up from Alberta too. We find only one listing for Bernese mountain dogs, and it's in the city where Parker and Kristen live. The ad says, "Puppies, eight weeks old with all their shots, $1,000."

"I think you picked a dog that we can't afford," I say.

"I got money. I'll buy the dog," he says, and despite my protests, he insists.

I phone Parker and ask him to go look at the puppies and pick us out the biggest male as Grandpère has specified. He agrees and phones us back two days later. "Those are the cutest pups I ever saw. The boys came with me and fell in love. We've got yours and we bought one that looks just about exactly like him for us. We'll drive up on the weekend. When we said we'd take two, she let us have them for eight hundred dollars each."

I'm eager to see our new dog, and Grandpère asks me about three times when they're coming, so I know he's eager too.

"Saved two hundred dollars on that dog already," he tells me.

I go in on Wednesday to see the home gardens, as I've been calling them. Everything looks perfect. There are hoses clamped on the ends of the beds and little rows of sprinkler heads down the centre of each one. To water, we just turn a valve handle halfway, and a spray of water covers each bed perfectly. I think it's a work of art, and when Rose comes by, I ask her who set it up.

"One of the maintenance men, Jim, did that."

"Oh, I met him last week. He seems nice."

"He seems to think you're nice too. Asked me a couple questions about you." She's grinning like the Cheshire cat in Wonderland. "Only told him good stuff, don't worry."

I tell her my plans for the other garden beds. I want to wait two more weeks, then plant pumpkins and squashes in one bed, fill another with potatoes and fill a third with salad greens and carrots. The last bed would get planted later with fall crops. She doesn't pay much attention to what I'm saying, just keeps telling me it's my call and whatever I plant there is fine with everyone.

Bertie tells me that some of the seedlings are germinating in the salad green bed. Sure enough, radish seeds and some of the spinach seeds are starting to sprout. "Good management," I say to her, and she beams with pride.

"Where's Jack today?" I ask her.

"He didn't want to come out. He doesn't want to get out of his chair. He's happy just sitting there, so I left him." She sounds put out by his laziness and shakes her head disapprovingly. "It's just sitting around that makes him like that. He spends too much time inside his own head and forgets to pay attention to the here and now. I'm not going to get like that. Your Grandpère, he's a lot older, but he's still a real person. I'm going to keep myself busy so I don't get like them."

"Good for you, Bertie." I'll bet it's scary for Bertie in there, seeing people younger than her lose touch. I feel sorry for her; she could almost manage on her own. I wonder how she got here and where her family is. I wonder if I'll get to know her well enough for her to give me answers to satisfy my curiosity.

I show her which are the radishes and spinach and point out the weeds. They're just as quick to germinate as the seeds we planted. She helps, and another older man joins us. He compliments me on the fine job, and then he too helps pick the weeds. There aren't many, and we're done everything there is to do before lunch. Bertie tells me and Grandpère to stay for the meal.

I am hanging around, hoping I'll see Jim so I can tell him how good the watering system is, but Bertie says the maintenance guys had to go into town to get a fountain, so I know he's not around. I feel kind of disappointed. Oh well, I don't have to listen to Grandpère on the way home. It's going to be my turn to tease. I start on him before we even leave the parking lot.

"That Bertie is probably twenty years younger than you, but I think she has her eye on you. Says you're still a real person."

"I'm more than a real person. I'm a love machine," he says, and we both crack up.

Once home, I decide it's warm enough in the greenhouse to trust that the rest of the plants in the house can go out there to stay. I spend the afternoon traipsing back and forth with the bike and trailer, transferring all the plants. I plant the tomatoes and peppers right into the soil, and the rest stay in their plug trays, waiting to be set out in the garden. We have a bench at the back of the greenhouse, and they all fit on it.

I'm just finishing and closing up the greenhouse when Blue starts barking, and a strange car pulls up. A woman gets out and stands looking around. She looks as though she's about to get back in, then changes her mind and starts walking toward the door of the house.

"I'm over here," I yell, and she turns to meet me. I wonder if she's a saleslady, but we don't get many of them anymore. She has short hair, cut straight at about ear length. She's wearing jeans, a sweater and sneakers and carries a bag over her shoulder. She appears to be about forty and looks kind of hard. She is very pale, as though she never gets outdoors, and is holding her sweater closed as though she's cold.

"It's Anzel, isn't it?" she says, holding out her hand to shake. "You probably don't remember me. My name is Jane. I was friends with Ben."

As soon as she says her name, I instantly know who she is.

How dare she drive into my yard and act as though she has a right to be here? I shake her hand but am instantly angry.

"What do you want?" I am kind of short with her.

"I want to talk to you, Anzel. Can we visit for a while?" Her voice is pleading.

I tell her to come in the house and we'll have a cup of tea. She doesn't look me in the eye but nods that she will, so in we go. I stay silent. The accusations are flying around in my head, and it's all I can do to be civil to her.

I serve the tea and sit at the table across from her. I don't need to be nice. She came here, and if she wants sympathy, she's not getting it from me. The silence stretches. She's looking at her lap. Finally she begins, "I owe you an explanation. This is the first time I've been back here since Ben died." She is silent for a while longer, but I say nothing.

"It was a horrible time for me. I didn't come around here because I felt so badly."

"We all felt badly," I say. "It was a hard time for all of us."

"But you don't understand." Her voice goes all quavery. "It was my fault he died."

"Nonsense. He died because he drank too much and thought he could still drive," I say. It's hard to accept even now that Ben would drink so heavily and climb in his car to drive home.

"I'd just found out I was pregnant, and I told him in the afternoon. We had a big fight. He said he wasn't ready to get married or have children, and I told him I wouldn't have an abortion. That's why he was drinking. It's my fault all of it happened."

"Jane, you can't blame yourself for what Ben did. He wasn't a child anymore. It's not your fault any more than it's my fault. No one forced him to do what he did." I can't believe I'm saying this to her, but to carry around a guilty feeling like that is not right. People make their own choices.

"Everything fell apart for me that day," she continues. "I never told anyone about my baby till after the funeral. Then I told my mother. She was so angry that she kicked me out of the house and told me never to come back. So I left and moved to the coast. I worked in a restaurant, waiting tables, till I was too big to do it anymore. Then I had a baby girl. I named her Angel." She looks right at me when she says this, but I say nothing.

"Everything went well for us for a long time. I had a boyfriend, and he was like a dad to Angel. He made us seem like a family. But I drank a lot in those days, and he didn't like it. Sometimes I stayed out all night and partied, but Robert got angry and didn't like me much, and after a while he was there more for Angel than for me. One time I was gone for a few days. When I came back, he'd moved out and taken Angel with him. I found them, and he had to give Angel back to me. I made sure he didn't get her again.

"Things got really bad after that. My friends were alcoholics and drug users, and I started using hard drugs. My life these last three years has been a blur. I wasn't a good mother, and Angel pretty well looked after herself. I kept promising myself to quit, but I never lasted longer than a week. Then I was out looking for a way to get high again. Last winter Angel ran away, and I haven't seen her since. At first I thought she must be dead. But she isn't. I put myself into the rehab centre and got clean. While I was there, I was served a restraining order that means I can't go near her. I can't even find out where she is. All I know is that she's alive."

She starts sobbing while she tells me this. Anger and pity are warring inside my head.

"Why didn't you come to us?" I ask her.

"My own family didn't want me, why should you be any different?"

"I would never turn anyone away because they were pregnant. I would have cherished your baby for Ben's sake."

"I thought you would turn me away because you would know it was my fault Ben died."

"Quit saying that. It is not your fault. Did you force him to make a baby with you?"

A hint of a smile crosses her face, quickly gone again. "No," she says, and we're both silent for a while. "In rehab they told me I had to make peace with my past. I guess that's what I'm trying to do." She picks up her bag from the floor, and fishes a picture out of it. She hands it across the table to me. I've seen it before, in the centre of a missing children's poster.

"She's pretty," I say.

"She's a really good kid. I wasn't a good mother to her, I'm afraid. After she got to about eight years old, sometimes it seemed like she was the grown-up one. I wish I could have gotten straightened out before she ran away. I hope she's happy. I would give anything to tell her how sorry I am."

"Things have a way of working out," I say. "What are your plans now?"

"I moved back here two weeks after I got out of rehab, and I got a job in the kitchen at the seniors' home. Right now I'm staying in a room at the motel, but I need to find a place pretty soon. I couldn't stay down south anymore or I would have fallen back into my old life. They have meetings here that I go to. It helps me remember the way I want to live." She sits quietly for a minute, then says in a wistful voice, "Maybe Angel will come here. She always wanted to know about her father after Robert left, and I told her he used to live here. If she comes here, I want to be the kind of mother she deserves."

I wonder if I should tell her where Angel is, but some part of me will not give her the satisfaction. If she'd decided to straighten out before it got so bad, they would never be in this situation. Anger is winning. Pity has to stay away for a while yet. "Well, you've made some good choices now. Good luck to you, Jane," I say.

"Thank you." She pauses for a bit. "I've been dreading facing you. I thought you'd be so mad at me. Over the years I imagined myself telling you, and in my mind you were a lot angrier. I loved him so much." She starts crying again.

"If I was mad at anyone, I was mad at Ben. He was a grown man. He knew better than to do what he did. You can quit blaming yourself." Here I am comforting her. In my imagination I was going to rip her apart if I ever saw her again — for Angel's sake, not Ben's — and here I am, patting her shoulder and comforting her.

Grandpère comes out for a cup of tea, and I introduce Jane to him. She remembers him from before and tells him she never imagined that he was still alive. Then she gets embarrassed, and tells him how good he looks.

"Old but good," he returns, and we all laugh.

"I should go. I borrowed the car to come out here from one of the ladies at work, and I promised her I wouldn't be gone long," she says. "Can I come out here and visit again?"

"If you want to," I reply. Then I tell her I work at the home on Wednesday mornings, doing the gardens.

"Are you the lady who's planting the vegetables? They look

really nice, and we're going to use them in the kitchen. Some of those lettuces are nearly ready. Maybe I'll see you there." She puts on her sweater and leaves, patting Blue on the head and lighting a cigarette before she gets in the car.

I stand looking at the driveway for a long time after the car pulls out. Jane back in town. Wanting to be friends. Crap, what a weird situation.

"The Great Spirit has its own reasons for the way things turn out," Grandpère tells me. He's sitting at the table, nursing his cup of tea. "She seems like a nice person. Maybe it is good she came back here."

"All these years she's blamed herself for Ben dying," I say. "She looks way older than she is."

"Pretty hard life. It makes people old before their time," he replies.

I make supper and we eat, but my mind is wandering all over. I decide to phone Angel after supper and talk to her.

She tells me she got an A in math and that she'll be caught up in English and science by June. She chatters on for a while, then I break in and say, "Angel, your mother was here today."

She is silent on the phone, then in a quiet voice, "Is she okay?"

"She's moved here and has a job cooking. She went to rehab and says she doesn't do drugs anymore."

"Is she looking for me?"

"I didn't tell her that I knew you or where you were. She knows you're alive, but she doesn't know where you are."

"How does she look?"

"She looks fine."

"Last time I saw her, she had sores all over, and she kept picking them till they bled."

"Well, I didn't see any sores. I think she's making a better life for herself. But you, chickpea, shouldn't worry. She can't find out where you are, and if you don't want to see her, you don't need to."

"I kind of miss her."

"You'll be here in the summer. Maybe you can see her then if you want to."

"I think I want to. But I don't want to live with her."

"Let's cross that bridge when we get to it, then," I tell her, and we talk for a while longer. Later I ask to talk to Faith and tell her about the visit.

"Poor Jane, what a load to carry all this time. It's probably good you didn't say anything. The restraining order runs out at the end of the month. I'll talk to Darcy and child protection services and see what they think about renewing it. We have legal custody, so she can't make Angel go with her. Don't worry, Mother, nothing more bad is going to happen to our Angel." She's so matter-of-fact and unworried that by the time I get off the phone, I feel better.

# Chapter Eleven

Friday night rolls around, and we're waiting for Parker and Kristen to bring the new dog. We have a bag of dog food — special formula for puppies — and I bought some chew toys. We put the big wire cage that we used when Blue was a pup just inside the door, and I put a soft blanket in the bottom. I soak the dog food in a bowl and set it inside. When the new puppy arrives, we'll be ready.

The kids left the city at noon and said they would arrive by dark. At dusk I'm getting up every few minutes and peering out the window to see if headlights are coming.

Grandpère laughs at me. "If you watch the kettle it never boils," he says. "Sit down and have a hand of crib."

We are halfway through the game, and Grandpère is way ahead, when Blue starts barking. I fold up my hand and put it back in the deck.

"Don't want to get skunked, eh?" he teases me, but folds up his hand too, and puts the pegs back at the start.

As soon as the car stops, Cameron and Coby put the two pups on leashes, and they walk to the far side of the driveway, where both pups squat and pee in unison.

"Good boys," the boys praise the dogs. Ezra tells them to undo the leashes, and the pups run back to the car.

"No, we're here now, no more car rides," Ezra says, pushing the pups away from the car. "Grandma, we should leave them out for a while, they never pooped all day."

Blue is sniffing them all over, and though his tail is wagging, he keeps jumping toward them, and they seem scared.

"Should I put Blue in the house?" I ask Parker.

"No, they'll be all right. We'll just stay out here for a little while till they're comfortable enough to do their business," he says.

We watch them for a while. They're not sure about Blue, but when he finishes sniffing them and trots across the yard, they follow him. At the edge of the bush he sits down, and they go their separate ways to find places where they can poop. They are little balls of fur, hardly bigger than the chew toys I bought.

"Their parents were both there when we picked them up," Parker tells me. "They are huge dogs. Very gentle — they just sat there and wanted to be petted while the boys picked out the pups. The woman said they were very good watch dogs."

"Our pup got sick in the car. He puked all over Mom, and she puked too," Ezra says.

I look at Kristen, and she's grinning. "Lucky I had extra clothes. I usually can clean up barf, but today Parker had to stop fast so I could do it outside. Don't know what came over me."

"Maybe you're pregnant," I say.

"No chance of that. I think it was the combination of the heat and the smell." She shudders. "We stopped and bought some Gravol, but we were close enough to here that we didn't give him any. But on the way back, he's getting some before we leave."

Both pups have done their business, and we go into the house. The pups are happy to be inside. They wrestle with each other and check out the house with a trail of boys following them everywhere they go. When the pups bite on things they're not supposed to, the boys tell them no and move them along. I give the chew toys to the boys to give to the pups, and these distract them for a while. The little dogs are growling at each other and playing tug of war with the toys, and we're all laughing at them.

"What do you want to name him, Grandma?"

"You have to ask Grandpère. He chose this dog."

They look expectantly at Grandpère.

"What do you call him?" he asks the boys.

"We named ours Bandit because he has a mask and we called yours King. But Dad says you'll probably call him something else," says Ezra.

"King is a good name. It suits him. He can keep on being King," Grandpère says, and the boys look quite pleased.

"They said we should keep giving him the same food, mixed up a bit with the other kind, if you're going to change feed," Parker says.

I show him the food I bought, and he says it's a good kind. He takes a handful of the food they brought and mixes it in the bowl with the food I've been soaking. Coby spreads another blanket on top of the ones in the cage, and the pups go inside and curl up with each other, fast asleep and snoring in just a few minutes. We laugh about the snoring.

Cameron tells us they snore all the time. "They fart a lot too," he says, and all the boys giggle.

The boys are all going to sleep together in the big bed, so we say goodnight, and just like the pups, they're asleep in no time.

I haven't seen the kids since Christmas, and Parker and Kristen haven't even met Angel yet, but we've kept in touch over the phone, so they know what's going on. I tell them about Jane coming here, and they agree that it was right not to tell her we have Angel. "Let's just wait and see if she really has turned her life around. Rehab isn't all that successful, from what I have heard," Kristen says.

"I always liked her when she lived here before. She was a really nice kid, and I know Ben thought the world of her," Parker adds. "What kind of mother would have kicked out her daughter because she was pregnant? What would you have done if Nadine had come and told you she was pregnant?"

I can answer that question easily, because that's just what she did. I remember coming into her room where she was sitting on her bed, crying. When I asked what was wrong, she said, "Everything. I'm pregnant, and Darcy isn't even finished school, and he wants to get married, but I don't want him to quit school, and it's ruined everything." Darcy was in his second year of university, and Nadine had been working in the grocery store while he went to school.

I sat beside her, put my arms around her and told her it didn't matter. "You can stay here and have the baby. There's plenty of room."

Lorne had come in and was standing by the door of her room. "A baby in the house would be pretty nice," he said, and came and sat down on the other side of her, his arm around both of us. "Don't worry, princess, this baby must have wanted to come awfully badly. They don't always come just when it's convenient." He'd caught my eye over her head and winked. I was sure he was remembering me telling him Clint was on the way. We weren't married yet either at that time, although before another month passed, we were. We just went and got married by the justice of the peace. Grandpère, Esther and Lorne's parents were the only ones who came to the ceremony, and after we spent two nights in a motel, he moved into the house that my brothers and I shared after Dad and Mom died.

Nadine stopped crying. She said she'd been afraid to tell us, but if we were happy about it, she would try to be too. Darcy had different ideas about that, though, and insisted they get married right away. He said he was lonely in the city and would probably be able to study more with Nadine there to cook and clean. By the time Tammy was born, they'd made a home there, and Sarah was born the following year.

Parker and Kristen are looking at me expectantly and I realize I've been lost in my memories. "Nadine did get pregnant, and your dad and I were happy about it, and so was Darcy," I tell them. "I don't know Jane's mother, but what she did was wrong. She has only robbed herself. Babies are a blessing, and she is poorer for not having her daughter or her granddaughter."

"Are you going to tell Angel?" Kristen asks.

"I already did. I phoned her on Wednesday, the night after her mother came out here. She sounded like she kind of missed her."

"What a weird year. Just when things settle down, it seems that something stirs everything up again." Parker is turning philosophical. "It keeps things interesting though, eh?"

We have a great weekend. King and Bandit tumble and wrestle and gallop everywhere after us. They pee on the floor indiscriminately as soon as they're in the house, and the kids tell me the pups are paper-trained. I tell them King has to be bush-trained. So we get into a routine of feeding and watering the pups in the cage. After they eat and have a sleep, as soon as they wake up, we put on the leashes and take them to the edge of the bush, where they go to the bathroom. As soon as they squat to pee, we unhook the leashes and praise them. At night we lock them in their cage.

Kristen is a real fan of the cage. The puppies like it, and it gives some control of what a pup can chew in the house. I have a smaller plastic one, and I send it with them when they go. The weekend passes too quickly, and before we know it, they're packed in the car and heading home.

King whines softly on the leash beside me. Now that his foster family has gone, he pays more attention to Grandpère and me. Blue still maintains a dignified distance but wags his tail when King sniffs him from end to end.

I've been able to serve fresh salad from the greenhouse, and so much spinach is ready that I decide to pick a big bag and take it to the home on Wednesday. I take the pup with me to the greenhouse and teach him not to jump in the beds. He's a quick learner and a sweet dog. If I'm sitting still, he comes over and flops at my feet. When I'm walking around, he follows along. He's clumsy and falls over his own feet a lot, but he doesn't mind us laughing at him. When he follows Grandpère along, he tries to chew on the cane. "Quit that," Grandpère tells him and gives him a little whack with it.

When we go to town on Wednesday, we lock the pup in the cage on the deck out of the sun. Grandpère doesn't need to be talked into coming. He's ready first thing in the morning and comes to the breakfast table with his town clothes on.

I take a ten-pound bag of sprouted potato eyes and flats of

zucchini, pumpkin and butternut squash. The trees are budding in earnest. The leaves are out on all the shrubs, and you can't see the forest floor anymore. The arnica is in full bloom, and the dandelions are starting to put on their sunshine show. It's so warm that I put the back window down partway to enjoy the spring air.

At the home lots of the people are outside already. The garden beds are looking fine. There isn't a single weed in any of them, not even in the ones I haven't planted yet. All the seeds have germinated, even the carrots.

"Who's been doing all the weeding?" I ask.

Bertie answers, "We've all been doing it. Well, not all, but whoever wants to just pulls a few when they go by. I show them which ones are weeds."

"Show me your hands," I say to her.

She holds her hands out, and they're stained brown from the plant juices and the dirt. I laugh and show her mine. Bertie's hands look good compared to mine, but it's still obvious that she's pulled a lot of weeds. I give her a hug. She feels stiff for a second, then hugs me back. A quick squeeze, then she backs away. I don't think women have hugged her much.

She and Grandpère start talking a mile a minute, and I take off to find Rose. "How's it going over?" I ask.

"Everyone is impressed. It's great to have the lettuce and chard started like that. Six-inch-high lettuce on the day of planting was great. Those garden beds are the best looked after in this whole town. Bertie puts in so much energy that they should be spectacular."

"Maybe I need to invite the old folks to come home and look after mine," I tell her.

"Not the same. No pride of ownership," she tells me. "Besides, I'd get in trouble if I sent the old folks out to a labour camp." This sends us into gales of laughter, with much speculation as to what the charges could be. She comes with me, and we're still laughing when we get out to the garden.

Jim is there and has brought all the plants from the back seat. He's just as good-looking as I remember, and he tells us there is nothing nicer to see than two pretty women laughing. Oh, he's a big flirt, but I get a warm glow just being around him.

Grandpère and Bertie, walking side by side, are discussing where to plant. Grandpère knows the plan that we worked out at home. We plant nine zucchini in three groups of three down the centre of the bed. The butternut go at the ends, and the two centre spaces get two pumpkins each. I tell Bertie to just let them spill over the edges and to use the garden blanket for these ones now as frost will hit them the hardest.

By lunch we're all done. We're served outside again, and Jane is one of the servers. She seems efficient and greets some of the old folks by name. When she comes to our table, she's smiling and pleasant. "I hoped I would see you today. This is very nice, Anzel," gesturing over at the raised beds.

"I can't take all the credit. Jim here built the beds, filled them and hooked up the watering system. We'd better give him some credit too."

"Hi, Jim. You know I give you credit too."

"And I deserve it, girl. Nice to see you here, Jane. Is everything going well?"

"Yes. This is a good job, and I like it here. But I'd better get moving. I don't want anyone to have to chase me down with their chair to get a meal."

She laughs easily, smiling at us, and away she goes.

"How do you know Jane?" I ask Jim when she's gone back into the kitchen.

"I just met her. She comes to the meetings. I might become her sponsor. I'm just getting to know her."

"The drug meetings?" I ask.

"Yes. Once I was where she's at now. I cleaned up my life, and it helps me to appreciate it more if I can help other people out. I've been going to the meetings every week for over twelve years now. How do you know Jane?"

"She lived here when she was younger. She was my son's girlfriend."

"You're Ben's mom?" he asks in surprise.

"Yes."

"Oh my God, how the world turns," he exclaims. "Say, we need to talk. Privately. Do you want to come and have coffee with me in town after I get off work one night?"

"Why don't you come out to the farm? You can come for supper on Friday if you want to."

"Sure, that would suit me just fine."

We grin at each other. We've just made a date. Weird.

On the way home Grandpère talks about Bertie. "She shouldn't be in that place. She is pretty capable. She just didn't have anyone to help her and she was lonely. She tried staying with her boys, but she felt uncomfortable there as though she was intruding. She offered to go to the home, but she hoped there was someplace else that she could go. It's pretty boring there for her."

"Jim is going to come here on Friday. Maybe he could bring her along for a visit," I tell him.

"Maybe next week. I'll tell her next week when we go there and see if she wants to." Then he starts in, "Ho, ho, the sexy man and the goo-goo eyes get together."

I can't think of a single rejoinder, so I just laugh along with him.

The next days pass quickly. I bake and cook. Grandpère is filled with glee, teasing me as everything gets done. "Is that for us, or are we saving it for someone special?" he asks. "Should we set out the silver?" And he says, "I hope he brings us lots of horses."

"Go take your dog for a walk," I keep telling him.

I watch him through the window. Blue walks sedately beside him, and the pup gallops circles around them. Grandpère seems spryer than he was last year, and sometimes he's gone for several hours before they wander back into the yard. The pup sleeps for a long time after their walks, and he's getting better coordinated. He asks to go out now, and we haven't had any piddle on the floor for three days.

On Friday afternoon at about five, Jim arrives in his pickup. It's an older truck, quite loud, but it's clean and shiny; he tells me under the new paint the rust holes are all filled with body filler. "Had her since she was new," he tells me. "Gone down many roads together." He pats the truck as though it's alive and can return his affection.

He looks really nice. He has on jeans, a soft plaid shirt and a leather vest beaded with rose vines up the front and a whole bouquet of roses across the back shoulders. He wears sneakers and a baseball cap, facing forward this time. His hair is braided and done up with leather lace.

He compliments me on every dish, and Grandpère keeps

telling him what a great cook I am and listing my accomplishments as though I'm a prize horse he's selling.

"All right, all right," I say to him. "Enough already." He's embarrassing me but seems quite unrepentant.

After supper Grandpère decides to take the dogs for a walk, and Jim and I go out to the greenhouse with our coffee. We look at the garden along the way, and he seems interested in everything. In the greenhouse we settle down on the chairs in the potting room and talk about Jane.

"She came out here to talk to me. She thought it was her fault Ben died. But it wasn't."

"We don't talk about the stories people tell in the meetings. But you already know her story, so it's all right if we talk about it. Do you know where her daughter is?"

"Yes, we have her." I pour out the whole story. "But I never told Jane, and I think right now it's best left that way."

Jim is silent for a while, then he agrees. "She seems like a nice girl, and I think she's really trying to stay on the recovery path, but you never know. Addiction is strong, and she's still at the stage where she could easily give in to her cravings. I know she's had at least one relapse since she got out of rehab; it's why she moved. I think I will sponsor her. She has a lot to live for, and I can help her out." He nods to himself for a while, then says, "Come on. Show me your favourite place here."

We walk up the trail to the lookout and sit down on the rock. The fields are all bright green with the new alfalfa, and the leaves are big enough to fill in the bush canopy. Everything everywhere is green and lush. Jim says he sees why it's my favourite spot, and we sit in contentment, chatting away till dusk. He tells me he's been single since his marriage ended in his early thirties.

He says he's wandered all over the country, even moved down to Texas when he was in his forties. He says he had a rough time of it for a while, but ever since he left drugs and alcohol behind, his life has steadily improved.

We are quiet for a while, then he moves closer and puts his arm across my shoulders, and I lean into him. For a time we just sit there, letting the peaceful surroundings fill us.

Jim gives me a squeeze, then says he guesses we'd better get back before Grandpère sends out a posse. That makes me laugh, and we hold hands going down the hill. I feel like a teenager, and when I look at him, he just grins. When we get down to level ground, he tucks my arm under his, and we walk close.

Grandpère is back with the dogs, and we play with the pup for a while, then put him in the cage and shut the door. We play a few hands of crib, and it's nearly midnight when Jim says he should get home. The evening passed quickly; that's the latest Grandpère and I have stayed up for a long time.

"You come back and see us soon," Grandpère tells Jim as he's leaving.

"I'll be back. Thank you both for a wonderful evening," he says as he puts on his shoes. I follow him outside. He hugs me on the step and kisses my cheek. "Thank you especially, Anzel. Thank you for trusting me."

"My pleasure. Thank you for coming," I say. "Any time you feel like it, drop by."

I wave till he's out of the driveway and dance back into the house. I really like him. Grandpère is still sitting up. "Pretty nice guy. He might be a keeper."

"Oh Grandpère. I'm not fishing. But he's pretty fine, eh?"

"Yep. Pretty fine," he agrees.

The next day Jim drives in around ten in the morning. "You did say any time," he says when he gets out of the truck. "All I could think of, when I thought about what to do today, was to come out here. Is there something I can help you with?"

"Today I was going to rototill the rest of the garden and plant out more of the starts," I tell him, and he helps me do everything. He does the tilling and helps me plant out the little plugs. By suppertime the rest of the garden is not only tilled, it's planted too.

He helps me make supper — lots of leftovers from yesterday — and a fresh salad. After supper I tell him to go and have tea with Grandpère, but he helps me do the dishes before he will. We talk and visit and play cards, and he seems like an old friend.

When he leaves this time, it's my lips he's looking for and not my cheek. I return the kiss with pleasure. A passion I thought was gone rises in me like a wave, and he leaves me gasping for breath on the step when he leaves. A glow stays with me long after his tail lights fade.

June starts with a week of rain. It sprinkles for a few days, and the flowers all look heavenly, then it pounds down for a couple of days, knocking the petals off the daffodils and tulips and spattering the other flowers with mud. Then it sprinkles for another couple of days. I can't even step into the garden, which is boot-deep quicksand. I can see the carrots have germinated, and well. They are the hardest crop to start in this clay-based soil, but once they have popped through the soil crust, they're hardy.

I don't go to the home on Wednesday, one of the pounding rain days. I talk to Rose on the phone, and she says it doesn't matter.

Jim has been out every weekend and some weeknights. Today he phones right after lunch to ask if it would be a good day for Bertie to visit. She'd looked forward to us coming there today and was sad we didn't come.

"Sure," I tell him. "Grandpère will be happy. I'll let him know."

When I tell him Bertie's coming out with Jim, he goes right into the bathroom, combs his hair and scrubs up; he's in clean clothes when he comes to sit at the table. He wonders if he should go out and take King for his walk.

"King can walk himself," I tell Grandpère and turn King out of the porch.

Sure enough, he trots right across the yard to the edge of the bush before he squats. We are both proud of how smart that dog is. Blue puts up with him, but I notice that he's never too far away from the pup. I think Blue is establishing who's boss in the pecking order, and it's a good thing, because King has doubled his size already.

"Should we get him fixed?" I ask.

"No need for that. It just makes them fat."

"Grandpère, that's an old wives' tale. They don't get fat because they're neutered. If they get enough exercise, they stay trim."

"Makes them lazy, then they don't get exercise. Old wives knew some sense."

How can you argue with that logic? The dog gets to keep his jewels. Soon King is back whining at the door to get in. His cage is in the mud room, and the room is living up to its name; a layer of sloppy mud has come in on the boots and drooled itself onto the floor on every trip in and out for days. We have a baby gate across the door to confine the dogs to the mud room. King runs indoors and settles himself in the cage. He's happy to sleep for hours, and the rain seems to make him even sleepier.

Dinner is ready when they arrive, and everyone declares it the best meal ever.

"Are you going to be my fan club?" I ask them, embarrassed about all the praise. It was a good meal, but not exceptional.

"I'm a fan club of one," Jim says. He comes over to the sink and hugs me and kisses me, right in front of Grandpère and Bertie, who laugh. That's how things are going lately. It feels natural and right for him to be here, and every time he leaves, I look forward to him returning.

Bertie is a great guest. She is only eight years older than me, but I feel as though she's a lot older. She's grandmotherly, but like an old grandmother, not a young one like me, I say to the voice in my head that's laughing at me calling someone else grandmotherly.

Jesse arrives a few days later after phoning to say he and Aaron are coming just for the weekend.

"Jessica?" I ask.

"Not this time. She has to work. See you Friday, probably around suppertime."

Jim is there when Jesse and Aaron arrive — I want him to meet them — then he leaves shortly after Jesse arrives. After Grandpère and Aaron both go to bed, Jesse and I sit up at the kitchen table and drink tea and talk.

"It's not going to work, Mother. Jessica and I are getting a divorce. We both want to. I don't like who she is right now, and

I don't even think she's been faithful to me. I don't buy all the late nights in the office. It's the only time her cellphone is turned off." He sounds bitter.

"Did you go to counselling?" I ask.

"Yes, we went separately, then together. Even the counsellor thought we should probably get a divorce. How bad is that?"

"Pretty bad," I concede. "What will you do?"

"We'll go to court and ask for a divorce. It doesn't matter whose fault it is; all our property gets split fifty-fifty, and our pensions get split. We've agreed to joint custody of Aaron. Right now I'm not working, and she is, so I'll get him in the day, and he'll go to her place at night. She's going to look for an apartment this weekend and should be moved out by the time we get home."

I am shocked at the suddenness of it all. "Did you decide that or did she?"

"She did, but I'm glad, Mom. It's driving me crazy, living with her. Maybe when we spend some time apart, I'll like her more. We have to do this. I'm just sorry for Aaron. How do we tell him? He's so little and he loves us both." There is such pain in his voice.

"It happens to lots of kids now. You just have to love them through it. You have to make sure he knows it's not his fault. His little world revolves around himself right now, and at first he'll be pretty sure it was something he did. Just make sure he always feels safe, and he'll just accept things the way they come along." I can't think of any other advice.

He sits forward in his chair, his elbows on his knees, with his head resting in his hands. He looks like a lost little boy. I sit in front of him and lean my forehead down to rest on his, then

I hug him for a while as he cries. And so do I.

"One door closes, one door opens," I tell him. It's my way of saying life goes on.

"God, I hope I do better in the next room," he says, and we laugh a bit, sniffing our tears away.

# Chapter Twelve

On Sunday the company rolls in. Jim brings Bertie, and when the phone rings, it's Jane. She wonders if today is a good time to visit. She says she bought a car this week but hasn't driven it on the highway yet. "Sure, get in the car and drive," I tell her.

Jim has sponsored her in their meetings and has told me she's doing really well. "She's a strong-minded girl. When she decides to do something, she does it," he told me. "She's kicking the habit cleaner than anyone I ever met. Still only one relapse so far — though it's early, and most recovering addicts slide a few times before they master sobriety. As a rule they use most of their energy just looking after themselves. Full recovery usually takes years."

So I am more kindly disposed toward Jane than I was a while ago — though I still think she is unfit to be anyone's mother — and I don't speak to her about Angel, nor do I intend to. I tell Jesse not to talk about Angel while Jane is around.

We have a pleasant day. As Jane and Bertie help me get lunch together, they joke around a lot, and I can see they are friends. Jesse and Jane are friends from long ago, and they talk a lot about the people they used to know and where they are now. Between them they know where almost everyone is; Jesse knows more than Jane, but she knows about a surprising number of them. "Sooner or later almost everyone from here passes through Vancouver for a while," Jane says.

Everyone wants to see everything. Aaron loves the four-wheeler as much as Pierre does and we all get rides from Jesse. Aaron sits in front of him, his little hands on the handlebars. When I refer to it as a bike, Aaron says to me, "Not a bike, Gwamma, bike means two wheels. This is the four-wheeler." He's right, but I'm old enough to call it what I like. "Gramma still calls it a bike, love," I say.

"Cwazy Gwamma." He grins at me and shakes his head. So darn cute. We all start laughing, and he looks around puzzled, wondering what's funny.

Jesse looks at the motor in Jane's car, and she drives it over to the shop, where he tinkers with something under the hood. That reminds me, the battery is still in the snowmobile. Jesse says he'll take it out, and Jane helps him by entertaining Aaron in the shop. Bertie goes everywhere with Grandpère, and Jim and I walk up to the lookout to be alone for a while.

"Jesse is sure a nice guy. Jane said all your kids are nice. I'm happy to see her here today," Jim says.

"I see her at the home every week, but this is only her second visit out here."

"It's good for people in recovery to feel they belong somewhere. Work is good for that, it makes them interact with other people, and when the social urge is still there after work, family is best."

"She's not exactly family," I say.

"If her daughter is your granddaughter, I'd say she's some kind of relative of yours," he tells me.

Well, I never quite thought of Jane as any kind of relative to me. But what he's saying has some truth. I've claimed her daughter as kin, but not Jane. I narrow my eyes at him, to see if he is manipulating me, and he narrows his eyes and peers back at me. We burst out laughing. Maybe he is, but I don't care.

At supper it seems as though Jane has come alive. She's talkative and can hardly do enough for anyone. She jumps up and serves everything, takes our dishes to the sink and is cleaning up before we're all finished. Grandpère is only halfway through; he might be making sure he chews every bite fifty times. He read that it's good to do that so your body doesn't have to work so hard to turn the food into energy. I tell Jane to sit and relax.

"No, you relax. I like doing this," she tells us, so we let her go to it. She has the tea made and served by the time Grandpère is done eating, and Jesse says he'll help with the rest of the dishes. We can hear them talking and laughing from the living room.

Jim and Bertie have to go right after tea. "Ten o'clock curfew. We don't want to ruin Bertie's reputation," Jim says. He has to help Bertie into his truck, as it's too high for her to just step in. Jesse says he and Aaron have to go soon too, and Jane leaves right behind Jim and Bertie.

"She's really nice, Mom, just like I remember her," Jesse says as she pulls out of the driveway.

"Nice is as nice does," I reply.

"I know what happened was pretty bad. But the only thing people can do is try to do it differently the next time."

"That's true, Son." I'm thinking that this kid is gaining wisdom while his life falls apart.

He grins, and what he says next startles me. "Look at your computer screen. Then let's talk some more."

I know right away what he means. The girls had put a screen saver on my computer that showed their three faces put together like a kaleidoscope, but it's still obvious who the faces belong to.

"Did she see it?" I ask.

"Yes. I turned it on to show her the site where she can get parts at cost for her car. When the screen saver came on, she gasped, and I looked at her. She reached out and touched the screen. Then she just looked at me with a wide smile."

I start swearing. I'm out of practice, so I end up repeating myself. If you're repeating swear words, you need to stop. I add a couple of the more outrageous ones I can think of.

"Don't freak out. Think about it. She knows where Angel is now. I think maybe she already did. She didn't seem all that shocked and never mentioned a word more to me about it. I don't think you have to worry about Jane. Maybe you should talk to her now, you know, now that we know that she knows what we know." He gets all tangled up in who knows what.

"'Oh! What a tangled web we weave when first we practise to deceive,'" I recite, and we laugh. I decide I'd better have a private word with Jane.

Grandpère stays home on Wednesday, but I agree to bring Bertie here for the afternoon. Everything at the home looks great. This may be the best-tended garden in central BC. I have made pea supports out of wood strips, and the peas are getting tall enough for me to start them up the bottom row. I worry that the wind will blow them over once the vines are heavy on them, so Jim brings over some wooden dowelling and helps me tie the tops of the supports together. Nothing less than a hurricane will be able to topple them now. He always tries to find something to do to help me while I'm at the home.

At lunch I tell Jane to meet me for coffee after work. She suggests the coffee shop at the motel.

We sit down at a table by ourselves, and I don't waste any time on pleasantries. "Jesse told me you saw Angel's picture on my computer."

She looks down at her hands. "Yes. At first I was just shocked. Then I was glad. I knew she was safe somewhere. Jim told me not to worry about her, to get myself cured and prove I was able to be a good person before I tried to be a mother again. I hoped she came to you, but I'd lost that hope till I saw her picture. You don't have to tell me where she is. But those other girls must be Darcy and Nadine's girls. So I think I know she's with them."

"Do you know what happened? Why she ran?" I ask her.

"No. She didn't leave a note or anything. She was gone when I got home. I'd been gone for a few days. I wasn't a good mother then." She starts quietly crying, and doesn't look at me, just stares at her hands.

"Some guy came looking for you, and when you weren't there, he raped her." I have a hard time saying this — my words sound accusing — and she cries more.

"Who did it?"

"She said it was an old boyfriend of yours. She didn't say a name." My patience snaps. "Jane, you were about as irresponsible a mother as anyone could possibly be. Don't think for a minute you're going to get another chance until you prove yourself — to all of us — and don't you dare try to convince her to come back to you. If you do, I will try to make sure you never see her again. Do we understand each other?"

She doesn't look up or stop weeping, but she slowly nods.

I take a few deep breaths, sit silently for a few minutes and then continue. "She came to me, but then we saw her picture on the missing children poster, and she went with Darcy and Faith. Darcy married Faith three years after Nadine died, and she's a lovely person. Angel is happy there. She's doing really well in school, and she and Tammy and Sarah are good friends."

"Does she know I moved here?" Jane asks.

"Yes, I told her on the phone."

"Does she hate me?"

"No. She wanted to know how you were."

"Will I ever be able to see her?"

"Jane, you're doing everything right. Jim says you're determined to make the rest of your life count, and I believe he's right. If you continue doing things right, there's no reason you can't be part of her life again. The restraining order runs out at the end of this month, and maybe I can ask them not to renew it."

"Would you do that?" she asks, the hope in her voice evident.

"Yes. I will."

"Oh Anzel, it's all I'm hoping for. I love her so much. It's for her I'm cleaning up my life."

"Jane, you're cleaning up your life for yourself. What kind of life was that for anyone?"

"A bad one," she replies with a bitter laugh, but her tears dry up, and she looks at me with a weak smile. "Anzel, I will do anything, anything, to see her again."

"Just keep doing what you are doing. It seems to be working pretty well," I say to her, patting her arm.

I pull out some pictures we took in the winter and spring. There's one of Angel sitting on the porch with Blue and Duke, one of her in the greenhouse, turning the soil with a shovel, and another with her cousins, standing in front of the tent when they had their camp-out. Jane takes them and studies them intently.

"Can I keep them?" she asks.

"I printed them for you. They are yours," I tell her, and she tucks them into her apron pocket.

"Thank you, Anzel, thank you for this."

I leave her and walk back to the home to pick up Bertie. I have promised her a visit to the farm this evening, and she's waiting by the car when I get to the parking lot. Jim comes over and tells me he'll be out after work and will give Bertie a ride back in the evening.

"Don't make supper. I'll bring pizza from town."

"Sounds great. I haven't had pizza for a long time."

"See you then." I wave at him and see him in the rearview mirror, waving till we're out of sight.

Bertie is in great spirits. "I love coming out to the farm. It's such a welcome break from this place. Not that it's so bad here, just kind of boring."

She has brought a bag with wool so she can sit and crochet while Grandpère whittles. They have become great friends, going for long walks together and inspecting all the plants in the garden and greenhouse. She knows a surprising amount about gardening; she says she used to keep a small garden. When they walk, she takes King on the leash. He is well-behaved for a puppy, which is a good thing, because he's already a very large puppy. They're teaching him to be calm and gentle when he's on the leash. I love watching them. They walk along slowly, stopping and chatting every few feet. She holds onto his arm, and Grandpère points to things with his walking stick. She waves her other arm about as she talks and every once in a while bends down and pulls a weed or straightens out a plant. My gardens have never had such care. They're out of sight on a walk when Jim arrives, and I meet him out at the truck. He's brought two large pizzas. We put them in the oven and wait for Grandpère and Bertie to return.

"I talked to Jane today. I told her where Angel is," I tell him.

He grabs me in a big hug and kisses my face all over. "You really are an Angel," he says. "What do Darcy and Faith think about that?"

"I haven't talked to them about it. I told her only because she already knew. She saw a picture of Angel on my computer screen when she was here on the weekend."

Jim's eyebrows go up into his hairline. "Maybe you should have talked to them first."

"I'll phone them later on tonight. I just told Jane for her own peace of mind. She still can't see Angel till the restraining order runs out. I told her she won't get her daughter back anytime soon."

"That is good," Jim says. "She needs to learn to look after herself first. I have a good feeling about this." He dances me over to the couch. We haven't slept together yet, but the kisses we exchange promise that it's only a matter of time. He awakens urges in me that I had thought were only things of memory. I am flushed and excited and sorry to break off when we hear the old people coming back to the house.

We put a surprising dent in the pizzas for supper, then we play crib till it's time for Bertie and Jim to go. I pack up the rest of the pizza and send it with Jim when they leave. He says he'll be out on the weekend and kisses me goodbye. I tell him to bring an overnight bag, and he grins and makes wide eyes at me.

"I will at that," he says, and we stand there for a while, grinning at each other.

"Come on, you lovebird, I'll be late and they'll kick me out of the home," Bertie says. We all laugh as Jim helps Bertie into the truck.

We watch till they are gone from sight. Then I go into the house and phone Darcy and Faith. The girls are already in bed, so I talk just to Darcy. I tell him about Jane coming out here on the weekend, and how she saw the picture, and then tell him about our talk in the afternoon.

"We'll talk to Angel in the morning. She has been talking more about her mom and has been going to counselling. We both think it'll be good for her to be able to visit with her mother, so maybe we can arrange it in the summer." Darcy sounds happy to hear that Jane is doing so well. "What about this guy Jim? Jesse thinks you've got it going on with him." A teasing note creeps into his voice. "Says Jim is making himself pretty much at home there."

"He's a really nice guy. He's been coming out to visit Grandpère and me a lot."

"Yeah, he probably likes to visit the old guy." Now there is no hiding the amusement in his voice.

"Yes. They get along well." I'm not giving him any satisfaction, but he starts laughing, and I join in.

The next morning it's raining hard, and we stay in the house. "Grandpère, we haven't written down your memories for a long time. Do you want to tell some more?" I ask.

He settles back in his chair and thinks for a minute. Then he sits up straight, lays his walking stick across his knees and grips it with his hands, leaning forward. He rocks back and forth and nods at me.

"I will tell you a story of revenge. For our people, pride was very important. When people rose to speak at a gathering, they first told of their deeds that they were proud of. From what things they told, you knew what kind of a person they were. Some told of how many horses they took in a raid. Some told of how they found food when everyone was hungry. Some told of how many wives and children they were looking after. I remember one stranger who stood before the fire with human scalps on his stick. He told of how he had killed his enemies with honour. My mother told me afterward it was nothing to be proud of, but I remember thinking of him as a very brave man.

"When one of our people thought someone had wronged them, they expected something in return. Usually there was a council. Each person got to speak, but only in their turn. The council listened to the elders in it, and they would decide what the compensation would be. It was always just, and when the outcome was decided, everyone smoked for peace.

"I remember in one of the next villages there were two boys who fought so hard that one was killed with a blow to the head. The family of the dead boy claimed compensation, and the people had to give their son to take the other boy's place. The people called him Son of Two Families. He hunted for both families, and they both claimed him as son. It was just, and everyone gained from a situation that could have left them enemies for life.

"I had a claim on a man who moved into our territory. Your mother and the boys were all grown, and Clementine and I had decided to take the pack horses and go on a trip. We were going to go to the edge of the lake to follow the old path back to our village, then carry on to the edge of the mountains. Our youngest son came with us, but he wanted to see only the old village.

There was nothing left to see, just a clearing in the bush by then, but he wanted to come anyway. Then he was going to come back by himself.

"The trouble began when we went to round up the horses. We had turned them out as soon as the grass was green, and they were a fair way away by the time we started looking for them. We found the herd, but one of the saddle horses and one of the pack horses were not with the herd. We tracked them back for a long way till we found the remains of a small camp. There were tin cans in the bush, a place where there had been a fire and a pile of spruce boughs where a man had slept. We could tell that he had two horses tied up, and we suspected he had taken ours.

"We followed his tracks for a while, but they were old, and we lost them at the edge of a rocky mountain. We knew by then he was headed west, so we borrowed two others from the herd and went home with three saddle horses and two pack horses. The other horses were Alex's, and he said he didn't need them all summer, so we set out, hoping we would find our own horses on the way.

"It was a beautiful summer that year, and we took three days to get to the old village. I showed where the lodges used to stand and the cache pits where we kept our food for the winter. The cache pits were all caved in, just small holes in the soil covered with grass. We camped there for almost a week. Then your uncle left with his horse to go home, and we set out in the opposite direction, going north above the Lake Whose Waters Flow West.

"We went that summer to all the places we wanted to see. We went farther north, and camped beside the Neck of the Giant. We stayed a week there, then started back home. When we got back, we had been gone all summer. We turned the horses back out with the herd when we found it, and to our surprise, our other horses were already there. We turned the others loose and took our packs home.

"No one had been in our house while we were gone. Everything was just as we left it. That was strange, because your uncle was going to stay there while we were gone. I went to find Alex to see where our son was. Alex, with much grief, told me that he was dead. He said a stranger showed up and said he found a man shot to death in the bush. He took the RCMP and showed them, and it was our son. Alex said he went looking for the horse and found it with the herd but still saddled. He said our other horses were back there too; they had been used, as there were sweat marks on them from saddles and packs. There was no sign of any person that he could find. He couldn't find the tracks where those ones joined the herd. The only stranger around was the man who found him.

"I asked Alex if he thought it was that man who had used our horses, and he said he wondered if he had something to do with the shooting too. He said the man had said he found him shot in the bush, but no one knew of anyone else in the bush, and it was just too much coincidence. He said maybe he got found with the horses by your uncle, and maybe there was a fight. Your uncle didn't have a gun, so if there was a fight, it wasn't a very fair one.

"We could not prove anything, and we were much grieved by our loss, so we spoke to no one about Alex's suspicions, but he pointed out the stranger, and from that time on I was always aware of him. His name was Melvin and he was a big man with a bushy black beard, very strong, and he took work around town. He always had work, as he knew his way around in the bush, and he hired out with packers. He wasn't kind to the horses, but he knew how to make them work. He reminded me of George, who I worked with many years before. He didn't like dogs and would boot them out of his way if they blocked his path. One time, when I went to the herd with him and some others to catch horses, I noticed my horses would not go near him, and my suspicions increased.

"Melvin drank a lot and bragged a lot while he was in the village. One day while he was drinking, he said he had been out west a couple years before, and I knew he was the one who had taken our horses. You know when you suspect someone of something, you always look for proof, and the day I heard him say that, I suddenly knew he was the one who had killed my son. I don't know how I knew it, but just at that minute, he realized who was listening to him. And he looked right in my eyes and was embarrassed, and suddenly I was sure.

"I decided then and there to get compensation. I didn't want him to be my son. I wanted vengeance. Maybe it wasn't right, but I wanted revenge. From then on I paid close attention to where he was. I didn't know what to do, but I was waiting for an opportunity that I knew would come if it was meant to. One spring he needed a ride across the lake in a boat because the spring waters had taken out the bridge. I offered to take him. We took a hide-covered boat that the boys had made. I never even coated it with grease. He was nervous when he got in, since he had never used a hide boat, but when he saw it floated well, he started paddling, and so did I. We were about halfway across when the hide got wet and the water started coming in. He had a bucket that he bailed it out with, but soon he could not bail fast enough.

"When the boat was half-full of icy water, I said to tell me about my son. He said that the only thing he had done was find my son's body. When the boat was nearly full, and he was bailing furiously, he started yelling that it was an accident, that he didn't mean to do it. Then I jumped out of the boat and swam to shore. By the time I reached land, there was nothing to be seen of the boat or him. I reported a man drowned to the RCMP."

I catch up to where he is with my note taking, and I look at him. His air is forbidding; his brow is furrowed, and his hands still grip the walking stick, white knuckled. His lips are sucked in tight, and he has quit rocking himself. He looks frozen.

"Grandpère, I will surely not be able to repeat this story while you are alive. I don't think there is a statute of limitations for murder, and that sounds like a premeditated one. If you think the old age home is bad, what would you think about jail?"

"Much the same thing to me," he says. "I didn't kill him. If he'd learned to swim, he might still be alive today. Not knowing how to swim killed him."

A pretty fine distinction, I think to myself, but to him I say, "Well, that's all in the past. Right now let's get some lunch."

While I am typing this up in the afternoon, I have qualms about writing it. Is this a story I want my grandchildren to know? I decide to type it up anyway, but I file it in a different folder and try to decide what to call it. I finally type in "Folly" and put it in with the recipe folder. Probably hiding it from myself, I think, as I shut down the computer.

Jim comes out right after work on Friday. He brings a small bag with him, and when he wants to know where to put it, I point to my room. We have a nice supper, and afterward Grandpère goes out for a walk with the dogs. Jim and I clean up the kitchen and walk up to the lookout. It's his favourite place to sit now too. He knows that this place is more than just a pretty spot. He knows who all the people are who have their ashes scattered here, and he says this spot makes him closer to the gods. I'm glad to share it with him.

We sit snuggled against the rock, watching the sun go down. Suddenly I feel nervous and embarrassed about asking him to stay the night. He catches my mood and says, "Don't worry. I think Lorne would have wanted you to move on. He would have wanted you to be happy."

I can't quite meet his eyes, but he takes me in his arms and kisses me till I feel relaxed again. Then we head down to the house. Grandpère is already sleeping when we get there.

Jim picks me up in the living room and carries me through the bedroom door. I go to shut off the light, but he says to leave it on. I am self-conscious and shy to undress in front of him. He laughs at me and undresses first. Seeing him standing there naked, in his sixty-five-year-old birthday suit with a big hard-on, makes me laugh, and I take off my clothes. He holds me at arm's length and turns me around. "Better than my wildest imagination," he says. He takes me in his arms, and everything feels all right.

When we wake up in the morning, it still feels right that his head is on the pillow next to mine. I wake up first and am just looking at him when he opens his eyes.

"I have died and gone to heaven," he says and smiles at me.

"Me too," I say, and we snuggle together till we hear Grandpère stirring.

He stays all weekend, and puts up with the teasing Grandpère gives us. He keeps telling Jim he didn't see any horses tied at the hitching rail. Jim tells him there is no hitching rail, but if he gets time, he'll build one.

"That one will cost a lot of horses." Grandpère must value me pretty high.

Jim knows how to use all the tools in the shop, and soon he has all the gates hanging straight and has done all the little repairs that I've been putting off. We have a great weekend, and when he leaves on Sunday night, all I can think of is when he'll be back.

# Chapter Thirteen

The next weekend Jesse comes out again. This time it's Jessica's turn to have Aaron for the weekend, and he says he doesn't like to stay at home alone. It's nice to have him here, but I don't quite know how he'll react to Jim spending the nights with me. He seems to take it in stride, and while he doesn't tease like Grandpère, Jesse is a pretty appreciative audience for Grandpère's teasing.

On Saturday night he leaves before supper and says he's going into town to take Jane to the movie. He doesn't get home till after midnight; we wake up when the dogs bark. King has such a little puppy bark that it's funny to hear him helping Blue warn us of approaching vehicles. Jesse comes in as he always does. *Clump.* That's the sound of his boots hitting the floor. A few steps, open the fridge door, peer inside for a snack. *Glug, glug.* That's him drinking milk out of the jug. Tiptoe to the end of the hall, quietly close the door, then silence. In the morning he'll still be dressed. So much of the boy left in the man.

"How was your night in town?" I ask him at the breakfast table.

"It was fun. We saw a really good movie. Then we rented another one and went to watch it at her motel room. It's just one room and a bathroom with a tiny kitchen. She pays a flat rate of eight hundred dollars a month. That's pretty expensive for what it is."

Jim says to him, "I've been thinking about asking Jane if she wants to share my rooms. I don't use even half the rooms in my apartment. The whole rent where I stay is only six hundred."

"Does she know? Because I said I would help her look at places today."

"No, I never spoke to her about it yet." Jim fishes his keys out of his pocket and takes the key to his place off his key ring. "Show her up there too. You can tell her about it, and she can decide if she wants to share the place."

Jesse grins at him and puts the key in his own pocket. He leaves right after breakfast, taking his bag with him so he can head home directly from town without having to come back here. Jim tells him to stash the key in the entrance under the rock.

Our lives settle into a routine. On Wednesdays I go to the home to do what little work needs to be done there and bring Bertie home. Jim comes out after work and takes her back by curfew. On the weekends Jim comes out Friday and stays till Sunday night. Sometimes Jane comes out on Sunday and brings Bertie. Jane move's in with Jim, and he says she's neat as a pin and a pretty good cook too.

Angel always asks about her mother when she phones, and I can tell she's anxious to see her. When the restraining order runs out, it doesn't get renewed. I ask Angel if she wants to come down on the bus by herself for a couple of days to visit with her mother. “Oh yes, please,” she says and we arrange for her to come on a weekend when the school is closed Friday for a Pro-D day. When I ask what that means, she explains that the teachers have to go to school, but the students don’t. So we arrange it, and when she arrives, I tell Jane to meet the bus and then bring her out.

They come out to the farm about four hours after the bus arrives. Jane keeps hugging Angel, and both of them are fairly glowing. We leave them to themselves as much as we can. They both know the farm pretty well, and I see them walking about out in the garden and the greenhouse, talking constantly. Jim and I are sitting on the bench in the shade behind the house when they come to the porch and sit down just around the corner. I am just about to get up and say hello when I hear Angel say, “I won’t, Mom. I just can’t. Where I live now, it’s how things are supposed to be. They’re so nice, and they’re always there. There’s always food. I feel safe there. I don’t trust you anymore, Mom. Sometimes you forget all about me.” Her voice breaks, and I can hardly make out the words.

I freeze and look at Jim. He grabs my hand and squeezes it, and I sit in tense silence. Then I hear Jane say, “I understand. I just wanted to know if you wanted to be together again.” Her voice sounds choked too. She continues, “I’d deserve it if you hated me.”

“Oh Mom, of course I don’t hate you. You’re my mother.” Angel says.

Jim grins at me. We get up quietly and walk around the house the long way.

Later Jane asks if it’s all right to take Angel home to her place to spend the night, and we say it is. Darcy and Faith phone that night to see how things are going, and I'm able to say, "Splendidly."

"Do you think she'll want to stay there?" Faith asks, the distress in her voice evident.

"No, I don't think you need to worry about that," I tell her. "No one is talking about her moving. They're just catching up."

Sure enough, on Sunday night Angel is catching the bus, cheerfully hugging her mother and telling us all she'll see us in the summer. We all wave till we can't see her anymore, and then Jane hugs us all, tears streaming down her face. At the same time she has a wide smile and tells us these are happy tears. "Thank you, thank you," she keeps telling us.

When Bella stops by to visit, she's full of news. She tells me about Jane being back in town. "She was a friend of Ben's, wasn't she? Do you know she was a drug user? She and that old man she lives with. He was too. I don't know where he came from, but he is sure a lot older than her. It's obscene, a young girl like that living with such an old guy."

It amuses me that the gossipers have got things turned around, so I don't correct her on any of it. Bella is full of praise for the gardens at the home and thinks it's a nice place. She worries that she's going to lose her driver's licence. In the spring she was stopped for not signalling and got a ticket. Then she got another one when she didn't stop at a stop sign. "I could see no one was coming, but he gave me a ticket anyway." She got a third ticket for going too slowly on the highway. "Imagine that, a ticket for going too slow. They let all the speeders go rushing by, then stop an innocent person for going too slow." The result of all those tickets is a letter from the motor vehicle branch to report for testing for licence renewal. "And I have to rewrite the test. It took me three tries to pass it when I was young. Shame on them, harassing an old woman."

"You'll do fine, Bella, you know so much more now than when you were younger," I try to reassure her.

"I don't like to read and can't remember what I do read. That book could be written in a different language for all I know." She gives a snort of a laugh and repeats, "Shame on them."

If she loses her driver's licence, which it sounds like she's going to, she plans to sell her house and move into the home. There's a waiting list, she explains, and sometimes it takes a couple years to get in. "They do everything for you there. It's like an all-inclusive resort."

"Yeah, to get in you just wait till someone dies," Grandpère tells her.

Bella misses his humour and starts telling us how old some of the residents are and who she thinks will go first. Mrs. Daly is on the top of the list; not only is she over one hundred, she has cancer "riddled through her."

"Do you think her ghost will stay in the room?" he asks her innocently, and Bella just looks puzzled by the question. I stand behind her and give Grandpère a scowl to let him know not to bug Bella. He just grins as though he's glad to get a rise out of someone.

"I saw Jesse in town. He was by himself. Are he and Jessica still a family?" she wants to know.

"They have separated," I tell her, knowing that I'm giving her gossip to spread. She wants to know all the details, but I change the subject and ask her how her kids are doing. As usual, they are all "doing great" and successful. But I wonder, if her kids are so great, why don't they ask her to live with them?

It's a question I don't ask out loud.

"I have to worry about my health. My cholesterol is too high, and the doctor says he has to put me on different medicine," she tells me as she helps herself to another cookie from the dish I've set on the table with tea.

"Does he tell you to change what you eat?" I ask.

"Heavens no, I eat very well," she replies with a merry laugh and tells me how good the cookies are while she eats another.

When she leaves, she walks heavily and struggles to get into the car. She putts off down the driveway with the car just idling. She leans forward, peering over the steering wheel, with both hands gripped on it as though she's ready for anything.

"The question is, does she lose her licence first or does she quit fitting in the car?" Grandpère observes. He chuckles all afternoon about Bella's driving.

On the weekend Jesse comes again, and this time he brings Aaron. The child is delighted with King, who has grown as heavy as he is. King is gentle with him. Jesse, Aaron and the dogs play out in the yard most of the day. They're trying to teach the dogs to fetch sticks, but the dogs are not retrievers and don't catch on to the game too well.

Jesse teaches Aaron to call Jim "Papa Jim," and Jim is pleased as punch. He takes Aaron for a long ride on the four-wheeler and wins his little heart. At bedtime Aaron sits on Jim's knee till he falls asleep, then Jesse takes him and puts him in bed with all his clothes on. "No need to wake him up just to change his clothes. These ones will be comfy to sleep in," he tells me. I can see Jesse has far different ideas about child-raising than Jessica did; she would never have let the boy sleep in his clothes. For the first time I think maybe it's good that they're apart.

Jane comes out on Sunday and says there's a party at the home, so Bertie doesn't come with her. Jim and I take Aaron to the lake. We put the canoe in his pickup and take a picnic lunch. It's a wonderful day. Aaron catches the only fish. It's tiny, but he's so happy about it that we clean it and take it home so he can eat it for supper. He shares it with all of us and is puffed with pride when we all say how great it tastes.

Grandpère, Jesse and Jane are sitting in the living room when we get back, and there's a funny feeling in the air. I look closely. It looks as though Jane's been crying, and both Jesse and Grandpère have odd expressions. I ask them if everything's all right, and they assure me it is.

Later, when they leave, Grandpère says, "Remember, you are like the smoke."

They both nod at him as though they know what he means. When I ask him what that was about, he just pretends he didn't hear my question. I puzzle about it for a while, then put it from my mind.

The week before the girls are to arrive, Jane takes a week of her holidays, and she and Jesse make plans to drive down to the coast. I'm concerned that they're going into a relationship too fast. I speak to Jesse about rebound romances, and tell him they seldom work.

He laughs. "You got it wrong, Mom," he says. "We're just friends. She isn't ready for a relationship, and neither am I. She wants to pick up some of her things from a friend's place. Everything will fit in my pickup, and I'm going along to help her out, more like a big brother or a good friend. Don't worry about me, Mom, I'm a big boy."

I smile and let it go. He truly has seemed much happier lately.

They're back in five days, and when I ask how it went, Jane says she's sure glad that she made the changes in her life that she did. "Going back and seeing it now, I can't believe I wasted so much of my life down there. I am never going back."

Jim comes over that evening, and Jesse and Jane take Grandpère up to the lookout on the bike. Jim and I putter around in the yard till it's almost dark. Then we decide to walk up to meet the kids and Grandpère. We walk up in silence, and when we get close, we see they're sitting around a fire. For some reason I feel as though we're intruding and pull Jim into the trees. We stand silently watching.

Jesse and Jane are sitting on the ground, and Jesse has the pistol that Grandpère has been carving. He's put a lot of detail into it, and it looks very real. Jesse is pointing it at the fire. Jane has what appears to be an arrow and is pointing that at the fire too. Grandpère is chanting; it sounds like the same chant he was singing when we had Angel's fire. He has his arms held out from his body, and when he drops his arms, they both throw their objects in the fire. They all yell, "Smoke!"

I pull on Jim's arm, and we quietly make our way back down.

"Do you know what that was about?" he asks me.

"No. If we're supposed to know, they'll tell us, I guess," I reply. I tell him about Angel's fire and how she felt so much better after, and he tells me he thinks Grandpère is pretty wise.

When they get back to the house, no one mentions anything about what they were doing, and neither one of us asks.

Grandpère and I meet the bus when the girls arrive and take them to the home, where Angel introduces her mother to them.

They go with her on a kitchen tour, and when they come back, all the girls are helping with trays to bring lunch out to the garden. Jane tells everyone Angel is her daughter and the other girls are her nieces.

The garden beds look spectacular, full of vegetables. A lot of the luncheon ingredients have been harvested from the garden, including peas still in the pod and baby carrots. I give Bertie all the credit for it whenever anyone tries to compliment me, and she is proud. She points out that the salad all comes from the garden, and so does the zucchini, which the kitchen has cut in rounds and fried with cheese on top. It's all delicious.

Rose comes out and has lunch with us. She makes a big fuss over the girls, and Jane and I are both brimming with pride. The girls go to help clean up at the end of the meal, and Rose turns to me. "So you and Jim really hit it off. I hear he spends weekends out at the farm," she says with a look that tells me she really wants to hear it all. I tell her I think I'm in love again and go on about Jim for a while till she holds up her hand to stop me and starts laughing. "Nobody deserves it more," she says as she hugs me.

I feel a bit guilty to be so happy when she's probably still lonely. "You deserve to have someone special in your life too."

She laughs, "Don't be too sure I don't," and evades my direct query till I threaten to phone Bella and find out. Then she spills it. The administrator at the hospital, who lost his wife to cancer about the same time Rose's husband died, has been calling. They've been going out a couple times a week for dinner and are going on a vacation together in the fall. She sounds as happy as I feel, and we sit there giggling.

She waves her hand at Bertie. "That one should not be in

here. Still quite capable of living on her own, but her children won't hear of her moving out, so she stays."

"I thought once you got hold of them here, they could only leave on a stretcher."

"Oh Anzel, you are too funny." She thinks I'm joking, but I'm not. Finally she realizes I am serious and she says, "For heaven's sake, Anzel, she signed herself in here. She still tends to her own finances. Her children pay for her to live here, but if she wanted to move out, she could do it tomorrow."

I thought about Bella looking forward to moving into the home, and realized that till now, I'd always imagined people being coerced into living here. I ask Rose if she knew Bella was planning on moving into the home.

"Oh my God. If she becomes a resident, I think I am really going to quit." We burst out laughing at the thought of Bella here. "She'll have to keep a notepad to keep track of the daily scandal in this place."

"Maybe you could get her to write a weekly scandal sheet," I suggest, and we laugh some more about what the headlines would be. Then she looks at her watch and bids me goodbye. "My break ended fifteen minutes ago," she exclaims, then heads back to her office. I round up the girls and Grandpère, and we head back to the farm.

The girls settle in at home as though they're staying forever, their stuff spread all over the house. They spend a lot of their time talking about boys, but they still follow Grandpère and me around and try to help with everything. They love to cook and tell me they're going to cook every other day to give me a break.

Sometimes I sit at the kitchen table and direct them while they try something new. I get out all the cookbooks, and we cook things none of us has tried before. They print Grandpère's stories that I have in the computer, and we talk about them. If we really want to know if Grandpère or Sven was my blood grandfather, they point out, we could get DNA tests.

"It's not necessary," I say. "It wouldn't make any difference to us. Grandpère is my grandfather. Sven is just a name in a story."

I show them the family tree in the album, and they like it so much they copy it out, complete with the question mark branch with Sven written on it. They draw a dotted line from Ben and add in Jane, then Angel. They tell me they'll make copies at school and we can all have one.

I don't give them the story filed under "Folly." That can wait till they are older.

They go camping again and leave the tent set up for the rest of their stay. They say they weren't even one bit afraid this time and they're going to sleep up there again before they go.

When Jim comes on the weekend, he suggests we sleep in the tent, and I agree. We pack a supper that can be cooked over a fire. The girls bring Grandpère up on the four-wheeler, and we cook sausage over the flames and have potatoes that have been blackened by the campfire inside their wrappings of tinfoil. The potatoes taste different cooked like this, their flesh soft and sweet, the skins black but oh so good.

After supper the rest of them go back to the house. Jim and I sit by the campfire, and he talks about his wife. He got married young, just out of high school. He felt as though she wanted to have a husband and children just to show she was successful. It was all so boring for him that he felt trapped in a life he didn't want. He wanted to travel and see the world, she was only happy surrounded by her home and the two children. He loved the kids but grew to resent her, and by the time he was thirty, he had strayed from the relationship in all ways. She caught him being unfaithful, and the divorce was bitter. He ended up just driving away, leaving her the house and the children. He went to northern Alberta and worked on the oil rigs. He stayed in camp and worked long hours; that's when he started using hard drugs. First he just used them to stay awake, but then he needed them all the time.

"I'm not really proud of that part of my life," he says. "I quit even sending child support."

He credits Alcoholics Anonymous for his recovery. He wants to repay them by helping other people recover, and he's committed to this goal.

His wife remarried, and when he saw his girls again, ten years had passed and they were like strangers. He felt as though they were judging him and finding him inadequate on all fronts. He thought their mother had blamed him for everything and taught the kids that he was not a person to be proud of at all. He says that he's on better terms with them now, and they have children of their own who call him Grandpa Jim. His wife divorced again and died young — in her early fifties — of lung cancer. By that time Jim had recovered from his addiction and made peace with his ex-wife. He returned to look after her while she died. "She left me the house, but I couldn't live there and sold it as soon as she passed on. It was worth ten times what we paid for it. I gave each of the girls a hundred thousand dollars and put the rest in the bank. I continued to live as I always did."

I don't know why he's telling me all this. I have no intention of telling him more about Lorne. It's a chapter of my life that's mine and Lorne's, and it feels wrong to talk of him to Jim. I am silent and comfortable in my silence. But he isn't telling me confidences to entice *me* to tell them. He says, "I just want you to know that I'm not as poor as it may seem. I like to work, and this job suits me. They don't need as many maintenance men in the winter. At the end of October, my job there is over."

"And then what will you do?" I ask, half-fearful that he'll tell me next that he's moving on again.

"Till now, I've never found a place where I want to stay," he says, grinning at me. "This winter I think I'll remodel the apartment. Jane has her own ideas of how to make it more livable, and I think it will be easy and fun to do."

I am relieved that he'll still be here, and to my surprise, tears well up in my eyes. I don't know if they're tears of gratitude or happiness, and I surreptitiously wipe them away. "I'm glad you're staying. You're very dear to me," I say, pleased that my voice is steady. I want to tell him I love him, but for some reason, I want him to say it first.

But he doesn't. "Well come on, love, let's hit it," he says. His lovemaking, which is always gratifying, seems more tender and sweet than usual. The campfire smoke, the sleeping bag smell and his man scent blend together in the small tent, making me feel like a gypsy in a caravan, bunked down for the night.

I dream of Lorne, my parents and my two lost children. They rise up out of the ashes and dance around the campfire. Duke comes out of his box like smoke and coalesces into his old form by the campfire. All of them swirl together and become a rainbow, which fades out and turns to ash, then falls like snow all around us. The sound of orchestra music accompanies the dancing, and there is a tremendous crash on the drums while the rainbow fades. I wake up to the sound of rain on the tent and thunder crashing in the distance.

We stay snuggled up in the tent. The rain is starting to pass in a fine mist through the fabric when we hear the sound of the four-wheeler coming.

Sarah yells at us, "Do you want a ride back to the house?"

We gratefully pull on our clothes and speed back to the warmth of the house with her.

"Thanks a lot. We would have gotten soaked if we walked," I tell her, and Jim echoes my thanks.

We have just finished breakfast when Jesse and Jane arrive together. He doesn't have Aaron this weekend. He brings the *Vancouver Sun*. They sit together on the couch in the living room, looking through the paper. I hear Jane give a small gasp, and look up to see what is the matter. They are reading the middle pages.

"Oh my God," Jane says. "A few weeks ago no one knew where he was. Now he's dead!"

She suddenly realizes she's talking out loud and has everyone's attention. She focusses on Angel. "Come here, read this."

Angel goes over and sits beside her mother. Jane puts her arm around her shoulders as she reads.

"I'm glad. I hate him!" Angel says defiantly.

"The guy who hurt Angel — he's dead," Jesse says to the rest of us.

There is a long silence.

"I hate him, too," I say into the silence to stick up for her. Then, because I know better than to hate, and with my mother's stricture "Never speak ill of the dead" echoing in the back of my mind, I add, "But he's dead now. He can never hurt anyone again. And hating him now is pointless. It can't hurt him, so maybe we should just let it go."

Angel holds my eye and nods at me, agreeing.

Jesse changes the subject, and soon he has the girls laughing again.

My thoughts keep coming back to the dead man. I'm trying to sort out my feelings. I have to admit to a certain satisfaction in knowing that guy can't hurt anyone anymore. I wonder if Grandpère felt like this when he gained the lakeshore in his last story, and I feel that maybe we're not so far apart on the issue of vengeance.

# Chapter Fourteen

Parker and Kristen arrive to spend a week while the girls are visiting, and Ezra has his birthday while they're here. We let him decide what we should do for the day. He wants everyone to go to the lake swimming, then hike up to the falls for supper. Jim offers to take the four-wheeler along so Grandpère can get to the falls, and Parker and he load it up into the back of his pickup. They prop two boards up on the tailgate of the truck and tell me to drive it up.

"No way," I say.

Jesse drives it up.

"I thought you weren't afraid of anything," Jim says to me.

"I'm not afraid," I reply. "I just have more good sense than to try to drive the bike up these skinny boards."

"Mm-hmm," is his only retort. He crinkles his eyes as though he wants to laugh but knows enough not to. He's getting the teasing habit from Grandpère.

"There's a difference between fear and common sense, eh," I say.

"Mm-hmm," he agrees, smirking.

We put the canoe on top of the car — it has a roof carrier —

and tie it to the front and back bumpers. Viewed from the side, it looks like a giant mushroom. We take the car, the pickup and Parker's car to fit everyone in. The giant cooler that we strap on the bike's carrier we fill with the food we need for the day. We have beach towels, sunscreen, beer, pop, junk food and a chocolate cake with "Happy Birthday, Ezra" written in blue icing on the top. The cake was made by the girls, who let Cameron and Coby write the greeting. "Happy" is written in big letters, "Birthday" has a hyphen and takes up most of the last two lines and "Ezra" is written in tiny letters in the last corner. The boys point out they had a hard time fitting it all on, but Ezra assures them it's a really good job, not as good as Mom might do, but pretty good for boys. His ten-year-old maturity tickles me, and Jim catches my eye and grins. I can tell he thinks it's pretty cute too.

Jane comes with us. She, Parker and Jesse talk for a while of old times. Kristen came into our lives after Jane left, so she's meeting her for the first time. She's heard the story from the family, so she knows who Jane is and where she fits in. She keeps looking at Jane, then she blurts out, "You're nothing like I imagined you."

"What did you imagine me to be like?" Jane asks.

"Harder. Meaner. More depraved. I don't know." Kristen looks embarrassed, as though she wishes she'd just said that to herself.

"If you knew me last year, you would have said I was all those things." Jane's voice is quiet, and she's looking at the ground. "I have promised myself to never become that desperate person again."

"Well, I'm glad I met you this year. I think we're going to be friends." Kristen, always impulsive, leans around Parker and squeezes Jane's shoulder. "Did anyone warn you I seldom think before speaking?"

"No. They all speak very well of you," Jane replies, and we all laugh at how seriously she says it. "Come on, you guys, let's jump in the lake. Can't let the kids have all the fun," says Jesse. Grandpère, Jim and I decline. Instead we sit at the picnic table and watch them all in the water. Jim tells me how much he likes Parker and Kristen, and I can tell him the feeling is mutual, for they've both told me already how much they like him. We sit and hold hands. I'm becoming attached to him. I wonder what it will be like to meet Jim's children.

Even Cameron and Coby can swim well, and they all swim and play and eat the afternoon away. For supper we walk up to the falls. It is only a half-hour hike, and Jesse brings Grandpère and the cooler on the bike. The bike is allowed only on the designated trail, which fortunately is wide and smooth. The cake is still fine when we get to the falls. The creek spills over its rocky bed and drops about five feet into a pool, pounded out by time and spring floods to make a beautiful swimming hole. The men dive off a rock, and the girls, not to be outdone by their uncles, follow suit. Ezra stands on the rock for a while, then says he thinks he will walk in, and the smaller boys follow him. They don't stay in long. The creek water is cooler than the lake, and soon everyone is gathered around the fire, where we've spread out the birthday supper on the picnic table. We all sing "Happy Birthday," then eat our cake quickly, for the wasps have discovered our supper and are particularly attracted to the icing. We pack up everything, and this time the girls take the bike — with Grandpère and the cooler — back to the parking lot.

When we get there, the park warden has stopped them and

is asking for the bike licence and registration. The girls are very happy to see me. Grandpère is mad. He calls the park warden a parasite and mutters about someone who doesn't have anything better to do than harass young girls and old men. He keeps banging his walking stick on the ground for emphasis, and I notice the warden is standing out of range of the stick, looking as though he wishes he were somewhere else. Parker steps right up and is so pleasant and reasonable that the warden, with noticeable relief, says he'll let it go this time. He admonishes me to make sure I have the bike licensed before I bring it to a public place again. I assure him that I will, and he drives off.

Jesse tries to tease Grandpère out of his anger, but he's still mad. "Goddammit, what's the world coming to, when you can't even take a bike down a trail anymore?"

"Grandpère is swearing, Mom." Coby looks at Kristen.

"Grandpère, it's not nice to swear," Kristen says, and that finally makes him laugh.

"Just gets my blood up," he says, reaching out to ruffle Coby's hair. "Your mom is right, it's not nice to swear."

"My dad swears too, when he gets real mad, doesn't he, Cameron?" Coby looks at his brother for confirmation.

"Yep. When people get mad, swearing comes out," Cameron says matter-of-factly, nodding his head, and this makes all of us laugh.

We tease the girls on the way back about getting stopped on the bike and tell them they could all be in jail for driving a bike with no licence on a public road. Jim tells us that the girls still couldn't be driving it without drivers' licences, even if the bike was legal. I have to agree with Grandpère, silently though.

The summer races by, and soon it's the end of August. Darcy and Faith come to get the girls in the middle of the last week of August. They are happy to see each other. Faith tells the girls they've changed so much in only three weeks, and they want to know in what way.

"You just all look so much more grown up," she tells them, and they all puff up.

I want Jane to talk to Darcy and Faith without the girls present, so I send them in to town to visit her at the apartment she shares with Jim. I ask the girls to help me in the garden. Jim tells Darcy he'll leave, but Jane tells them she wants him to stay. "He's practically my father," she tells them.

Darcy and Faith stay in town all evening, and in the morning they tell me it's all settled for this year. Jane told them that she and Angel had agreed already that Angel would go on living with them. "It's best for her to stay with you. She's doing so well and she's happy."

Jane promises to let them keep custody, and they promise to let Angel visit during school holidays. They tell her she's welcome to come there and visit any time she wants. They part on good terms, and later Jim tells me that Jane cried for a long time after they left. He says she still has some work to do, healing herself.

"She is really nice. I'm glad things are working out for her," Faith says. "Still, I'm glad she's leaving Angel with us."

When they leave, Grandpère, Bertie, Jane, Jim and I stand in the yard and wave till they disappear. Jane bursts into tears after they're gone, and we all try to console her.

"Christmas will be here before you know it, and you'll see her then," I tell her, but she just cries harder.

"I'm feeling sorry for myself. Just let me cry for a while," she says, and Jim nods to us over her head. She goes over and sits on a bench by the garden, and we leave her to her grief. After a while she wanders off, and when she comes into the house, she's feeling a lot better. She tries to apologize for "losing it," but I assure her it's a natural thing and tell her sometimes a good cry is not only called for, it's downright refreshing.

"Well, I guess I am refreshed," she says, and we settle down to a quiet supper. After supper Jane takes Bertie back, and Jim spends the night.

It is so quiet that we go to bed early and lie talking for hours about the kids and the summer. He has met everyone but Clint and Patty and likes all of them. We talk about Bertie, and he says he has a plan but won't tell me what it is. "I don't know if it is going to work out yet," he says.

When he leaves in the morning, the house is quiet. Grandpère gets up late and comments on how quiet it is with everyone gone. The sun doesn't come out all day, just hides behind a bank of grey cloud cover, and we both spend a lazy day.

The boys have sawn our firewood again, but Jim has been widening the trail and says he will help us haul the wood to the shed with the pickup. I make a list of the things I need to get out of the garden but don't feel rushed. We have all fall to do them.

I've been wanting to ask Jim if he'd like to move in here, and I mention it to Grandpère.

He snorts. "He might as well be living here, he's here all the time anyway. What are you waiting for?"

"Maybe he won't want to," I say.

"Maybe the sky will be green tomorrow," he replies, as though I'm supposed to know what that means.

On Wednesday I go for my usual stint at the home and find Bertie in tears. Jack has died. "He was just sitting in his chair, smiling," she says. "He was fine, then he was dead."

Bertie is far more upset than I think she should be, since Jack has been giving up on life since before I met him. She's always looked after him, wheeling him out to the yard and making sure he ate his supper, and I wonder if it's just one more thing missing from her life or if she truly will miss the person he was. He couldn't have been much company for her; he hardly communicated, unable to remember from one moment to the next who people were or even where he was.

I ask Rose if I should take Bertie home with me.

"Yes. If you don't mind, take an overnight bag and keep her for a couple of days. It'll get her mind off Jack and do her good," she says.

Bertie definitely wants to come. Ten minutes after I ask her, she's waiting in the parking lot by the car, suitcase in hand. She regains her composure by the time we get home, and she and Grandpère visit in the living room all afternoon. I hear them laughing once when I come in, and by the time Jim arrives for supper, she is able to tell him about Jack without tears. He already knows but lets Bertie tell him about it again. "It's good for her to talk it out," he tells me later.

After we have Bertie installed in one of the spare rooms, and Grandpère is snoring softly in his own, we sit on the couch. He's talking about the changes he's making to the apartment, but I'm only half-listening. I want to ask him to move in with me but I'm nervous. What if he says no? Finally I just say, "Do you want to move here?"

"Say that again," he says, and I repeat it in a slightly clearer voice.

He starts grinning. "I thought you'd never ask. It's what I want more than anything. I never want to go home. I wanted you to ask — I couldn't just ask you. I love you, Anzel, more than I've ever loved anyone in my life."

I am limp with relief. "I love you too, Jim. I couldn't say that before. I wanted you to say it first," I say, and suddenly we are both giggling. We wrap our arms around each other and we keep whispering "I love you" to each other and laughing.

He tells me he hasn't said "I love you" to anyone except his daughters and grandchildren since his marriage ended. He says he waited thirty-five years to find me.

That night our lovemaking is different. Our kisses carry commitment along with the passion. There is new tenderness in our caresses, and I feel as though we have passed a marker that we have been racing toward all summer.

We make plans for him to move as soon as he finishes the renovations on the apartment. We keep looking at each other and smiling. In the morning he tells me the rest of his plan. He wants Bertie to move out of the home and into the apartment with Jane. He says Jane and he have talked about it already, and she thinks it's a great idea. When he leaves for work, I'm full of ambition. I clean the house; the dust bunnies are thick in the corners, and none of us has dusted for weeks. When Grandpère gets up, he asks me if the Queen is coming.

I am dusting with the feather duster, so I go over and pretend to dust him off. "Yes," I say, "she is. And she doesn't want to see any dusty old men."

"Get out of here," he feints at me with his stick, and I dance out of range.

When Bertie gets up, she tells me to go do whatever I

want, and she will finish the housework. At breakfast she and Grandpère make plans for the day. She's brought her crocheting, and he is finishing the last walking stick from the shop. They're going to gather more sticks from the bush, he says. They're all close enough to walk to, and the sticks need to dry for a while before he can work them. I tell them if they want me to take them anywhere, just holler for me.

On Friday Rose phones to tell us Jack's funeral is on Saturday and asks if we want to come. I ask Grandpère and Bertie if they want to go. Bertie does; Grandpère doesn't. Bertie says she should go back to the home so she can get her clothes ready. I drive her into town, where a bus will come and take them to the church and the reception.

When I get home, Grandpère has made lunch.

"Bertie is a good influence on you," I tell him.

"She's all right, but a steady diet of her would make a man old before his time," he says.

I'm surprised. "I thought you really liked her."

"I do. But I'm not Jack. I don't need her to get my slippers or hold my arm when we are walking. She hardly lets me go to the bathroom by myself," he complains.

I understand. He needs to have his own space. Bertie likes to look after people, and he hates feeling as though he needs to be looked after.

I change the subject. "Jim is moving in here at the end of the month."

He gives me a self-satisfied look as though he's the one who arranged it all. "The Great Spirit searched the world and sent you a good man," he tells me, and he keeps nodding to himself, smiling away. He looks the way I feel.

That day Grandpère goes for a long walk with the dogs. I stay busy in the garden and the greenhouse. I pick all the chili peppers that have turned red and set them out in the screens to dry. If they're not dry enough, they'll get mouldy during storage. I found this out the first year I dried them. Even the chickens wouldn't eat those mouldy dry peppers.

I thin the carrots for the last time this year. I always pull the biggest ones, and by the time I've thinned one row, I already have a five-gallon bucket picked. I wash them and lay them in the shade to dry. I clean the root cellar; only one small sack of potatoes is left from last year. The sack looks as though it's alive, covered with long sprouts reaching out through the burlap in quest of light. I take the potatoes and give them to the chickens, then sweep the cellar floor. By the time that's done, the carrots are dry. I put them in a plastic tub with the lid on and set it on a pallet. These are the first vegetables in from this season, and I survey the cellar with great satisfaction before closing the door.

When I get into the house, I can hear Grandpère talking, but I can't quite hear what he is saying. It sounds odd, so I go into the living room to see if he wants something. He is sitting bolt upright in his chair, talking in Carrier as though he's having a conversation with someone.

When I come into the room, he looks at me with a smile. "Look, Anzel, they are all here," he tells me in a voice full of wonderment. He looks beside him, and speaks again in Carrier, gesturing toward me. He laughs again, then looks at me.

"Who is here?" I ask, for obviously he can see something I can't. The hair on the back of my neck prickles, and goosebumps cover my arms even though it's warm.

"My family. My Clementine. All of them. They are coming

for me. Don't go!" he cries and stretches out his hand. He sits there for a minute, then in a dejected voice says, "It isn't time."

He looks up at me and says, "You couldn't see them?"

"No, but I felt them. It gave me goosebumps." I want to reassure him that he's not going crazy. There was definitely something in this room that isn't usually here.

"My time is coming. I see them more and more when I am awake now. The veil between the worlds is thinning out for me." He sounds melancholy.

"Oh Grandpère, you've got a lot of life in you yet," I say, trying to cheer him up.

"I am getting tired," he says. "I don't care about dying. I am looking forward to it. This old body is tired. There I have a young body. When I sleep, I go there. I think the spirit world is the same as the land of dreams. You can go anywhere just by thinking it. Things change into other things, and your body can be old or young, just however you want it to be. My friends are there. I spend more and more time there." His voice sounds yearning, and I reach over and pat his hand.

"Do you want a cup of tea?" I ask.

"Sure," he says. When I bring him the tea, he tells me he thinks he knows what is happening to the people in the home. "When you get old, you get abilities young people don't have. When you are young, you are focussed on learning things and need a strong focus to be able to learn. When you get old, you can do most things by habit. Your body knows how to do almost everything without your spirit directing it. Then the spirit can wander, and other senses can be learned. I can see things that aren't in this world, sometimes when I am wide awake now. I think some of the people in the home have wandered off in their spirit bodies and are living in both worlds at once. I think that's what Jack did."

"Yeah, probably," I agree. That's just how it seems, their bodies are present but nobody is home.

"Thank you, Grandpère, for remembering to stay in your body," I tell him, and that makes him smile. We drink our tea and have a quick meal, and right afterward he goes to bed.

In the morning he wants to go up to the lookout. I ask if I should pack a picnic, but he says no, he just wants to sit up in the sun for a while. I take him up on the bike, and he tells me to come back for him in a while. I put a woollen blanket on the ground, and he sits on it facing the morning sun, his legs bent up and his arms wrapped around them. One dog sits down on each side of him and they stay there when I leave with the bike.

I sweep the mud room and the porch, then pick all the ripe tomatoes in the greenhouse and freeze them whole. I can stew them later in the fall when the weather isn't so nice. It's nearly noon by the time I finish, so I go back up to get Grandpère. It looks as though he and the dogs haven't moved. He hears me coming and gets slowly to his feet. He doesn't say anything, just smiles and climbs on the back. He looks peaceful and happy. I grin back at him and take him down to the house.

He eats a big lunch. We both like to fry the ripe tomatoes and have hot tomato sandwiches, and the new row of spinach has given us its first tender leaves for a salad. We linger over lunch as he tells me how good it is that Jim will be here for the winter. He thinks Bertie and Jane will be good company for each other. He says it's kind of good for us that Jesse and Jessica have split up, since we've seen more of Jesse this summer than in the last three years. He wonders if everything is all right with Clint and

Patty; we haven't seen them since Christmas. I tell him they are most likely just busy. Patty is off maternity leave, and travelling with four young boys can't be too much fun. "I'll see if everyone can come for Christmas again," I say.

"Maybe I'll see them then," he says. "Right now I think I will have a short snooze." He goes into the living room and lies down in the recliner chair. Within five minutes I can hear him snoring away.

I go outside and play in the flower beds for a few hours. I dig up some of the daffodils and split the bulbs apart, then replant them spaced out better. They have multiplied so much that I have to dig another spot to plant them all. It is an enjoyable task. Knowing each bulb carries the promise of spring flowers makes each one precious. I deadhead the rest of the spent flowers on the annuals; they will keep blooming right till freeze-up if they can't set seed. By the time I'm finished, it's nearly suppertime.

When I go into the house, Grandpère is still sleeping in the chair. He hears me in the kitchen and comes out to sit at the table while I prepare the meal.

"Clementine and I were on the horses. We were going to pick berries. We had a pack horse, and we were going to the meadow to pick strawberries. We had your dehydrator on the horse," he says.

"What?" I say. "When was this?"

"Right now. It was what woke me up. I knew the dehydrator shouldn't be there. I said to Clementine that it wasn't right to have that on the horse because it took electricity. She started laughing, and then she disappeared. Then I woke up. It was so real." He sits there for a bit, then adds, "I wanted it to be real. I was disappointed when I woke up."

"You will see her again, don't worry," I say to him. Then I think that is a silly thing to say. The only way he's going to see her again is if she's waiting for him when he dies. If that is really how it works. But he doesn't find anything wrong with my words. "Yeah, they are waiting," he says and starts talking about other things.

In the evening we play crib. I haven't had a game with him for a while, and he wins the first two games. I win the next two, and we play one more to break the tie. The first hand in the last game, he gets a perfect hand of three fives and a Jack, which matches the five turned up on the pile. He says it's the first time ever that he got that hand. He skunks me, and is happy when he goes to bed.

I wake up early, and he is not up. I make the billing for my time this month for Rose, who has been reminding me to bring it in. I make pancakes for breakfast, and he's still not up, so I put some in the oven for him and go outside. It is a gorgeous day, not a cloud in the sky, cool in the morning but not yet cold. The dogs are starting to get their winter coats, and King has such long fur that it's getting a bit matted, so I groom him for a while. He's not used to it and wiggles around a lot, but finally he's soft and fluffy again. Blue has shorter hair but really likes being groomed, so I brush him for a while, too, so he doesn't feel left out.

When I go back in the house it is midmorning already, and there's still no sign of Grandpère. I go to check on him. He's lying on top of the blankets, completely dressed in his clothes that he wears to go to town. He looks as though he's sleeping, but I clear my throat, and at the sound he opens his eyes. He gestures me closer.

"I have been waiting for you," he says in a voice that sounds as though it is coming from his toes. "They are here. This time I'm going."

# Chapter Fifteen

I go to Grandpère's bed and sit down on the edge. "Do you want me to stay with you, or are you coming for breakfast?"

"I just wanted to say goodbye."

His eyes close and his head sinks into the pillow. My skin prickles, and I reach for his hand. I hold it and squeeze it a bit, but there is no answering squeeze. His whole body goes limp, and a cloud of silver grey seems to gather about him. The cloud hovers above Grandpère for a few seconds, and the room seems briefly illuminated. In that strange light it seems as though I hear voices and music. Then the light swirls into the cloud, and all of it disappears.

"Did you see that?" I ask.

There is no reply. A weird smell is in the room, and when I look at him, I realize he is gone. I put my head down on his chest, but there is no heartbeat to hear.

I sink to the floor beside the bed, holding his dead, limp hand. Gone. Gone so quickly. He just held on long enough to say goodbye. I lean against the bed and hold his hand to my cheek. My tears get it wet, and it feels wrong to get his hand wet with my tears. I pat his hand for a while, then tuck it beside him on the bed. I look at him for a while, then cross his hands on his chest. That looks wrong too. I pick up his walking stick and put it under his hands. One hand curls around it, and the other lies on top. That looks better.

I go make a pot of tea. I put two cups out. Then I put one back in the cupboard. As I drink my tea, I think of the promise I made. Should I haul him out to the landing and give him the same end as old Duke? The more I think about it, the more I think that it's the right thing to do. I imagine him in the chair, making me promise. When I am thinking about him, I can feel him right there, and I imagine his voice telling me to get on with it.

I go back into his room, half-hoping he would not still be dead. But he is. He looks peaceful, as though he's sleeping, but that sweet-sour smell is still in the air, and I want to do something. I take the top blanket and fold it up around him. Then I think I should sew it closed. I start at the feet, and using the packing needle and sinew thread, I sew big looping stitches to hold it closed. As I get to the top, I open it and put his hat on his head. I kiss his weathered old cheek and say, "Goodbye, my friend, goodbye. I hope you are at a party in the spirit world." I close up the blanket again and stitch it shut. I cover him up with another blanket and tiptoe out of the room.

I take the bike and go out to the landing. The kids have sawn a huge pile of wood, leaving pieces about ten feet long. I take these for the bottom of the pile. I put two rows flat, parallel to each other, then cross them with the next layer. I build up the deck, layer by layer, till it's as high as my chest. "You need moss," says a voice in my head, and I remember him saying, "You make a nest with a layer of moss."

I take the bike and trailer to the tall trees and gather up a trailer full of soft moss, which I lay in a fluffy pile in the centre of the wood. Now what? "You need the body," says the same voice in my head. I go back to the house. It seems wrong to drag him out to the bike trailer, and he won't fit in the trailer unless I fold him up. I wonder if the car will make it to the landing, so I take the bike back out and eye up the trail. I don't think the car will make it. There are too many stumps. I go back to the house, trying to think of how to get Grandpère to his funeral pyre with dignity.

I think of the long toboggan in the garage. I can strap it on top of the bike trailer. I go get it and lay it on the bed beside him. I lift him on to the toboggan; he is lighter than I remember. I get four rubber snap straps and strap him down so he can't roll off. Then I put a blanket on the floor and pull the toboggan off the bed onto the blanket. The whole thing slides out of the room, down the hall and to the door, where I've backed the bike trailer up to the steps.

I pull the toboggan up onto the top of the bike trailer and tie it on with rope. I bring matches and a knife for making feather sticks to light the fire. Then I hear Lorne's voice saying to never mind the feather sticks; take along some paper and diesel, that's the best way to start a good fire. I feel as though he's helping me and approves, so I do.

I drive very carefully back to the landing with my precious cargo. The dogs trot alongside the trailer like an honour guard. When we get to the landing, the dogs start barking and run back toward the house, barking as though someone has come. I have a sinking feeling that it might be Bella, but they come back with Jim.

"I just asked the dogs where you were, and followed them,"

he cheerfully says, then takes in the pile of wood and the bike. "What are you doing?"

My voice is not good, but I croak out, "Grandpère," and indicate the toboggan with its shrouded occupant.

He stands looking at it for a long minute, then comes to me and puts his arm across my shoulders and leads me over to a log, where he pulls me down beside him. My tears, which have dried up since morning, start running again. He is silent, and we sit there till I quit sobbing.

"Are you sure this is the best way?" he asks, and I can hear the reservations in his voice.

"I promised him," I say. "He made me promise."

"A promise made is something that has to be done, then," he answers. "I'll help. What do we need to do?"

"We need to get him on the pile. He's pretty light. I can almost lift him myself."

Jim goes over to Grandpère, and undoes the rope that I have secured him to the trailer with. "Is the toboggan going or staying?" he asks.

"It's wood. It will help him along," I reply, and he waves me away. He picks up the toboggan and slides it to the centre of the pile. I climb up and arrange the moss around Grandpère. I take off the snap straps, as it doesn't feel right to have him held down. "We need to make a teepee over him with wood, and put things he might want inside," I tell Jim.

He raises his eyebrows. "What things?"

"I don't know." I think about what he might want to take along.

"You get what you need. I'll lean up the teepee," he says, and I take the bike back to the house. I go into Grandpère's room.

His carving knife and the carving he is working on are on his night table. I put them in a box. Then I get his moccasins that the girls gave him for Christmas and his winter jacket. The pancakes from breakfast are still in the oven. I put them on a paper plate, butter them and cover them with syrup and berries. I put them all on the bike, then I go back and get the twenty-two. I fill it with shells but don't put one in the chamber. I drive back to the landing.

Jim has covered him up with a wooden teepee, and I take a slab off and slide the stuff inside. He looks at what I am putting in, but doesn't comment on any of it.

"Now we completely cover everything. It takes a lot of wood to burn a body," I say, echoing the words Grandpère said to me when we burned Duke.

We build the pile till even Jim can't reach the top.

"Now we say our last goodbyes, then we light the pile all around," I say. He bows his head, and so do I. In my mind I see Grandpère walking down the trail. He doesn't have his stick, and he's walking with the stride of his younger days. At the edge of the bush he turns and waves his hand. I wave back, and I say out loud, "He's really gone."

"He had a good, long life, and he stayed good till the very end," Jim says. We stand there for a while longer, then I get the jug and pour diesel around the base of the wood pile. Jim lights it with a match, and the fire starts instantly. We sit down on the log and watch the fire. Within a half hour the whole pile is blazing. I am not prepared for the smell. When the smoke wafts our way, it smells as though we're cooking a roast. It disturbs me, and I get up and walk a bit farther away. Jim comes, too, and soon we are walking circles around the pyre.

"We are supposed to sing him to the spirit land, but I don't know any of the songs," I tell Jim.

"I know a medicine chant for catching fish," he says.

"Let's sing it, then," I tell him, and he starts. It is simple, and soon we're singing the fishing chant, walking circles around the fire. It is getting late; the air is cooling off away from the fire. We stop singing the fishing song when we hear a loud explosion from the fire.

"What the heck was that?" Jim asks.

"Probably the bullets exploded," I say.

"You loaded the gun?" Jim looks surprised.

"What good is a gun with no bullets?" I say to him.

He shakes his head and laughs. "You've got a point there." He wants to know if I want to eat, but I'm not hungry. I tell him to go to the house and get himself something, and he leaves on the bike.

I sit on the log to watch the fire. I think I can see Grandpère's outline in the centre of the fire, so I pile on more wood. I throw on a lot more till I can no longer see him. It doesn't smell like roast anymore.

When Jim comes back, he's brought two sleeping bags, a thermos of tea and some sandwiches. He pours tea, and I drink some. I try a sandwich and am hungrier than I thought. I eat both the sandwiches, as he says he ate at the house and brought these for me. We wrap up in the bags and watch the fire burn. When it starts to die down, we pile another big heap of wood on top.

Jim sits on the log and drapes the sleeping bag over his back. I sit on the ground in front of him and lean back. He wraps his arms around me, and we sit in silence, listening to the crackle of the fire and watching the flames leap into the air. I drift in and out of sleep. It seems that sometimes there is a whole crowd of people around the fire, but each time I open my eyes, the crowd fades, and it's just me and Jim sitting there.

Daylight fades, and the stars appear one by one till the sky is ablaze with stars. The only sounds are quiet cracklings from the fire. Occasionally the fire collapses, and sparks fly high up into the air, leaving red streaks behind. When the fire gets low, we heap on more wood. It's getting cold, but I don't want to go to the house. "Let's just sleep here by the fire," I suggest.

Jim goes back to the house and brings the foam mattress and two pillows. We make up a bed where we figure the sparks won't land, and I fall asleep right away, sleeping in my clothes. I dream of Grandpère. He is young in my dream, and he is dressed in leggings and a tunic cut to a point in front and back. Grandmère Clementine is with him, and they are going in a canoe. She has on a flowered dress, and she is helping him pack the boat. He has the twenty-two, but the wood is burned off it. They're excited to be going on a journey, but they stop and eat pancakes that I bring to the shore. He picks up a smooth red rock and gives it to me, and tells me to save it and call him on it if I need him. They climb into the boat, which has changed into a motorboat, and he starts it. They wave and yell goodbyes till they are just a dot on the water horizon.

When I wake up, Jim is building the fire up again, and dawn is breaking in the east, turning the sky brilliant red. I lie there quietly. Yesterday floods back into my mind. I realize I am holding something warm in my hand and look to see what it is. It is a smooth, round red rock, the one Grandpère gave me in my dream. I look at it with astonishment.

I sit up. I'm definitely awake. I stare at the rock. Jim sees me sit up, and comes over to plop down on the mattress. "What do you have there?" he asks, looking at my rock.

"Grandpère gave it to me," I say and hand it to him. "In my dream," I add.

"He gave it to you in your dream?" His eyebrows go up, and he turns the rock over and looks at it closely. "Looks like a real one to me."

I don't have any explanation, so I just shrug. He hands the rock back as though it has suddenly become too hot to handle, and I tuck it into my pants pocket.

It feels all right to leave the fire now, and we go back to the house. I explain about the box and the bones to Jim, and he says he will make a box. He goes out to the garage, and comes back in right away with a wooden box. It is about two feet long by one foot high and wide and has a lid held on with hinges. It's the same kind of box we used to collect Duke's bones, I know it's one Grandpere made. It makes me grateful, and I thank him in my head. It's just the right size, and I tell Jim that when the fire is dead, we will collect the bones.

The phone rings, and it is Rose. Jim talks to her, tells her Grandpère has died, then says to give us today and not come till tomorrow. When he gets off the phone, he comes over and sits by me. "You should phone the kids and tell them. They'll want to know," he says.

I haven't yet thought about phoning them, but agree that I should. I phone Clint first. He isn't home, but Patty is. She wants to know what I'm having done. I tell her he is being cremated, and she says it's just as well; she hates those open-coffin funerals. I tell her we'll have a memorial service, and she says they'll be down as soon as they can get away. She offers to phone the rest of the family, and I thank her and tell her I'd appreciate it.

Jim is listening while I talk to her, and when I hang up the phone, he's nodding. "He is being cremated. I wondered how we were going to explain what we did. We'll hope no one asks for details. Just pretend you did it the normal way," he says.

I agree. "I think we can get into big trouble for doing it Grandpère's way. It's good, what we did, but it isn't like it used to be. Before he died, I thought I wouldn't do it. But now that it's over, I'm glad I kept my promise."

Jesse arrives in mid-afternoon. When Patty phoned him, he says, he just got in his truck and drove straight here. He has tears in his eyes, and keeps saying it's the end of an era. I tell him how Grandpère stayed in this world till he said goodbye, and that he'd told me he was getting tired and was not just ready to die, he was eager. "He even put on his good clothes to die."

Jim and I were heading out with the empty box. We look at each other, then at Jesse.

"What can I do?" Jesse asks.

"Come in to the house for a while," I say. We sit at the table and drink tea while I explain about how Grandpère didn't want me to send his body off to strangers and made me promise to send him off in his own way. I explain about the funeral pyre, how much wood we used and how it smelled like roast.

Jesse's eyes get big, and he keeps saying, "Holy shit."

Jim says we aren't going to tell anyone else how he was cremated.

"Good thing. I don't think you're allowed to do that. Don't worry about me, I can keep a secret," Jesse says.

They tell me I don't need to come out, but I feel as though I should, so all three of us go out to the pyre. It's just ash now but still hot in the middle. Jesse stirs in the ashes; there isn't much to find. I'm puzzled not to find the gun barrel, but we stir and stir, and it doesn't show up. There are fewer bones than we found for the dog, just a round part of his skull and some small pieces of other bones. At one point Jesse finds a tooth and holds it up to me with an inquiring look.

"Not Grandpère's," I say. "He had no teeth left. Maybe Duke's."

The box is not even half-full. We shut the lid and close the hatch.

Jesse takes it to the shop and nails the lid down tightly. He asks, "What now?"

Grandpère's remains should go up to the lookout, I tell him.

"Any place in particular?" he asks.

"You're supposed to look around, and the right place will feel right. You leave it there," I say. "Do you want to do it?"

"I will be honoured to take the old guy to his final rest," he says. He doesn't want the bike and says he will pack it up. "It is better if I walk and take Grandpère for his last walk."

I don't want to go with him, I just pat the box for a while and then go into the house with Jim. The telephone keeps ringing as the kids call, one after the other. They will all be down on the weekend and wonder what day the funeral will be. I tell them maybe Monday, and Jim phones to book the hall.

We hold the memorial service in the Elks' Hall. So many people come that there's standing room only. My boys give the eulogy; they tell stories about Grandpère's life, and some of them are funny. People laugh, and most are not full of tears and sorrow. Clint has told them not to cry, as Grandpère's life was long and good and he is with his family again. No one asks me anything about the cremation, and I'm glad.

When it's over, we all go back to the house. All of us go up to the lookout and are there when the sun sets. Jim stands beside me with his arm around my shoulders. Even the little boys are quiet while the setting sun turns the sky orange. I don't see Grandpère's box anywhere, but I feel his spirit telling me that life goes on.

A quiet peace fills me, and when we make our way down the hill in the fading light, I echo Jesse's words. "End of an era."

# Acknowledgments

To properly acknowledge all who contributed to this story would be to thank everyone and everything in my life. But there are some that deserve special recognition, so I thank my grandmother for making me wonder about Gitchi Manitou, my parents for teaching me values, my family for their unending support, my husband for his love and commitment, and our children and grandchildren for the blessings that children bring.

Thanks also to the late Gus Raphael for telling me stories about the giants; my friend Lynn to whom I turned to for information about abused children; elder Emma Baker for reading the draft and telling me where I strayed; my sister Rene for reading the first draft and still encouraging me to carry on; Harold Isaac; the Prince family; Edgar Ketlo; and all the others involved in the wonderful sweat lodge experience.

A big thanks to my agent Carolyn Swayze, publisher Vici Johnstone and Caitlin Press, and editors Susan Mayse and Patricia Wolfe whose insights and questions helped make this a better book.

Information comes from so many places, and I have to thank God for search engines. It is such a luxury, having a world of information at your fingertips. The other luxury is books. Here are some that helped me along the way; *Inkonze – The Stones of Traditional Knowledge*, Phillip R. Coutu and Lorraine Hoffman-Mercredi, *Fort Fraser (Where the Hell's That?)*, Lenore Rudland, *Deeper Roots and Greener Valleys*, Fraser Lake and District Historical Society and *Harmon's Journal* (Touchwood Editions), Daniel Williams Harmon. All these books are gems.